Killing Waldo

A Belle's Revenge Story

Victoria Helen Rose

CONTENTS

For Granddad

"The only person you are destined to become is the person you decide to be."

Ralph Waldo Emerson

Chapter One: Belle Jones

"Cuff me to the bed. Now. Knock me out," I
ordered the men guarding me in the hospital.
Minutes earlier the medical officer at my site had
broken into tears and confessed that everyone's
worst enemy, Omar Al-Zahrani, had successfully
escaped from the site I had tracked him to in
Saudi Arabia.

My name is Belle Jones; at least that's what I
call myself. I'm basically the opposite of what
you think a spy would look like: tall dark
handsome and male? I look a lot more like Lois
Lane than James Bond; twenty–four years old,
about four months into a hellish pregnancy, and
a globally wanted and feared operator. Call me a
spy.

Technically, I'm a prisoner. Nothing lasts
forever; and once I realized my condition I knew
I needed to choose between staging my death
and letting myself be captured. I'm an American,
so I went home. FBI Agent George Tomapolis
was there waiting for me and we finally met in
person after all those facts and files I'd mailed
him.

The only thing you really need to know is that I
hate terrorists. The striped rat bastard stole my
mother from me and I was determined to get him
if it was the last thing I ever did. Honestly, if I'd

never gotten pregnant I wouldn't be in this mess because he'd be dead by now. I searched, I fought, and I found him after years of training, fighting, and generally raising hell.

I found myself in a hospital bed in November of 2010 because of some incredibly scary complications to my pregnancy. Everything was clearing up now and they'd probably transfer me back to the secret base prison soon. At this exact moment I have bigger problems than my delightful parasite wiggle-worm. If O.Z. is in the wind, we need to find him all over again. Assets will need to be pressed for information. Footage will need to be reviewed, lines tracked, ideas spawned and pursued, and a hunt would begin.

Time was not on our side; time is such a bitchy mistress, always running out. Somewhere in the back of my brain a fact registered so I gave the order.

Please understand: I'm more of a collaborator than a prisoner. I belong with team USA in this particular set of games. I've been working with three-letter agencies for months now putting my diverse professional skills to use. The guards have it set up so I have a little band around my left ankle which can shock me like a shock collar if I misbehave. It's our usual alternative to handcuffs.

These people have been taking care of me and I've connected on a personal level with many of them. I am loyal to this team, but even as the guard slapped a cuff on my left wrist and hooked it to the bed rail I knew that my desire to pull the trigger would override my personal feelings. Damn the team, damn the baby, damn the hospital staff: my blood boiled and my adrenalin surged. If we're not all very careful, hate will trump love every time.

"Belle, Alexis," Susan, the medical officer onsite broke into my whirl of panic. I was born Alexis Johnston; they like to remind me every once in a while. "Listen to me." She bored holes in my eyes with her own. "They will shoot you dead. Let's go home. We'll get you well; you can get back to work. You've done it before; I have faith in you."

"Yep. That's why I asked for the cuffs. Am I well enough? I'd like to get the hell out of here," *to someplace I can't escape so incredibly easily.* My hands twitched and I recognized the code calling for soft backup when Staff Sergeant Andrews called it in.

A young man with no signs he had ever smiled came in armed exclusively with incapacitation gear. I read him from head to toe while he avoided eye contact and scanned my body. His gear was primarily from the knee down; perhaps a few zip ties at his waist but the good stuff was strapped on his calves like boots. His long sleeves were skin tight and his rippling muscles aroused my overactive hormones. No name tag; that's fine, I like them anonymous.

"Stay calm," Muscles ordered me firmly in a normal speaking tone. I felt a little like a dog but given the moment wanted to obey him. I took several exaggerated breaths and slowed my heart rate. No one moved in the room for a moment and I realized how incredibly tired I was again.

I rolled slowly onto my left side and pulled the blanket up over my chest with my free arm. I sensed Andrews step back out of my range and didn't care. Al-Zahrani wasn't going to show up in the next ten minutes so I slowly drifted off to sleep.

"Jane?" a loving woman's voice summoned me from my sleep. "Jane, I need you to wake up now," she called and I opened my eyes slowly remembering I was Jane. Dr. Gloria Morales was there and I realized that her scrubs had changed color.

"Hi Gloria. Can I go home yet?" I yawned and stirred slightly. I could swear that Muscles had frozen in place: he looked like a giant GI Joe doll TM.

"Soon," she promised. "I need another look at your cervix first though." Gloria turned to the others while getting a sheet. "Can we assume exam stance, please?" she requested with professional aloofness. The boys moved around and Muscles came in very close to my neck and head. He hadn't touched me yet but I already knew his playbook. As far as I could tell, he'd be cool with me as long as I was cool with him.

"Nice and calm," Muscles restated his earlier line. The exam was brief.

"It looks very good," Gloria assured me as she discarded her gloves and washed her hands. "There's a man here to see you, but Sara is going to bring you a change of clothes first."

My spunky little nurse came in and helped me change into some scrubs; she didn't even blink at my scars or shock device and I loved her for it. I was all ready for George to come through the door, probably with flowers. Instead, John from the CIA came in bearing my favorite stuffed dolphin. Muscles took it from him and effectively groped it to examine it for contraband. He must have satisfied himself because I was given my toy. Andrews unlocked me from the bed and I hoped John would be here to see me out.

"Hey princess!" John greeted in the awkward overly-happy forced way people greet hospital patients. He looked tired, like he had gone to sleep and been woken up too early. His horseshoe hair was less than pristinely smoothed down.

"Hi John. Baby's fine," I offered.

"Excellent. Really, excellent." John at least faked relieved well and I knew what had brought him.

"I'm not leaving, John," I assured him in a flat voice. I watched his face twitch and spasm while he tried to say something reassuring or helpful. "We going home now?" I cut the torture short.

"How do you guys want to handle this?"

"We don't want to knock her out if we don't have to," Susan spoke.

"Speaking objectively, I don't see a need to," I offered. I was physically weakened by my health and in no condition to pull off an escape from tight control.

Susan came around and removed my saline drip, leaving in the needle for convenience later. After a debate they decided to let Muscles do what he does best. He was surprisingly gentle as he strapped my ankles into restraints. Then he lifted me onto a gurney like a dance partner and immobilized my elbows before strapping me to the padding. By then most of the people were gone from the room and it was just John and two soldiers besides Muscles.

Muscles came to face me at the foot of the gurney. "Are you listening?" he asked in a near-monotone. For anyone else it would have been condescending but something in Muscles triggered acceptance in my mind.

"Listening."

"You've stripped me down twice," Muscles stated and made eye contact for the first time. "So you're probably familiar with my gear. I don't know you. Don't study you, not my thing."

"You're here because they want me back alive," I understood. "We share the goal."

"Just so you know, I have everything I need," Muscles stated.

"Noted."

"So here's how it goes. Right now, you're as restrained as I need you to be. I need you calm. I need you quiet and I need you to obey instantly. They will let me do whatever I need to; but we can have a two-way respect here. Let's put the blindfold on until you're in the vehicle." He lifted the blindfold he had previously placed next to my foot and stepped around to slip it on gently. "Good job. Hands palms up and flat please," he directed and I felt him lift and hold the hand without the IV plug. His hands were kind, warm, and gentle. "You're doing great. We're going to roll backwards at first but they'll turn you around. I need you quiet; nod if you understand."

I nodded and after a moment's pause we began to roll out as Muscles had described. I felt an elevator ride and what seemed like incredibly long halls before a brief flood of cold air.

"You're doing well, just relax," Muscles coached and for a second I thought he might be my brother, long-since killed in action. They spun and lifted me and I sensed that I was in an ambulance. Muscles had released my hand for the lift and I started to fidget. I felt the vehicle jostling.

"Hey," Andrews said quietly. Two doors slammed.

"Hey!" Muscles said and someone snapped twice: I knew it was him. I heard myself whimper again and tried to take a deep breath. "You're okay. Calm down," he ordered and I put myself back where he wanted me. Two more doors slammed somewhere else and Muscles took my hand again. "You can speak now, no shouting."

"Okay," I acknowledged quietly. He took my blindfold off; the light was dim but I could see that I was in some kind of van.

Andrews and his gun were sitting by the doors behind me. Muscles perched next to me. I was sat up in the gurney and faced forward as the van maneuvered. Muscles gave me ginger ale and water to drink through a straw, patiently offering me the fluids and holding them while I drank. He also scratched an itch that was driving me crazy and I began to like him. I tuned out as we traveled, thinking about the Al-Zahrani situation. Every once in a while we'd hit a bump or turn and I'd strain my straps and change gears from being upset about the loss to being upset about my status.

"You're doing well," Muscles told me encouragingly. "It's late. Are you tired?"

I felt weak but not actually tired. I knew it would help him feel better so I leaned my head back and closed my eyes for a while. I totally lost track of time, which was likely their objective. I was sipping soda and eating bites of oatmeal when we pulled to a series of three short stops. Even weak and groggy I knew the signs that we were back on the base. We pulled around again in a loop to the left and stopped.

"Shh, nice and calm," Muscles said and subtly checked my restraints.

"Where did they find you, Muscles?" I asked drowsily. He didn't answer because the doors opened after some clanging.

"Blindfold's going back on," Muscles declared and slid it gently onto my head again. There was several minutes of nothing followed by the backward lurch and drop. They wheeled me quickly and at one point I wondered if they were wheeling or carrying; the angle of the bed kept changing.

"Take that off," Captain Stover, one of the heads of security at my little haven-prison ordered and the sleeping mask was removed. Muscles moved quickly and I blinked in the harsh florescent hallway light. "You look like hell," Captain Stover announced affectionately.

"I missed you too," I retorted. Muscles' hand twitched and I wondered briefly if I should shut up. They reeled me into my little apartment and Stover ordered the restraints off. Muscles freed my ankles and elbows and seemed to wait for orders on the straps.

"Medic will be here in a minute," Stover stated. "Want to hang around on the gurney until then?" he asked while clicking the release on the medical straps.

I knew it wasn't a real question, but with the straps gone I was able to stretch and squirm around to my heart's content.

"Hello Beauty," my friendly medic came in; there were several but I think of this one as the friendly one. He was fat and jolly and almost certainly gay if my detection skills are worth a dime. "Can you eat anything?"

"Is there pasta marinara anywhere?" I expressed my craving and heard someone in the hall moving.

"I'm sure they'll find something." He slipped on the sphygmomanometer and took my pulse, pressures, temperature, and had a good listen to my heart and lungs. "Are you ready to be totally grossed out?"

"Try me," I scoffed. My life's experiences had not been sweet or pretty and nothing about the human body disgusts me anymore. He simply directed me to go into my bathroom and replace my current underwear with fresh and bring him the old set. I found pads in the bathroom: I had never needed those before in captivity. After a few questions relayed through the glass walls I sealed the evidence bag and washed my hands, working around the IV.

"Careful on that IV site!" Jolly Medic cautioned me.

"Yes dad!"

Muscles was waiting for me right outside the door: he had lifted me down from the gurney and walked me to the bathroom. Some combination of hunger, fatigue, and the drugs made me quite weak and dizzy and Muscles walked me over to the futon.

"Drink," Muscles demanded after seizing an Ensure® and straw from the food tray. He seemed to like to mother hen me so I let him hold the can while I obediently sucked.

My cell is quite large: big enough for a full-sized bed, small bathroom, a futon couch, tiny round dining table with three chairs, desk, and dresser. I even had a small fridge for sodas. It was better living quarters than several places I had lived during my adventures. My cell was built from several cells and an excess door had been converted into a window with a ledge where they delivered food. The real door was impenetrable, even for me. Lots of technology accented by a stone-age bolt. Technology can be hacked, locks can be picked, but physics is a bitch.

Muscles wouldn't go away until I made the end-of-can sucking sound. My food arrived and everyone but Stover left.

"You know I like eyes at a level," I gestured for the captain to join me at the table. He pulled a chair away and sat.

"Is she okay?" Stover inquired after about half the dish was gone.

"She's fine. Some kind of infection," I replied and noticed that his face was honestly glad. "How much longer?"

"About five months," I let the silence speak while I finished the meal. "Tell me you know I'm not leaving."

"I know you're not going to do anything to endanger your daughter. You're too good a mother."

"I'm also a really good assassin," I confessed.

"No you're not," Captain Stover contradicted and stood. "Assassins kill whatever their target is with no emotions involved. You couldn't kill an innocent person like that. You'd never kill a child. All that being said, you understand why we have to keep or kill you, right?"

"I do." Bare facts have always been a friend to my thought processes. If I escaped into the world I could be captured and tortured for information. Humans are experts at torture and everyone gives eventually. The only thing worse than not knowing the target's location is for the target to know what you know about him. Knowledge really is power, and I had a lot of it.

"Sir?" a man called in the hall.

"Clear for entry," Stover replied and the door made all the noises of being opened. Officer Belot came in and checked the sensor on my ankle's shock device. She left and Deputy Director Elsa Goode came in. Stover got the hell out of there but Muscles came in to lurk by the doorway.

"Director," I pushed the table to try to stand respectfully.

"Sit!" Muscles ordered. I began to wonder if he was going to be a permanent fixture. I don't mind looking at him but I generally prefer the dominant role in an S&M relationship.

"Give us a moment, Sergeant," Director Goode directed and Officer Belot replaced him before the door sealed. "I want you to get some rest. They're going to give you a few more medications before removing the IV. I know you're aware that we've had a major setback."

"Ma'am," I said and my mouth was dry.

"You'll be able to rest for as long as it takes to get you better. You need to rest so you can recover. You might have some visitors tomorrow. *He* wants to see you."

"We need Agent Won to pull some chatter: Ozzie didn't just move on a whim."

Director Goode nodded knowingly and I knew she was on it. "We put some protein drinks in your fridge; feel free to drink as much as you can until we can get your health back. Goodnight." She left and Jolly Medic came back to give me three injections and a tube of topical cream. The annoying IV was pulled and he warned me that I would want to go straight to bed.

After a very long night's sleep and a hot shower I felt much better. I drank an Ensure® with the large breakfast they brought me. The food was gone and I had just finished braiding my long dark hair when I heard men in the hall. This is a fairly normal occurrence for me; there are always guards out there. I never know who or how many are in that hall but I think it's always two people.

"Sir, sir, that's a dead zone!" one of the guys sounded slightly distressed. They're Marines, it's hard to tell when they're upset. "Sir! Please!"

I almost tripped over myself making the bed when an old man poked his head and neck clear through the food tray opening. "Hello Belle!" Deuce's voice greeted in his smoky tone.

"Sir!" The guard fretted and I giggled.

Deuce is a man of great importance in the Defense espionage and covert activities arena. I never knew his exact name and so named him by his importance ranking. This worked for everyone involved.

Deuce pulled out of the hole and after a moment I heard the telling beeps that foretold the door opening. I decided to go ahead and sit at my table before the guards ordered me to.

"How are you feeling, Beauty?" Deuce walked in closely tagged by Lieutenant Shapiro. Shapiro had my shock device controller ready in his left hand and was fine with me knowing it. They get jumpy around the VIPs. "How'd you like Jack?" he asked and sat to join me.

"Captain Stover?" I guessed. I don't know many of the guards' or agents' first names.

"Is that his name?" Deuce looked amused. "No, Jack's my man. I brought him in special for you when we had to move you offsite."

"Average height, sharp cheekbones, green eyes?" I described Muscles.

"Think of Jack as a life preserver," Deuce replied.

"I've been calling him Muscles," I confided and he laughed. I thought about my experiences with Muscles with this new information in mind.

"Yeah, he's mine."

"He's fine." I folded my hands and then flinched at the IV bruise.

"I'm glad. I know the medic will be here soon, so I'll get right to the shooting," Deuce stated. "How do we find him again?"

"Find the leak and plug it." I stared right into his smoky old eyes. "Get the psychologists, figure out where he would have gone people-wise. He moved out of fear. He's still going to need to communicate with someone somehow. We've tagged a lot of his followers." I shook my head in depressed frustration. "Can you get me my original files back? Maybe they'll remind me of something; you know, situational memory." I wanted to cry.

"Beauty," the gravelly voice spoke quietly. "We'll get you what you need. You have a rare advantage here; you've breathed his air. You found him once; we'll find him again. Do you still think he's linked to Bin Laden?"

"He's one man in a sea of seven billion! It was half luck finding him the first time. I'm out of my element here," I took a breath. "Yes. You might check and see if there has been any activity on Bin Laden." A thought came to me but I kept it to myself. So far I had fed them some information about Bin Laden and his associates in order to secure the team's help in taking down Ozzie. They were all about finding Waldo even though I think I've convinced some of them that Omar Al-Zahrani is the real danger.

"You adapt fast, Beauty," Deuce stood up. "Give Jack a chance, he's a good kid."

I rolled my eyes when he turned his back and kept my thoughts on dominance to myself. Shapiro saw Deuce out and they shut me in again. I stretched out on my bed and stared at the fake window. It was a delightful little device, programmed to show me life scenes in perfectly simulated daylight. I set it to the Saharan dunes and studied the endless sands. I had intended to get back up in a few minutes but fell asleep instead.

"Ring Ring?" a woman spoke the words as though they were onomatopoeia. I blinked my eyes open again and found that the room's lights had dimmed and the sands were still shining in on me. "Belle?" the voice came again and I realized that someone was calling through the speaker.

"Speaking," I mumbled and rolled onto my back.

"Did I wake you? It's one o'clock," the lady said and I realized it was Agent Starr.

"It's what?" I sat up and experienced anemic dizziness. "Oh for fuck's sake, I've slept through the morning!"

"I did wake you. I'm sorry. I just wanted to check on you."

"I'm fine, I don't think they're letting me out just yet," I replied and hobbled over to strap on the ankle brace for my bad leg: some soft tissue had been damaged in an altercation several weeks prior. After the brace, I flipped the lights back on full blast while Starr started talking about maps and climates. "Screw the weather forecast!" I finally interrupted rudely. "He needs shelter, messengers, and money. The odds are very good he has no idea *how* I found him, just that he was found."

Now fully awake I felt the full range of pains, aches, and assorted ickyness. The cramps were now just aches and parts of my body were sore from being in the same positions for so long. Add a headache and pain from my foot to the side effects of medications, anemia, and pregnancy and I almost felt like curling up and dying.

"Hang on a minute, Starr, I think I need to," I grabbed the table and swung my butt into a chair before I fell down. "Oh god," I mumbled to myself and put my head on the table.

Starr started calling my name repeatedly and I missed the beeping clanks of the door opening behind me. Muscles pulled me to him and lifted me with what seemed like disturbing ease. I didn't see anyone else, just Muscles tucking me into bed, holding a can and straw while I drank it, and helping me swallow two blue pills.

I lay there for some time; too sick to get up but not tired enough to sleep. Muscles sat on the couch and started reading a book while monitoring me. When my brain got its shit together I started to think about what Deuce had said about Muscles, Jack, being a 'life preserver'. What the hell was that supposed to mean?

I turned around and seized the remote for the window, flipping through channels until I got to a park in the rain. I turned the sound effects on and stared at the rain. Each of the scenes was basically a film on a loop but the loop times were different. I counted seconds against the patterns and tried to determine the loop cycle time. I had just decided that I needed to get up when Muscles appeared next to me.

"This is an ear thermometer," Muscles stated and showed me the item before gently placing it in my upper ear. "You're still a little warm. Water or soda?"

"Coke," I pulled myself up. "Is it dinner?"

"What do you want?"

"I don't know. Salad?" I requested and gave him the details. I heard him talking to the guards outside while I used the bathroom.

Muscles stuck around while I ate my salad, the medic came and gave me some early PT exercises for my ankle, and apple pie showed up sometime that evening. I did the PT exercises and discovered that Muscles was reading a Russian phrase book.

"Really, Russian?" I commented.

"*Da,*" Muscles replied.

"*Tovarich,*" I flashed a peace sign and got back to point-and-flexing. This started a conversation about pronunciation and emphasis syllables.

"I've been saying that wrong for a year and no one corrected me?" Muscles laughed a little.

"I've known some pretty interesting Russians," I admitted with a grin. "They hate him as much as I do." If Deuce had placed Muscles on my case, it was reasonable to think he'd be read in. "Russians have a different mentality, I knew a family that had lost two thirds of the sons and cousins trying to fight the Afghanis and I asked one of the sons left behind why he was out there with me. He said, "The root is still there so we'll keep digging," It was weird."

"I don't know any Russians."

"I used to. They're probably dead by now."

"So, dolphins?"

"They're good animals; helpful to the innocent and deadly to the sharks," I shrugged. "So what's it like, working for the big man?" My eyes had taken up flirting with Muscles and I wasn't inclined to stop them.

"It's a lot more interesting these days," Muscles replied. "Want to play a card game?"

"I don't know any," I lied. "The only thing I know with cards is target practice and covert communications."

"I suppose you shoot the ace of hearts every time," his tone was dry and I couldn't tell if he was being funny.

"Hearts are meant to be ripped through. Diamonds are begging to be shot and the little clover one just makes me think of leprechauns."

"So what's your beef with spades?"

"You know we're being watched, right?" I asked him and pointed to a badly hidden camera in a fake smoke detector.

"How long did it take you to spot?"

"Last night I was too drugged, but this morning, well, come on. It's not exactly Versailles in here, I'm going to notice things."

"Can I talk you into eating something?"

I had a brief and profane thought and kept it to myself. "Where did he dig you up?"

"Who?"

"The man. The boss; the big guy. Deuce or Trey or is he the biggest cheese now? He came and saw me earlier, Jack."

Muscles cracked a lopsided smile. "They said you were smart."

"They lied, I'm brilliant. Make sure you do your homework, Jack. I'm a real piece of work."

"I confuse you, don't I?" Muscles replied and retrieved a small plate of warm chocolate chip cookies from the food delivery ledge.

I didn't reply but I did stop pacing; it was killing my foot. He did confuse me, more than a little. "What do you want, Muscles?" I shot him a short glare and snatched a cookie when offered.

"Well you can definitely keep calling me Muscles," he replied dryly.

"Cow."

"Moo," he snapped back. I burst out in genuine laughter and almost immediately recoiled in pain. For a moment there was nothing confusing about him; he looped an arm around my back and helped me walk to bed. Muscles brought the cookies and served them like a butler.

"This kid had better be worth it," I announced half-jokingly.

"The side effects of the anesthesia will be better tomorrow."

"Are you just going to hang around? I do have work to do."

"Not today. You're not well enough to work."

I pushed myself into a sitting position and prepared to stand. "I'm well enough to pee and I don't like being listened to."

We all heard the signal bangs on the wall above the food slot.

"I'll leave you to it then. Get some rest!" Muscles added sternly and I went to the separated restroom while he left. Susan was there when I came out, along with guards Benzion and Morgan. I like Morgan; she's a good egg. Susan checked various things and asked embarrassing questions. She gave me pills to swallow and then checked that I had swallowed them; it's so insulting. I made a few extra faces and no one reacted.

"Can I go back to work tomorrow?" I asked as Susan left.

"We'll let you know," Susan replied and the door sealed behind them.

I sat there in the silence for a few minutes, hearing their footsteps as they completed the hall and got into the elevator. When I was very quiet I could hear the guards outside and determine who was there. I sat and listened until the guard changed.

"So what's the deal with that?" a man asked very quietly.

"It's only when she has solo company. Goode wants it off otherwise. This is the switch," Someone muttered something and there was a pause. "No, that's his guy. I don't know. Kinda queer. She calls him Muscles. Good luck."

Someone walked away.

"Fuck it," I muttered and went to bed.

The dawn came the following morning, at least according to my artificial window. I stayed totally still for several minutes in hopes that I would drift off to sleep again. Finally the sounds of a drill in direct proximity to my cell interested me and I sat up in time to see a wooden flap of some kind swing down over the food window entrance. It swung open and closed, open and closed and then there were more drilling noises followed by the sounds of a vacuum briefly. I got up to look at it and the swinging flap felt like cork. Cork is good for a lot of neat things, but it is mainly a sound and heat barrier. I leapt to the conclusion that the installation of the board was connected to the installation of the camera.

Fury is an old friend of mine. He's gotten me through some truly ridiculous times and will probably pull me through any obstacle if I let him. I didn't want to let the camera know how I felt about all this so I calmly walked to the refrigerator, pulled out a protein drink and a bottle of water, and proceeded to the bathroom. I shut the door, briefly did the calculations and stepped into the shower. Behind the brief curtain I knew they would have no line of sight on me whatsoever.

I sat in the shower stall and got comfortable. I tried to guess how long it would take them to realize I was there and wasn't showering. If the camera actually was on then it would be just a few minutes. If it was genuinely off it would take longer. They would have to raise the flap to give me breakfast. They would expect me to take the food. They would expect me to flip the privacy screen on the proper door's window.

They could bite me.

I sat there in the dry shower and heard the repressed sounds of the arrival of breakfast. No one came. I heard muffled sounds of someone on the speaker briefly but no one came. I sat there and thought about this new dynamic where I am openly spied upon and anything I do can be used against me. They must have installed the board because they figured out my trick where I can listen in on the guards in the hall. I briefly wondered what they would do now that they knew I could hide in the shower.

Nope. We are playing in my territory and if they want my help with their precious quest to find Waldo they're going to play by my rules. Pregnancy might cause a temporary drop in IQ but I have plenty to spare. I could pop out a dozen babies at once and still make Mensa.

I sat there and began to think I should have brought a book. My mind wandered back to how bored I was getting when I actually did find Bin Laden. It was an accidental find, mostly courtesy of a nerd whose probable death I am now responsible for. My file on Bin Laden, well, unless he's moved too I can send him a Christmas card. That thought made me smile a little; how shocked would he be? If I handed the file to the US intelligence teams here they might find him and do whatever they want but there was no guarantee that they would then go after Omar. If I don't give them the file, they might decide to just flush me and Omar and pursue Bin Laden without me. People don't know about Omar, the quietest mastermind in history, the man who actually put the men on the planes that killed my mother.

I stretched out my legs and got comfortable in the tiled shower. My butt was going numb and I started to reconsider this whole prisoner thing. *Sometimes I think this team is full of idiots more willing to play the political games than interested people who want to get bad guys. Individuals seem fine, but when they're all together it's like the room is being pumped full of stupid gas.* This is how people like me get away with what we do: trampling borders, running underground markets, assassins and thieves for hire; intelligence tit-for-tat trading, single day alliances. There's money in it for those who can survive but the expected lifespan echoes that of a young black American gang member.

I figured out how to escape three weeks ago. The only problem is that people will have to die; at least seven by my best calculations. I actually like most of the people here; some of them are kind to me. Resolution arrived on the wings of boredom: the camera had to go. I looked around at my resources: they were scarce and I began to think about how to use the washcloth, floss, and a pair of tweezers in defense of my privacy.

I drank the protein shake: I was still so weak from losing the blood and from the drugs. *Oh, I had forgotten about the drugs. Damn. They'll be here any time to give them to me. I need to take them. Fuck. Fine, I'll take the meds and then come right back here. I already know how long I can go without food…*

I felt a vaguely familiar warmth in my nose and my vision blurred in my right eye. I blinked and the lid was wet, cooling rapidly in the air. *Oh for God's sake, this is not happening. This is not happening. I am not crying! I don't fucking cry!* My nose started running and I reached out and pulled in the roll of toilet paper. I opened the lid of the toilet so I could immediately dispose of the evidence. *I do not cry and people do not know about any incidental crying-related crap.*

My left eye started leaking and my chest did strange things: my breathing pattern became erratic. I blew my nose a few times and then just let it run. *Screw it; I'll just shower when this is over. This had better be some pregnancy related business because Alexis Johnston does not cry and Belle Jones sure as hell doesn't sob in a shower stall. In prison. While cameras spy on her. And she's too sick and weak and tired and frustrated to...and the bastard's gone. Disappeared. Out somewhere else planning his next mass murder. Killing people he's never met from a thousand miles away. Well, shit. I'm crying.*

Chapter Two: The Asset

It almost felt good, in a desperate to die sort of way. I hiccupped and blubbered and ran through piece after piece of snotty toilet paper until I felt like I better flush the toilet and start again. I sipped water when I could while trying to calm myself but trigger after trigger flooded me and I lost it over again. I started to realize that this had nothing to do with my little wiggle-worm but I promised myself no one would ever see me like this and I squinted my eyes shut.

"Hey," someone said very softly and gently and I felt strong hands behind my shoulder and around my forearm.

"No!" I shrieked and I sounded insane. "No! NO!" I thrashed my arms and scratched and clawed anything I could get hold of. I pushed and pinched and tried to kick Muscles because nothing was more important than not going back out into the room; not letting the world see my shameful state.

"Sergeant?" a woman asked from outside.

"Code, I don't know, Code Amber," Muscles replied, "Give me a few minutes." He closed the bathroom door while I scuttled into a corner and prepared to defend my position from my squat against the tile. To my genuine surprise he sat down, giving me a solid three feet of space.

I said nothing: there was nothing ready in my brain scripted for a conversation with anyone. I stared at him and he didn't stare back; he seemed more interested in the area around me.

"I don't know what the code is for 'curled up in the shower refusing to leave.' I mean, I'm sure they have one," Muscles said with a light note. I caught onto his game.

"I know what you're doing," I accused and my voice sounded pathetic.

"Do you?"

"No, no idea," I admitted. I was too fried to serve my own purposes.

"Do you want your breakfast? I think the bagel is still warm and that strawberry cream cheese looked delicious."

I squirmed a little, unwilling to give up my position.

"We can eat it right here. I know I've had meals in worse locations; I'm betting you have too." Muscles offered and opened the door. Officer Morgan handed over the plate of pre-shmeared bagel and he held it out to me. "Are you going to throw this plate at me?" he asked sternly before letting go. I shook my head and he must have believed me.

I ate breakfast silently and he indirectly watched me.

"Officer Morgan's your favorite, right?" Muscles asked and didn't wait. "She's going to chill out in your room but we can send the others away. Would that help?"

I nodded because I wanted as few witnesses as possible to witness my unraveling. Muscles gave the order and rolled the displaced water bottle back to me. I put the plate on the ground and slid it gently in his direction as we completed the exchange. I stared at him and drank the water. What did Deuce mean, 'life preserver'?

Muscles looked totally comfortable leaning against the door. His skin tight black shirt showed some evidence from my attack and his cheek was bleeding with a single scratch mark across his cheekbone. I felt bad about that: it may have been the first time I didn't mean to inflict harm on someone. I squared up some toilet tissue and held it out to him.

"So, I gather this is Alexis," Muscles said and lightly touched the paper to his face. I opened my mouth to deny it and was stopped by his eyes.

"Psychologist," I said.

"You want to talk to one?"

"No. You," I accused and blew my nose again.

"No. Not me. I'm not that kind of brainy."

"Sergeant."

"Yes. Well, no," Muscles replied. "I'm going to be honest with you because I'd like you to be honest with me. I was a Sergeant, Sergeant First Class, and they call me that here because they like to remind me that I'm beneath them. I'm not strictly Army. I'm in one of a few "special" units. I work for the man you call Deuce. I just call him sir."

"Jack."

"Yes, that's my name."

"Alexis."

"Yes, that's your name, your first name. Before Belle or Beauty. There are parts of the world now that shudder at the word, 'Beauty', parts of the world that need cleaning up."

I hid my face in my hands. We sat there for a few more silent minutes until someone lightly knocked on the bathroom door.

"Sergeant," Officer Morgan said quietly, "A moment." Muscles stepped out and left the door open.

"Can you get her out?" I recognized Captain Stover's voice.

"She's in no danger," Muscles replied.

"Are you?" Officer Morgan asked.

"What does she want?" someone else asked.

"She needs to take her medications. Slip a sedative in, at the very least she needs to be under observation."

"What do you think I'm here for?" Muscles asked. "You can let me handle it or you can call my boss. Your option," he returned and closed the door behind him.

"Omar," I greeted him. "Al-Zahrani. We lost him. They only care about Bin Laden, that's their game."

"The world knows about Bin Laden; not so much about Omar."

"I found Waldo: Bin Laden. I found him and I found Omar and now we've lost them both."

"The raid was on Omar's location; why would you be certain that we've lost Bin Laden too?"

"They cannot stay separate for long; Omar is the vine and Bin Laden is just a big loud grape off of that vine." I shook my head.

"Well, do we know what they were up to last? Maybe they went to blow something up," Muscles offered.

In the other room I heard a loud woman's voice. "Everyone out now!" Director Goode sounded irritated. A minute later she opened the door to the bathroom and handed Muscles a cup of pills. "She does need to take these. You'll hear from him," she said to Muscles and handed him an earpiece. "Let me know what I can do to help."

"Thank you, Director." Muscles was standing at that point and he sat on the toilet to hand me the cup of pills. I downed them all with a large swig of water, knowing that there may or may not be a sedative in the mix. "Sir," Muscles stared straight ahead into the wall near the door. "Negative. Affirmative." He paused and listened. "Environment. Affirmative. I," he paused and I heard a slight buzz in his ear. "I will take that under advisement. Understood sir." He checked his thin watch which was usually tucked under a sleeve. "Understood sir. We will." His body language told me when he was done with the conversation.

"Is it bad?" I asked.

"He's on his way. I have ten minutes to get your butt into a chair out there," Muscles told me openly. I tucked my knees in closer to my chest in childish defiance. "Alexis,"

"They'll see me," I mumbled explanation.

"I'm on your side. He's on your side. He hates Omar as much as you do. What if I sit you facing away from the door?"

Away from the door would also put my back to the camera. I assessed Muscles briefly but knew my decision. He was going to put my butt in a chair no matter what, so I may as well keep a little shred of dignity. I rocked onto my side and pushed my legs underneath me to rise.

"Thank you." He wet a washcloth in the sink and handed it to me. I wiped my face clean and washed my hands and peeked out the door briefly to see the empty room. All the lights, including the emergency lights were on and Muscles helped guide me to a chair at the dining table. My back was to the camera, as promised.

"Thank you," I said quietly and swallowed several times.

"Okay, listen. He's going to come in here and I do not want you to get hurt. So these are the rules: stay where you are, stay calm, and I think we'll trim those nails." Muscles took some steps behind me and returned with a black bag which he opened to produce a nail clipper and disposable nail file. I sat very quietly while he cut down my three dangerous nails and filed them smooth. "I moonlight as a manicurist," he joked and I smiled.

"I am sorry I attacked you. I didn't mean to; you didn't deserve that," I admitted. I really did feel like Alexis again, pre-vicious killer.

"Hazard of the profession. You could have done much worse."

"I won't make you hurt me. I'll do whatever you need," I confessed.

"What inspired this round of strange behavior?" Muscles asked.

I pointed to the food flap, which was closed again, and up to the camera. "They're spying on me now, and it's not just when you're here. I used to hear things, noises in the hall, people chatting, they used the camera to figure that out and this morning they put that thing up. I can't, I can't, I can't," the words were stuck in a loop and I couldn't move forward in the sentence. "I barely tolerate being here but I was okay because this is my apartment. It's my home. Now I'm a rat and they don't even, they don't give a damn about me or about Ozzie, they just want to look for Waldo and I'm just a tool."

"Alexis, I need you to calm down. Right now, deep breath," Muscles ordered and rubbed a spot on my lower ribs until my lung obediently expanded. "And again," he instructed and I heard the door prepare to open. "Stay put and stay calm."

"Muscles," my voice squeaked and I knew I wasn't ready for Deuce to come in. There was so much I needed to tell Muscles. It was too late.

"Hello Beauty," Deuce greeted and Muscles kept a hand on my shoulder to keep me in place while the older man walked around and joined me at the table. "Jack, you okay?"

"Yes sir," Muscles replied and subtly swept the fingernail clippings off the table.

"Beauty, I'm a little concerned. Tell me what's going on."

"I can't deal with the camera," I confessed to the table. "They're spying on me now and using stuff against me."

Deuce sat for a moment. "Did you attack any of them or just Jack?"

"Just Muscles. Jack," I corrected. "Sir. I wasn't, I didn't mean, I'm sorry." I spoke only to the table.

"Jack, do you want to be moved?" Deuce asked.

"No sir, I'd rather stay," Jack replied.

"What if we killed the camera and had Jack bring in a portable eye when he's visiting? That was the only accepted use of the camera to begin with," Deuce proposed.

"The other change was the flip board there," Jack pointed. "Perhaps we can try to keep that open; keep it from getting claustrophobic in here."

"Works for me. Now: Omar Al-Zahrani and Bin Laden," Deuce changed the subject.

"I think you need the second chip," I admitted. "I believe it will save us the time we need in relocating these two."

"Where is the second chip?" Deuce asked.

"The camera first. The chip is in easy reach from here," I assured him honestly.

"Any new ideas on Omar?"

"I really need newspapers. I think we can cross out Egypt, Israel, and Syria. They had a lot of ties in Afghanistan, so maybe Turkmenistan, Tajikistan; I doubt Uzbekistan because there isn't anyone in that country that he hasn't pissed off. Take a good look at Pakistan. A long look. They're smart, especially Ozzie. If I'm being hunted by the US, I'm heading to a nuclear country that the US doesn't want a war with. We made major advances with their cyber network; let's get locators going on all of those devices to see who's moving."

"We started on that; it's a lot of data to process but we're focused. People are starting to buy that they're linked."

"In the world, how many people know I've been captured?" I wondered.

"Just allies. UK, Israel, France."

"Not Spain?" I asked and he shook his head. "I know a man who sells a thing to a person."

"And…"

"Omar uses a specific set of software that isn't readily available in that part of the world. It lets him scan the people who work with him and do an automatic identity and background check against everything on the internet."

"That sounds brilliant."

"It is; makes it really hard to get close to him. If he had to leave his software or machines, he's going to need replacements."

"The Spaniard is a provider?"

I nodded slowly, basking in my own brilliance. "It's him or the Greek; the third provider is dead."

"Okay. Give me the name of the Spaniard and we'll rip that camera out right now," Deuce offered and I willingly gave up the member of the ambassador's staff. Deuce shook my hand and Jack stood on a chair to dismantle the camera's lame camouflage and pull the unit out of the wall. Fatigue swept through me quickly and I suspected that they had slipped a sedative into the cup.

"Jack," I called and set my head down on the table with a yawn.

"You're okay, sweet Beauty," Deuce passed and lightly stroked my hair. "We're going to take care of you."

I just knew I was so incredibly tired that I was about to fall asleep on the table. I heard beeping behind me and the lights dimmed down and I smelled Muscle's deodorant.

"You're okay, Alexis," Muscles said and I believed him.

"Sweetie?" A familiar maternal voice called. "Sweetie, its two p.m. Do you want lunch?"

I opened my eyes to see Agent Lisa Won, the sweet and beautiful DIA agent working the cyber side of things in this collaboration. I was in bed, which I didn't remember, but I felt well rested. My eyes were still puffy from the morning's hysterics and my head hurt the way it should when you go bat-shit crazy.

"Do we have something?" I remembered all of the other times she had visited me; it was always because they needed help with something or had made a breakthrough.

"Yeah, sweetie," she spoke quietly, almost too quietly. "I need your help with something."

"Sure. Where's Muscles?"

"He's just outside. I need your help. It's about the leak."

I was now fully awake. "Who is it?"

"We're not sure, but I know how to find out. Everyone knows you are brilliant and have had experience with tactics and programs we're not familiar with. If they believed you had developed a program which would track international transmissions,"

"It would have been a phone call," I shook my head. "VOIP line, but they work in cyber, they aren't going to risk being tracked like that."

"You're probably right," she sucked on her inner cheek. "How confident are you as an actress?"

"Stake my life on it," I replied.

"If they'll let me take you upstairs for an hour," Won said.

"Put me in a lab and leave the door open," I agreed.

Ten minutes later I was in a wheelchair with three regular guards and Muscles escorting me up to the IT section.

"Are you sure about this?" Agent Won asked in a normal tone.

"I'm positive. He told me the whole area's calls are monitored; the new technology, well, anyway, I shouldn't say anything about that," I replied on our premise. She put me in a lab booth and I started hacking away at the computer.

"What's up?" Agent Kmetz asked.

"There is a record in a database of all of our calls, including the internet and satellite calls. It's a little precaution someone upstairs took when we set up this task force. Anyway, it keeps the records for a month in case something happens," Agent Won explained.

"That's creepy," Kmetz stated but kept moving. I silently prayed that he wasn't the leak: I had grown to like the pimply prodigy.

"Lisa, I'm almost in. I need the passcodes," I called audibly. "Aw, hell, hang on. It's getting harder to hack America," I muttered and focused on fake-hacking. It was right around three p.m.: peak hour as the shifts met and people transferred in and out of their stations. "Can I get a little more bandwidth here?" I asked.

"She needs more bandwidth, the system isn't letting her in," Agent Won repeated into the main room and one of the geeks sat down to try to redirect computing power toward me using a throttle protocol.

"Agent Won, I'm hitting something," that geek reported.

"Aaaaaaannnnddd," I held the word out as I pretended to breach something. "Oh! Come! On! Comeon-comeon-comeon-comeon…Okay. No problem! Now we just pull them all up and," my screen went dead. Kmetz and Won snuck in with me and lit up the partnered computer to quickly trace the source of my computer's death. A number came up and a horrible expression crossed Kmetz' face. He's practically a teenager so it was interesting to see that depth of emotion on his mug.

"Cologne!" Kmetz shouted and was rammed over as the man made a desperate break for it. I don't know what he was thinking; it takes half an hour to get out of this section.

"AIIIIGHIIII!" I heard a deathly shriek and stood up to find Muscles standing in the doorway of the booth, blocking me in safely while he shocked the crap out of the traitor with a Taser.

"He was too close to you," Muscles said and gave him another jolt before letting the soldiers take over.

"Definitely too close to her," Won agreed. "I'd say she was in direct danger. Don't you think so, Kmetz?"

"I think he should have shot him," Kmetz replied. "Clean up on aisle one!"

Muscles cleared his weapon and holstered it before picking up the phone on his hip. "Sir? I have good news and good news. We have the leak and I needed to stun him into submission," he paused. "Cyber department, name Cologne. We're there now." Agent Won high fived me over his head. "Right away sir. Three sir? Yes sir," he hung up, "We need to go back right now."

They rolled my wheelchair right over the puddle of urine and we pushed through the halls rapidly.

"We're in trouble," I knew in the elevator.

"He was not pleased that you left the cell," Muscles admitted and once the doors opened we jaunted rapidly down the halls again until we reached my hall. I think we both thanked god that Deuce was not actually there. "Lunch now?"

"Definitely," I agreed and we sat at the table and ate a pair of salads. Lunch was gone before we received our next visitor by way of the speaker.

"Belle?" Director Goode asked.

"Yes ma'am?"

"I heard you identified the leak."

"Yes ma'am. Agent Won and I collaborated on that."

"And I understand that Jack neutralized the man during an escape attempt? A number of people were quite adamant that it was completely necessary to use non-lethal force; I doubt there will be much of an investigation."

"Agent Kmetz thinks he should have shot him," I shared. "Jack is here with me," I added.

"Yes, I expect so. You may expect some files regarding an earlier conversation you had with the man you call Deuce."

"I will be here."

"Good. How are you feeling?"

"I feel a little weird. It's probably the medicine."

"Let me know if you need anything. You can always ask for me." Director Goode paused and then I heard the click.

"Okay," I mentally regrouped. I usually just think in my head but Muscles showed no signs of leaving.

"Physical therapy?" Muscles suggested.

"Good," I got out the exercise band and started to use it. "We may have plugged the leak."

"They will need to clean him up before we can interrogate," Muscles replied.

I glanced across his body again and discovered that the yellow gun was missing. "You took it off," I observed, "How did I not notice that?"

"You're still drugged, there was a lot of activity. They have my stuff outside but I don't need that kind of force with you. You don't deserve that kind of force."

I stared at him again and realized that he made eye contact on purpose. Was there kindness or smarm behind those green eyes? "Do you do this often?"

"Do what often?" he asked, "do those exercises slower."

I slowed down and did them properly. "This! This weirdness right here."

Muscles sat down and crossed his arms facing me in my desk chair. "Tell me about the rest of the team," he requested.

"Okay, George, Agent George Tomopolis; he was my initial contact. FBI all the way; he even smells FBI-ish. John, CIA, looks like that cartoon character with the pointy hair. I thought he sucked for a while but I'm starting to warm to him. Agent Starr; FBI sniper with profiling skills, she's the pregnant blond one. Sweet kid. Agent Won, DIA, IT queen who lets me hack people. Director Goode," I pointed to the speaker, "you've met the medical staff and then there are a handful of others. There's a shrink who is only interested in my head and a different shrink who mostly wants to get stuff out of my head, that's Tom McEwen."

"Is John the one who came to the hospital?"

"Yes, he brought me the dolphin. I expected George. Has he tried to see me?" I asked.

"It's possible," Muscles replied.

"So what's the deal now?" Genuine curiosity reached me. This was all very strange: usually I'm not locked in a cell and if I am there's always visitors. Tom, Starr, George, Stover, SOMEBODY should have been here by now. Instead it was Deuce, Muscles, and Director Goode. "And while I'm asking questions, what did Deuce mean when he called you my life preserver?"

"Hold that thought," Muscles said and picked up a radio on the food ledge, which was open now. He spoke with someone and I went to the bathroom.

Okay, I have got to get my shit together. I thought as I graced the throne. *Muscles is not family; he's some guy I didn't know last week, some guy that someone is probably paying very well to keep me in commission. Yes, that's what it is! That's what Deuce meant! I'm just an asset they need. Alright, facts: I am going nowhere until both Bin Laden and Al-Zahrani are dead or captured. What I need is to find one of them and entice the other to visit. Seals in and out, or maybe Rangers. I don't know. I do like the Rangers better. Focus!* I pulled up my scrubs and realized that I had never actually showered this morning. I failed the sniff test and shucked off my dirty clothes to get into the shower.

The hot water and soap helped immensely. I was glad that my hair was already washed when someone knocked on the bathroom door.

"Alexis?" Muscles asked.

"I'm actually showering!" I replied and looked around to find my razor. "Where the hell is my razor?"

"They took it!"

"Well give it back, I need to shave my pits!"

"How do I know you won't hurt yourself with it?"

"It's a safety razor!" I rolled my eyes. "What am I going to do, nick myself?"

"Okay, I'm coming in," he replied after a minute. I cannot count how many men have seen me naked but it was always on my terms. Muscles' hand came in and delivered the razor and waited there until I put the handle back in his hand. "There is a meeting tonight at five; they're going to hook up the speakerphone."

I turned off the water. "Why not just take me up there? I mean, it is here, right? Everything on the task force is here."

"We're not going out," Muscles explained as he exited the bathroom.

"Don't think I missed you dodging the question about this weirdness." I wrapped myself in the towel and marched out to find a change of clothing.

"Hopefully they will explain "the weirdness"," Muscles offered and politely looked in another direction.

"Weirdness!" I took the clothes and slid back into the bathroom to dress. I came out and saw a huge accordion folder on the table so I tore into it.

"Those are from upstairs," Muscles stated.

"Pictures. They're all pictures. Dozens of them, hundreds," I observed and peered through them. "This is, this is, okay, that is definitely Libya. These are Israel, Tel Aviv and," I squinted, "That's me. And that there; but this angle, this wasn't a satellite capture." I sank into a chair and flipped through to photos that were more clearly of me in various guises but still Belle Jones out and about being an operative. Egypt, Libya, Israel, Lebanon, France, the horn, the Dead Sea, the streets of Iraq, the house I stayed in while in Syria. People: long perspective shots of people; friends, allies, enemies, marks, assignments. Some photos were just of locations but they all looked familiar. The table wasn't big enough, not for this kind of data explosion, so I swept up everything and dumped it all on my bed.

"Is that you?" Muscles looked at the photo closest to him. They were of varying sizes: some larger and some the ordinary size for something popped out of a photo machine.

"They're out of order. Or," I paused and stared, "no, they're sorted. Ozzie-relevant and everything else. This is insane. March, June, February, this is all the way back in October of last year. These photos are a year, yes," I glanced around manically. "This is almost everywhere I've been this last year. This is," I heaved in a breath because I seemed to have run out of oxygen. "Who, who sent these?"

"It could have been Director Goode or Deuce. Does it matter?"

"YES!" I almost shrieked and heard crazy Belle rising up. "Do you have any idea how creepy this is?"

"It is pretty creepy, but there's a decent chance they weren't targeting you, just the places and people. I was told you were like an army of one out there. The chief said that there are parts of the world where just using the word for 'beauty' can send people running."

"Deuce pretty much only calls me Beauty." I remembered and closed my eyes, trying to sort my thoughts. "Abba, my Israeli...person," I failed to describe a high-ranking avuncular Mossad official, "he called me Beauty. Director Goode calls me Belle, that's what I go by here," my eyes flew open and I turned to face Muscles.

"I need you to calm down."

"You have never once called me Belle. They all call me Belle, Belle Jones and you have never once called me by anything other than Alexis. NO ONE here uses that name."

"Well none of them ever saw Alexis Johnson."

The change caught my ear. "What did you just say?"

"None of them, the guards and agents, even senior leadership, none of them, you never let them see you. Never let them meet Alexis," Muscles replied.

"Alexis who?"

"Alexis Johnson."

"Who?"

"Alexis Johnson, what?"

"Where did you get that name?"

"I was briefed!"

"No, I mean, where. File? Paper? Fortune cookie? Phone conversation? Who gave you that name and how did they give it to you?"

"Look, I realize that you turned into Belle Jones for a reason, but," Muscles moved around the room to very indirectly get closer to me.

"Answer the question," I demanded.

"In person briefing in a contained facility. As far as I know, the information is Top Secret Compartmentalized and no one outside this room knows," Muscles finally yielded.

"Look me in the eye and say that again," I challenged.

"Why?" Muscles made eye contact and seemed genuinely confused.

"Because this," I pointed to the stalker fodder on my bed, "is creepy but that name is truly alarming."

"I was orally briefed by a high-ranking person in a secure facility. The briefing included your medical history's highlights and other information that I need to secure you without harming you."

"Why do they trust you so much?" I'll admit to anyone at any time that I am a pain in the ass, but questions keep me breathing so I ask a lot of them.

"Because they know me. Why do you trust me?" he asked and I didn't blink. "Look, I don't know your life story. I do know that they call you Belle Jones or Beauty. I know that Isabelle Jones was not your real name, that Alexis Johnson was and like many people who hide behind a persona and a name, a mask for the work they have to do, there's a real person behind Belle and that person is a scared, scarred, slightly desperate young person with some serious backstory that drove you where you are."

"I'm in a prison cell!"

"You are the person who found someone that no one else could and I mean, they have been trying."

"Bin Laden," I scoffed.

Muscles shook his head slightly, "No. Ozzie. You went out as a teenager and brought down some of the worst people in the world."

"I'm twenty-four and a murdering, lying, stealing, cheating, ice-hearted," I took a breath.

"I'm not saying that all that didn't happen. I'm saying that those were all Belle Jones and you don't really need her now."

"Alexis is dead."

"No, she was just hibernating."

"No, I killed her. There was a backstory and everything, drowned in a lake. I am Belle, I am Beauty. I am a monster and grown men wet themselves before me."

"Okay, maybe I'm looking at Belle Jones right now," Muscles was willing to concede.

"No, this isn't some schizoid bipolar multiple personality wig-on wig-off bullshit, there's only one of me," I resisted.

"Can I use your bathroom?"

"Of course," I immediately responded. It didn't take thought and besides, there was a whole bed's worth of my life in front of me. A thought struck me and I gathered up all of the photographs taken more than a week before I found the deadly duo. "This is what we need to look at," I informed Muscles as he wiped his wet hands on a napkin to dry them. "Someone took these pictures, and that's nice and all but we're looking for any common faces or things."

"Why?"

"Ozzie is smart, brilliant, and if he thought someone was close to exposing him or giving him to any of the nations that want him, he'd be interested. We can assume these photos were taken by the US or an ally. They were interested in me enough to put in the effort and the miles, why wouldn't Ozzie," I didn't have to finish the sentence.

"You said he checks out everyone through that system with the photos," Muscles agreed.

At least he catches on fast, I thought. "I took myself off of the internet three years ago when I realized that he had that ability, or that anyone had that ability. I had an arrangement with someone so they do a daily sweep of my names, photo, likeness, and so on."

"The US would probably love to get their hands on something like that program."

"Yeah, well I'm giving you Bin Laden and Al-Zahrani, as well as most of their upper networks. Don't get greedy," I smirked and flipped the lights all the way up.

We searched in silence for a while.

"So what do you want me to call you?" Muscles asked.

I opened my mouth to say, "Belle," but my tongue froze. "I don't know."

"I have a feeling we're going to see a lot of each other."

"Especially if you keep interrupting my showers," I joked.

"You wanted the razor," Muscles reminded me. "Am I a lot for you to process?"

"I just don't know where to sort you," I admitted casually and picked up two more photos.

Muscles' attention appeared to be on the photos as well. "Where are you?" he asked without looking up.

"Underground prison cell," my smart mouth replied. He didn't respond at all and the childishness passed. "This is all Syria."

"Are bicycles common in Lebanon?"

"Yeah, of course."

"Look at this one," Muscles pointed to a blue and silver bicycle with a distinctive water bottle in a brown basket. It showed up in several of the Lebanese photographs at different times of the day. "It could belong to the person who took the photos."

"They'd be an idiot to leave their transportation so close to the target. Okay; orange and green metal water bottle," I squinted.

"It's a huge network. It's not likely that the same person followed you internationally."

"Are you talking about the good guys or the bad guys?" I inquired.

"What do you mean by 'bad guys'?"

"Terrorists, child molesters, human traffickers, oppressors and those who are willing to help harm innocent people," I proposed the definition.

"With Ozzie and Waldo at the top of the list?"

We were on opposite sides of the bed and looked at each other for the first time in a while. "God can do his own judging. I'm not some angel or saint; I can't help everyone. They're at the top of the list because of what they did to me."

"What did they do to you?" Muscles baited.

"I had a chance once, a long time ago. I had a real opportunity to become a normal person in a normal world, to live in your universe where life is pretty uncomplicated. They robbed me of that life. They stole Alexis John-," I stopped myself because he didn't have the right name. "They stole her happy-ever-after. You know I didn't even get to bury my mother? No, Ozzie and the bastard took even that, even a gravestone, nothing!" I felt strange things rising and falling inside of me and it was almost dizzying. "She knew me, she understood me, she LOVED ME and they fucking murdered her!" I knelt first, leaning my head against the corner of the bed and then sat down on the rug there and leaned my shoulder into the mattress. "Hundreds, thousands, hundreds of thousands of innocent people are dead because of two men and their bullshit philosophy. Millions of people had the potential to turn into me, to turn into a heartless machine on a mission and I didn't even get it right! They are still out there." A thought lit up in my brain. "Oh my God," I scrambled to my feet. "Get me Deuce, get the Director. I know how to find them. No!" I realized. We didn't actually have the software. *Maybe from the Spaniard*, "I was going to use that internet identification program across IMINT but we don't actually have that software," I explained.

"IMINT can't cover the whole world," Muscles stated. He had started stacking the photographs. "Come on, we'll group these by location and date and have a team of nerdlings upstairs go through them. We found the water bottle; they can project and scan and do all kinds of analyses on these to find common factors. If we identify someone, we'll run them with what we have. Maybe we'll get the Spanish thing, maybe we won't, but we're not useless without you."

"Nerdlings?" I echoed the word but started to group the photos with him. I noticed when his back got a little straighter and knew that he was receiving instructions through his earpiece.

"Do you know a Dr. McEwen?" he asked as he checked his watch. "He is going to join us for the 1700 meeting."

"Dr. Tom McEwen, psychologist agent profile king," I explained in brief. We stacked the photos into a five inch pile crisscrossed because we didn't have a better way to separate them. The top of each section had a torn piece of paper from my notepad with the dates and locations to identify that section of the pile.

"Belle?" I heard one of the guards, probably Shapiro. "Agent McEwen is here to see you. Sergeant, he brought the eye with him."

"Clear for entry," Muscles replied; I was over by the food slot setting out the stack.

"Belle, you look good," Tom greeted me, "Getting around on that foot I see."

"Tom, have you met Mus--," I stopped myself from introducing him as Muscles. "Sergeant Jack Something."

"I'm read in," Tom greeted and shook Jack's hand.

"Anyone want to read me in?" I asked. I always view psychologists with suspicion. My brain is unique and deadly and I don't like sharing my thoughts.

"We're about to," Tom replied. He pulled my desk chair out to the other side of the room and sat. The eye, as he called it, was about six inches high and was set upon my desk. The camera was round and encased in a shiny black glass like they do in airports and banks. A bright blue light seemed to indicate its activity. "I came early to see how you were."

"Where is George?" I asked point blank. "Even Agent Starr gave me a call since they brought me home."

"Agent Tomopolis is on vacation," Tom lied.

"Bullshit," I called him on it.

"She is really hard to lie to," Tom addressed Muscles.

"Yeah, and she hates being talked over," I added and sat on the futon, "Try again."

"Director Goode will cover that," Tom eluded. "How are you feeling?"

I ignored him and Muscles handed me a bottle of water. I cracked it open and drank without thinking about it.

"Well how's this going?" Tom wiggled his finger to indicate Muscles and me.

"A hell of a lot better than this is going," I indicated him and me.

"I'm getting a lot of anger."

"You're lying to me, were you expecting laughter?" I asked bluntly. "If George doesn't care about me, I'm fine with that. Did you hear that I caught the leak earlier? Yeah. Jack made him pee himself."

"I'm glad that the baby is doing well. I'm a little more concerned about you," Tom did the psychologist lean-forward with his elbows. "Would you rather talk to Cyndy?"

"That's the other shrink," I explained to Muscles, "I'm fine, Tom."

There was a bee-bop sound and I glanced up at the speaker. "This is Director Elsa Goode with the," she listed off a whole bunch of letters and names. I gathered that Deuce and someone who works with him were in on the conference along with Agent Won, John, some IMINT specialist, someone who sounded like Agent Won's boss, and Leona Hampshire from the Department of Homeland Security. "The information we are about to cover is top secret compartmentalized need to know only," Director Goode added. I noticed that the flap over the slot was lowered quietly and realized its usefulness.

"Recent circumstances have forced us to make a number of changes," Deuce stated and Muscles stood up. "We are fully engaged on relocating Osama Bin Laden and at this time we are officially extending the manhunt to Omar Al-Zahrani. This manhunt will not be considered closed until we confirm capture of both these targets. Live capture continues to be preferred but death is acceptable," Deuce continued. "My office is relocating to this base until this mission has been completed. My team and my superiors recognize that our best asset in this war is in this building. We are dedicated to ensuring the health and well-being of this asset and for that I have brought in a specialist. All access to the asset will be run through my office. All resources required for the asset will be run through my office. We have already made significant gains under the new program," he continued and he talked for a while. Then he talked about Omar Al-Zahrani, the network we had identified through cyber, and the best bets to locate both of the bastards. Evidently they had run a raid on a location they thought Bin Laden might be at, but it was only mildly successful. Four dead terrorists are nice, but specifics really do matter. As I listened I was thinking at a million miles an hour and my brain and gut agreed that they needed that chip. When there was a pause I looked at Muscles and ignored Tom.

"Let's get the chip," I said quietly, unsure if they could hear me upstairs. Muscles nodded silently.

"The second chip? The Bin Laden's other file chip?" Tom tried to enter our world.

"Tomopolis?" I asked him pointedly.

"Everything okay down there?" Director Goode asked.

"Miss Jones wants to know where Agent Tomopolis is," Tom admitted.

"Agent Tomopolis is engaged on a different project now," Director Goode informed.

"Did he want to leave?" I asked.

"Yes, it was his request."

"We have chased Bin Laden for 9 years now. Lots of people get burned out," Tom tried to console.

Muscles looked at me and I saw a hint of compassion in his eyes. He wasn't a strange drone in a hospital room anymore and I now knew that his expressions were subtle to the point of robotic.

"Director!" I stood and stared at the green eyes while speaking to the speakerphone.

"Yes Belle?"

"I'm ready to give up the second data chip," I announced loud and proud.

"Excellent," I could hear her pleasure. "Where should we look?"

"My cell," I called out. "You're going to need a scalpel and a pair of tweezers," I informed Muscles and grinned.

Chapter Three: The Cards

At 0830 the next morning there were way too many people in my room.

Late last night after the meeting we broke the new cell confinement rule in a mass pilgrimage to the medical center. Agent Won stood outside with Muscles as they took a detailed X-ray of my left foot, specifically my medial calcaneus. They had to blow the image up a bit but there it was!

The chip was small, about the size of my pinky nail after being trimmed close. It had been carefully implanted under the tough skin on my heel and frankly my body is covered in scars so the little J-flap was unnoticeable. Feet are full of little lines like that and there isn't much in the way of blood flow in that part of the body. When I had put it there six months earlier, just before my trip to France, I had sealed the chip in a plastic coat and slid it under the skin. I used ice as anesthesia and super-glue as stitches.

"Mask?" Muscles handed me the surgical mask. They had rolled a gurney into the room and they expected me to hop up and let them slice my foot open. They made the marks before setting up their little operating room.

"I really would prefer to do it myself," I restated. "Look, it's not deep, come in at an angle from here," I pointed.

"This is going to hurt." Susan jabbed a needle into my foot. "Okay, masks, Belle, please just relax this whole leg. The anesthetic will kick in shortly."

Jolly Gay Medic attached the oxygen reader on my right index finger and slid on the heart monitors so fast I barely noticed he was in my shirt.

"Seriously guys, I got this covered," I objected.

"How about your MP3 player?" Muscles, now just a set of eyes and brows, offered. The nurse strapped my arms down on the sitting gurney.

"I strongly object to being strapped down!"

"Then I'll be quick," Susan replied.

"Don't damage the chip," Agent Won said from the doorway.

"Don't damage Belle," Muscles replied.

"It's just under skin," I assured him.

"You look exhausted," Muscles said and I focused on him instead of the hullabaloo near my feet.

"I didn't sleep well. Too much stuff. Weird dreams. Too much sleep yesterday," I yawned, "Did the nerdlings say anything about the photos yet?"

"I'll check on it. Why your foot?"

"Easy to operate on, tough skin to protect it and the inside of the heel sees almost no action. I knew I should plant it near a thick bone to hide it on x-rays. It worked." I looked down to see Susan signing off on something on a clipboard and the nurse finishing taping up my heel.

"We'd really like you to stay off of it for a few hours, Belle," Jolly Gay Medic requested as he pulled off his gloves. "The skin needs to heal. I'll be back to check on it tonight. Even if it didn't, you'll need to watch out for losing your balance." He unstrapped me and pulled off his mask. "While I'm here, your morning pills." He handed me a cup and I swallowed the four pills. The medic thanked me politely and gathered up the electrodes.

I swung my legs over the side and Muscles snugged in close and turned his back. I slid to ride piggy back across the room, his arms under my thighs and my shoulders over his. The baby forced me to curve my back like a cat.

Muscles set me down on the bed and I scooted back to sit against the headboard.

"Sergeant?" I heard a guard from the hall as they finished moving out the medical equipment. "Agent Starr here, she's on the list."

"Can I see her?" I requested. I had a sneaking suspicion that Muscles was in charge of me instead of just here to help me out.

"Yeah, can I leave you with her for a few minutes?" Muscles requested and left. A moment later Starr was sealed in with me.

"Where did that thing come from?!" I joked at her now-apparent baby bump. Her blond hair had recently been chopped into a bob and her face had filled out with her pregnancy.

"Well about six months ago," Starr teased and pulled up a chair. "How are you?"

I glanced at the eye and the light was off. "I was bat-shit yesterday," I offered. "They just cut a computer chip out of my foot."

"Jeez, I wonder what's in my foot. Probably nothing that exciting," Starr joked.

"Part of it isn't even decrypted; it was information I got and I'm pretty sure it's relevant but I hadn't had the chance to crack it. I went to France and tried to find a…contact who knows decryption; couldn't find him, took a break, got pregnant, took a few field trips and then, you know, pee stick of destiny. I came here to find George."

"And now he's gone. I'm sorry he left like that," she empathized, "I think this case was eating at him." Starr paused in respectful memory briefly before her expression changed to impish. "What's with tall, dark, and ripped?" she leaned in close in sorority.

"He works for the big guy. Have you met Deuce?"

"Uh, no. The head honcho? I may have seen him but I sure as heck haven't talked to him."

"Ah, well, he hangs out down here. Muscles is his, I don't know, Guy Friday?"

"Muscles?" Starr giggled.

"Jack," I blushed, "don't tell anyone I call him that."

"He's kind of scary."

"Yeah, he is," I conceded, "but I'm pretty terrifying too so it works." I wiggled my toes on the numb foot. "Damn it, I need to pee again."

"Can you even walk?" Agent Starr asked. It was a good question: they were right about me staying off the surgical site and my right foot wasn't up to hopping.

"Um," I dangled my feet off of the bed and thought for a minute. "Okay, get that chair. You can't lift me; hell, you're about to topple yourself, but we can still do this without my feet touching the ground."

Under my direction we lined up the three chairs from the table and the desk chair so I could scoot the seven feet into the bathroom. She couldn't get the bathroom door completely shut but promised not to look.

"Agent Starr," I heard Muscles as I finished up.

"Yes, um, I didn't catch your name?"

"Jack. Hey," Muscles knocked on the bathroom wall.

"I'm almost done," I called and had to balance on my right foot to keep my left off of the ground while hoisting my pants. "Okay," I flushed and knelt on the desk chair's seat to get ready to scoot back out. Muscles carefully opened the door and looked at my bizarre work-around. He didn't move or say anything for a moment so I leaned over and washed my hands.

"Could you stay put for a moment, please?" Muscles requested as I dried my hands. I watched him in the small mirror there and saw him move the chairs away. "Okay. This is an odd angle," he considered for a moment and went with a forward hug. I closed my eyes for a second and it felt like an actual embrace, like real people, like a family member who loved me. For a second there I felt like I might actually have a heart left.

"Thank you," I said politely as he set me back on the bed.

"You could have just called, I'm never too far away," Muscles said gently.

"So what is your MOS here?" Agent Starr inquired in her delightfully direct way.

"Here to help, Agent Starr," Muscles replied politely but vaguely.

"So, I thought I would visit for a while," Starr segued. "I know it's plenty annoying to be off your feet."

"How about you teach me a card game?" I proposed to Muscles. We moved to the round table I used for dining and meetings and I pretended to listen and learn ten card gin. There are only a few card games that can be played without chips or a fourth player so we played gin and then blackjack without betting. The game gave us a venue and a pretense for conversation.

"So, is your family from New York?" Starr asked me.

"No, we lived in Pennsylvania; mom sometimes had to travel into the city for business," I volunteered.

"I grew up in Texas," Starr informed.

"No way, I hear absolutely no accent," I objected.

"Accents can be deceiving," Muscles interjected, "how many cards?"

"Two please," Starr replied and swapped cards. "Lubbock, Texas: home to absolutely nothing."

"That does explain your comfort around weapons."

"I think I read that you are a sniper, Agent Starr?" Muscles inquired.

"Yes, it's my primary MOS, but I'm also training in profiling. That's coming in real handy right about now."

"Yeah, there comes a point where we won't be able to lay flat for hours," I joked, "Even if I could lay flat on my stomach, I'd have to get up and pee every hour."

"That's the truth of it," Starr muttered.

"Is this your first child, Agent Starr?" Muscles inquired.

"Yes, do you have children?"

"No; I work a lot."

"You look young. Gin," Starr said and we gathered the cards up for me to shuffle.

"I'll be twenty-five in January," I said. "I left home as a teenager."

"I'm twenty-seven," Starr announced. "Belle, you kind of went through life early."

"That's how we ended up here, isn't it? We went through our lives hot and fast," Muscles observed.

"How old is he, Belle?"

"Oy, Jack has one of those faces. He's really strong, muscles are still really together...I'd guess between twenty-six and thirty-three but I can't narrow it. Am I close?"

"I will request a file on what information I am allowed to give you," Jack offered firmly and checked his watch. "What do you want for lunch?"

"I don't feel like eating," I replied honestly and caught a stern look from Muscles. "I've burned no calories, I don't need to refuel."

"How about something small or light?" Starr offered. "You have been knitting a human all morning."

"I'm tired, nauseated and my foot throbs. How far in did she stick that needle?" The local anesthetic wore off and my bone began to object to its earlier invasion.

"The needle was short but she stuck it right into the foremost part of the calcaneus. It was a thirty gauge, very small. There was no blood during the operation," Muscles spouted.

"You saw all that while talking to me?" I was astounded.

"Are you a nurse? You are, aren't you?" Starr accused.

"Guys!" my head got a little buzzy. "I'd like to take a nap now."

"Bathroom first?" Muscles inquired straight-faced. He carried me there and left me balanced on one foot for a few minutes before coming back to retrieve me. In those minutes he had turned down the bed and dimmed most of the lights. Muscles plopped me down in bed but didn't attempt to cover me up or any other such nonsense.

They left me there and I closed my eyes to the sounds of rain falling in the park inside my fake window.

I woke because my foot throbbed and I felt the incision burning. Before I opened my eyes I stretched out and reassessed things. *I need to put some ice on it before that drives me crazy. Speaking of driving me crazy, what the hell is Muscles? Nurse? Guard? Interrogator? Long-term…something? He's young, but old enough to be an interrogator. He does know a decent amount about medicine and care. You know what this reminds me of? That book. That one book in Spanish about the really bossy guy and the stupid girl. Well, I could definitely deal with this ending in sex and leather.*

Luc doesn't even know I'm pregnant; he probably thinks I'm just out there, disappeared into the sands like I did before; like I always do. Like I always did. My many adventures in disappearing into the night came back to me: midnight trains, wells of planes, hopping on a bus, truck, or cart on my way to wherever. Mostly trains in Germany, lots of rental cars as well across European capitals. I used ships to bounce from port to port in the Mediterranean: sometimes legitimately and sometimes as a stowaway. I was caught once and pulled out my sweet naïve Israeli girl act for a Jewish Captain: by the time I was done they gave me safe passage all the way to Egypt, an offer of shelter once there with a cousin of the captain's, and medical treatment for my active wounds at the time.

Those were the tears I was comfortable with: those were the only type of tears I tolerated. Tears of deception, of convenience, of mission. Lying was my religion; lying and stealing mostly. Plus murder; about two dozen deaths so far at my hands. *Hands, guns, knives, an ax, multiple forms of explosive devices and the occasional poison. I headed out as a teenager because something needed to be fixed and I wanted to fix it. No, that's a lie. Good god, you're lying to yourself now.* I ran a hand through my hair and my foot throbbed a little louder. *Someone needs to suffer. Someone needs to pay for mama. Someone needs to pay for Keith; well, technically I already settled that debt.* The memories flooded: gunning a man down and blowing someone else up; Afghanistan's countryside full of war-torn recent ruins. Sometimes I think my mother would be horrified at my life choices; but she cared deeply about justice. *Mom wanted to fight the big guys; the oppressors, the cheats and liars. She would understand that fighting terrorists is for the greater good. That was her thing, what she cared about most.*

Keith; he'd be glad I got them. He would have wanted to be avenged. He would have been pissed that he was killed so quickly in his military career. He really loved the Army. He just wanted to fight the bad guys; guess it's the family mission. I wonder if Dad drank himself to death. A twinge of guilt struck but passed quickly. *I could find out. Agent Won could find him in a heartbeat. Hell, George could, oh, I remembered, right. No more George. Bloody hell.* I opened my eyes and looked around. I had sensed someone around but didn't see anyone until I sat up a bit. Muscles was doing push-ups on the ground near the door.

"Hi Belle," he greeted while in motion. "Need a lift?"

I shook my head but realized he didn't see it. "No, thank you. You were in the Army?"

"Yes; 2000-2008; then I got called up."

"My brother was in the Army," I revealed cautiously. "He was killed in Afghanistan."

"I know. They didn't tell me his name."

"Keith," I clutched my dolphin hard. "He was killed in 2002, January 28th."

"Do you remember the unit?"

"No. I got to talk to him though, on my sixteenth birthday. He got permission to call me; Keith promised that when he got home he'd help me get away from dad. Dad drinks," I explained and those stupid tear ducts got excited again. "The records may or may not show US forces in Afghanistan at the time he was there, but the records can go fuck themselves.

"I was gone by March. We were never far from the border and I learned how to drive when I was twelve. I looked older; I had a friend with a friend who got me the ID I needed for the paperwork for a passport. Small town post offices aren't hard to manipulate. I crossed into Canada and started breaking laws right and left."

"With some mishaps along the way."

"Lots of mishaps. I've stared death in the face so many times I could probably give it to a sketch artist," I joked weakly.

"We'll take good care of you; you're here now."

"So, are you a nurse? Or a guard, or an analyst, what are you, Muscles?"

"Muscles. I'm just a body to care for and help entertain you, protect and serve. I'm a really badass butler if that helps."

"Are you a trained interrogator?" I woke up my own interrogation skills and Muscles pulled up a chair and sat with his legs wide open.

"No."

"Are you a nurse?"

"No, but I have had medical training."

"Are you in charge of my care and life here?"

"Only as in charge as my boss leaves me."

"Are you living on base?"

"Yes."

"Nearby?"

"Reasonably."

"What's the weirdest thing about all this for you?"

"They're training me to be a doula; never thought I'd walk down that path."

I held it in as long as I could before bursting into giggles and guffaws. "Okay," I gasped for air. "One more question and then I will eat lunch, as you're about to demand."

"Done."

"How long have you been on this project? Did he just call you up a few days ago and say, hey, get your handcuffs and scamper on down to the hospital?"

"No; it's been a few weeks. Let me get clearance before I say anything else," Muscles requested and I respected his request. He carried me over to the futon for lunch and secured an icepack over my heel. I half-expected Muscles to cut the ravioli for me but instead his back stiffened. "Understood sir. Beauty, any ideas on the decryption of the section of the chip?"

"I was heading to a decryption specialist in France but couldn't find him. So I got knocked up instead," I added facetiously. "What about the Spaniard? Any luck?" I asked the clip that was attached to Muscles' shirt.

Muscles listened for a few minutes and headed over to make the bed.

Badass butler indeed. I pondered to myself and finished the meal. Muscles removed the plate and called to the guards that a visitor was coming.

"Hey Muscles, I'm wearing my pajamas," I observed.

"An excellent point," Jack went to my drawers and pulled out the top half of the uniform I wear; it looks like a short dress with stretchy pants and a fleecy jacket. "Bra?"

"Yes please," he gathered the items and then gathered me and took it all to the bathroom. "I'm already wearing panties, let's focus on the top half," I advised while balancing on one foot and a hand on the sink. "Just, don't look."

"Scout's honor," he pledged and I shucked my pajama top and he handed me the bra.

"Were you actually a scout?" I wobbled and he steadied me.

"Arms up," Muscles requested and pulled the dress over quickly. I sat on the toilet to change pants while he looked studiously over his shoulder into the room. "Done?"

"Done," I replied and stood carefully. Muscles came and crouched and I got on his back again to ride him back to the futon. *I have done some pretty weird things in life but this situation right here; the badass butler might be the weirdest.* I closed my eyes to think: a couple of things had been rattling loose in my brain and the loose ends were starting to bug me. *What changed a few weeks ago? The foot, that was a while ago, Ari,* I shook my head to get the thought out. *Powell?* A few days ago; it seemed like forever now, Agent Powell had seized an opportunity to talk to me alone and creeped me out. Muscles didn't set off my creep alarms, which are pretty highly honed.

"Clear for entry sir," Muscles called.

The Cyber breakthrough; that was a few weeks ago. That was…two weeks ago? Where did the time go? I had to focus because Deuce was here and he brought a lady. Deuce is a six-foot tall Irish-looking man in his early sixties who bears the evidence of decades of smoking. The woman was a fake blonde, forty-seven under her makeup and naturally tall. She wore three inch heels and could look Deuce in the eye. She wasn't slender, but she didn't roll in either. Muscles stood back while Deuce and the woman joined me at the table in the little dining seats.

"Hello Beauty," Deuce greeted.

"I would like to know where," the woman started in a barely-polite tone and Deuce raised a hand in interruption.

"Jack, Captain Stover would like a word."

Muscles left after handing me an ice pack and the door sealed behind him. The board had been lowered over the remaining window so it was a private party now.

"Beauty, this is my associate Jessica," Deuce introduced and Jessica squirmed slightly.

"I know your name isn't Beauty and you hardly merit the title," Jessica grumbled and I fought an amused smile. "Your name isn't Belle either, or Jones. I'll be addressing you as X-128 as that is your name as far as I'm concerned." She paused but didn't look for approval. "I would like to know where you got that chip."

"My left foot, Jessica," I used the tone women use when we hate each other.

"We'll be reviewing your x-rays for further hidden objects," Jessica stated, "I appreciate the pregnancy may prevent us from taking further x-rays until after the birth but we can wait."

I looked over to Deuce, "It was probably a mistake for Jack to leave," I informed him.

"You will address me," the woman stated.

"How many sets of shoes do you have, Jessie?" I inquired pointedly. "I have that many skeletons in my closet. Before you open your mouth to threaten me or my baby, and I sense it coming, you should know that if you give me enough cause there is nothing anyone can do to save you from me," I turned back to Deuce. "Call me anything you'd like; I respect you. I like you, sir."

"Are there any further objects?" Deuce inquired in a warm and quiet tone.

"No. I'm not in the business of hiding things in my body; you found the Deutchland locker, you know my system. You know me like a family member. Unfortunately," I turned my eyes back to the blonde, "my family is dead. I left home at sixteen because there was no home anymore. I went out as a teenager and did things your poor little gray brain cannot imagine. I've slept in palaces and I've slept with rats." I leaned back and crossed my arms at the wrist and stared into her eyes. Most people don't think brown eyes can be cold; they're wrong.

"Thank you, Jessica," Deuce dismissed wisely and the woman stalked to the door and banged on it. "I swear she has some form of autism; I don't know why I thought it would be different with you," Deuce said as the door sealed again.

"I can't speak for the autism but there's definitely an active case of bitch. No one has called me prisoner X-128 in months; technically it's not correct anymore. They give the prisoners tags according to their cell: level B4 starts the X level, we're in building 12 and the eight cell: X-128. They don't have a code for this section; it's all built-out recently. Let's be honest, sir," I offered, "If that woman so much as thinks about harming my baby or taking her from me; everyone dies."

"No one will harm you, Beauty."

"Okay," I believed him. "So, what's the deal with Muscles? Why the change? Was it the cyber breakthrough, Powell in the hallways, does it date back to the British invasion?"

"I do enjoy the honesty, Beauty," Deuce smiled a little. "The night we met, you were bound to a wheelchair like a patient in a psychiatric ward. They thought it was the best way to keep you from hurting yourself. I found you honest, blunt and helpful that night and I learned things I could not learn from a file.

"There are so many things you cannot learn about a person from a history or even descriptive terms. I haven't watched the tapes of every session they have had with you but I have seen many of them. You are more than an asset, Beauty.

"Muscles, as you call him," Deuce cracked a smile, "which is hilarious, is equipped with a specific and highly specialized set of skills and experience with dangerous people. You, my dear, are highly dangerous, and for all your willingness to sacrifice for others you seem to be missing a self-protective instinct."

"I am not suicidal, I don't endanger myself!" I objected.

"Your ribs are still stiff from your engagement with the guards on your arrival here and you are currently confined to a few steps at a time from an injury when you bravely and somewhat recklessly interceded with a former asset of the UK," Deuce pointed calmly. "Until we are completely sure it is safe for you to be back out upstairs, your perimeter is small. Let Jack help you."

"So he's company, sir?" I remembered the respectful intonation this time.

"Yes. Company is a good way to think of him."

"Company that carries me around like a badass butler," I mused and Deuce barked out a laugh.

"I would be very happy if you two got along well. He only needs to report what he honestly thinks I need to know."

"So he's like my partner, sir?"

"Yes, if you would take him as such. That would be ideal."

"As you wish."

"Tell me about Omar," he requested and gave me his full attention.

"He's brilliant. Annoyingly brilliant; he's also manipulative. In person he is irresistible; I've watched him weave his spell before on man and woman alike. It's like a snake charmer and once he's gotten into the person's mind he tends to stay there.

"His lieutenants spend time with him in person; less than a year, it may vary by person. I was never sure. There were four lieutenants: Aref Zaman in Palestine, Abdul-Malek Almasi in northern Afghanistan, Qaed El-Amin in southern Afghanistan and Pakistan, and Rahim Durrani in Algeria. I've never seen El-Amin or Durrani in person but I would not be overly surprised if Zaman is dead by now. He was a problem," I explained succinctly.

"For you or for Al-Zahrani?" Deuce asked.

"I was focused on Durrani and Almasi; I never got Durrani but I definitely gave him hell," a small, sick, demented smile crossed my face. "The Algerian man I blew up, the trafficker pedophile? Durrani's cousin, his first cousin. In fact, he came to my radar not as a trafficker or pedophile but because I was looking to hurt Durrani, to draw him out."

"What about money?" Deuce inquired in a soft but intense voice.

"Everything I knew about their financial movements was in my computer."

"I think Jack briefed me about the photograph trail idea," Deuce probed.

"Ozzie is brilliant and highly personal. If he thought someone was after him, and I think he'd have gotten that impression, he would need to know who and why."

"He knew the western world was interested in him," he stated.

"Yes, and he's spent great deals of time screwing around with institutionalized intelligence. Turning agents on each other, having people killed or otherwise disposed of as he needed. He would probably send some of his messengers; low-ranked men for hire. They may not even know who hired them or why." I stole the opportunity to gaze into his eyes, steely by nature, and try to guess what he knew. A feeling welled in my gut that he had seen as much death as I had and my eyes found something better to stare at.

"Love interests?" Deuce inquired.

I shook my head, "I've never seen him with a woman. It would probably interfere with the gospel he preaches. Bin Laden's got wives like I have passports, but I don't know of any love for Ozzie."

"What could you tell me about the disk we recovered this morning?"

"Part of it is encrypted; I felt like it was important but never got it cracked to see."

"Important enough to embed in your skin."

"You know what's on the chip; you know what precautions I needed to take," I almost chided him. "Knowledge is power and whoever thinks the fastest lives the longest."

"If you had one man to send one place to look for him," Deuce asked.

"I would send them after Qaed El-Amin. Wish I had an address for you," I said with genuine regret. "Ozzie placed his lieutenants with logic and insight. The best men went to the best places and El-Amin is a nightmare on the brink. He was my winter plan: that was my next stop after France when I started throwing up."

"It's a dangerous part of the world," Deuce observed and his body language signaled the end of the conversation.

"Sir," I said as he was about to shift to stand up, "Something feels off about your associate Jessica. I don't just not like her; something," I wrinkled my nose. "I could be wrong, you know, hormones, confinement, but something…"

"Thank you, Beauty," Deuce thanked me. "Let Jack know what you want or need. He's your badass butler for now." He laughed on his way out the door and I wondered if he would share the joke with the guys in the hall. Muscles didn't return immediately and I turned my attention back to my laptop to pull up files I had previously worked on. The Field Surgery Guidebook looked more interesting than the notes from the terrorist's handbook.

Where did that thing go; it was in my office. I wondered when they would let me out of this strange level of confinement at least enough to go to my office. I crawled on the futon to the food slot as the flap was raised again. "Hey guys," I called and heard three steps.

"Yes Belle?" Lieutenant Branch bent his knees to come to my level in the hall outside. There was a dead zone painted onto the floor to warn people to stay out of my potential reach.

"Hi, haven't seen you in a while!" I greeted the familiar face. "Any chance I can go to my office?"

"None. Sorry; do you need something from it?"

"Getting bored, thought I might get back to work for Captain Stover's project."

"I'll pass that on. Anything else?"

"Thanks." I turned back to my room and delved into my thoughts. *One man to send one place; El-Amin. Definitely El-Amin.*

It was hot, but not horribly. May of 2005: it took me more than a year to identify which group of men were responsible for the attacks on US forces in January of 2002 in that section of the country. I was still an unusual asset for Israel; that's where I got the intel tools and gear. I considered tracking someone to the capitol but followed that truck instead. God, I walked for four days straight but I found the camp. Then I walked back with some photos and linked up with a contact. If it had been up to me I'd have done something stupid. Instead I perched on the mountainside with a pair of binoculars and watched as the rockets started to land. The feeling rushed through my blood again; accomplishment tainted with a hollow filthy guilt. That guilty feeling that I shouldn't be this proud of killing a camp full of people; it kept me up that night as I mentally repeated that they weren't my rockets, not my deaths. If they counted, then my overall count would at least double, making my death count close to fifty. *I never planned to turn into a serial killer. Stover was right though; I wouldn't kill an innocent. Hell, I never even took orders on assassinations.*

The door binged and beeped and opened and Jolly Gay Medic came in with Officer Morgan. They left the portal open: with my purse-sized belly I was hardly going to dash by them.

"The anesthesia wore off. The needle hurts worse than the incisions," I informed them frankly.

"So it's like dental work," Jolly Gay Medic replied. "I've come to take a peek." He crouched down to look at my feet. "We're going to need to loosen the band, officer. Normal feet swelling," he informed.

"I'll pass that on," Officer Morgan reported.

"So, the holidays are coming up. What's your religion?" the medic asked. "I mean, what do you celebrate?"

"I guess I'm a Christian," I reflected aloud. "I haven't celebrated anything in a decade. The

Christmas after mom died was just horrible: Keith was in Afghanistan so it was just dad and me. He was hung over and forgot…everything. Over the years I took on religious observances of convenience; Judaism, Islam, whatever I needed to be at the time."

"Have you been doing your exercises?" the medic asked.

"Yes. Can I walk on this thing now? The baby gets restless when I'm sitting."

"Sure. Let me tape it up real well; then you can take him for a stroll." The medic set to taping the wound's gauze securely to my foot but his eyes froze as he realized his slip.

"Him?" I asked. No one had actually told me, confirmed the baby's gender but…a boy? "I'm having a boy?"

"Now Belle," Officer Morgan approached lightly.

"Congrats?" the medic had finished his work and he backed away slowly maintaining eye contact. "He's healthy; the tests were great. Clearly I'm too early here, so I apologize," he edged away.

"Shut up! Get out!" I shouted with rage. "She's a girl! She's my baby girl and she's going to be strong and amazing and look like my mother!" My emotions were like fireworks.

"Just get out," Officer Morgan directed the medic quietly and he obliged. "We'll come back to loosen the strap," she told me and left.

"She's a beautiful little princess, fuck you!" I screamed in case they could hear me.

Muscles returned and found me sitting in the shower. I had left the bathroom door open; I didn't care that he knew what I was doing.

"They here to loosen the strap?" I asked without looking up.

"Can I have your left foot please?" he requested and I saw a strange looking tool in his hand. I extended it silently: I had fitted a sock over the gauze and tape. When I looked again the band had been completely removed. "We're going to take this off for a few days."

"How are they going to threaten me now?" I asked and closed my eyes before resting my head against the shower wall.

"Forget them. We're in lockdown; they don't need to handle you in any way right now."

"Baby's really a boy?" It felt like a nightmare.

"The baby is healthy; all the tests came back excellent. There are millions of things that can go wrong that didn't," Muscles pointed out.

"But I'm having a sweet little angel!" I whined and tried to hold onto the tears. "What am I supposed to do now?" I demanded and Muscles stepped out and didn't immediately return. *Oh for god's sake.* I scrambled around for several minutes trying to use the floor, toilet, and shower wall to get vertical. I wasn't sure if I should laugh or cry at my predicament. "Muscles!" I called with a slight tremor in my voice. I started laughing at myself. "I can't get up!"

Chapter Four: Christmas

I stood before the large mirror in my room; a new addition, and gawked. At twenty-five weeks pregnant I could not believe how big my belly had become. There had been no further complications after the early November hospital scare: my feet had both healed completed but were big and puffy to the point where I had to change shoes.

Christmas had officially invaded even the strict military base, from candy canes being passed around in Cyber to paper chains and strings of light up at Natalie's desk. My pregnancy complicated every factor in my life but it gave me a venue by which to track time. It was two days before Christmas but the place was buzzing for a different reason.

"Belle, are you ready?" Captain Stover called as the door opened. "They want to talk to you upstairs."

"Did Deuce make Natalie take down the lights? I thought they were delightful," I grinned my chubby cheeks at him and he smiled back.

"How are you feeling?"

"Back hurts, hip hurts, and I haven't been able to use my nose properly for a month," I reported, "But everyone seems to be doing well. I still cannot believe this is happening," I pointed to my protrusion.

"Well, couldn't happen to a nicer girl." Jack joined us as I stepped into the hall. He was a regular part of my life now: he was gone once for three days in a row and I discovered that I missed him. That was an exception, just the one time. Every day he was at my side; my constant companion if I left the cell and internal company most days. "Shall we?" he offered his arm.

I took it because my balance was crap. My brain knew that he would probably feel better with both of my hands on his arm in case he developed a need to control me. My silly heart liked the feeling of being on a man's arm, but what the hell does she know?

"I can't believe I'm going to get bigger," I muttered in the elevator.

"You look fantastic!" John greeted me as the doors opened. He backed away smoothly and I mentally connected that to Jack. Muscles had evolved within the task force and base since he first rode in on my ambulance van. Whatever the guards or agents might have thought about him, he was unquestionable and at least outwardly respected by everyone I had witnessed. The Taser incident in Cyber was well known and I had the impression there may have been some other territory-marking behaviors while I was still grounded.

By the time they let me out it was Hanukkah. There were some changes in those four weeks: Agent Powell was gone (rumored to be related to Muscles), Agent Starr was waddling, the CIA geek Fred had lost twenty pounds while working twelve hour days on Operation Waldo, and I had never heard from Deuce's Jessica again. There were some new faces when I returned to Cyber; I hadn't gotten back into an interrogation control room and I took the time in my cell to finish the translation of the Terrorist's Handbook for Captain Stover. I had also tried and magnificently failed crocheting while trying to make peace with carrying a soldier instead of a princess.

The second and third weeks of December were exciting for everyone as we caught a lead through some DNA profiling. Deuce had confided that Qaed El-Amin was being hunted by the best and a wave of general optimism swept through the weary team. Deuce and I continued to have meetings in my cell; as did Director Goode and I. It felt like a huge accomplishment when I stepped back into her office for the first time in two months.

Muscles lightly brushed my hands with his left hand and I fought a smile. "Sir," we entered the room to see Deuce and Director Goode, "ma'am." We entered and closed the door behind us. I grabbed the back of the sofa and let go of Jack's arm. His right hand lightly touched my back and I corrected my posture to the proper position.

"Agent Won's team came across some interesting information," Deuce greeted. "This led to an asset coming to our attention. Come sit."

I joined them at the table with careful steps. Director Goode opened a folder and passed me a photograph. "The Canadian?" I recognized the man.

"He seems to have taken a page out of the Belle Jones playbook and his prime goal is to blow up stockpiles of weapons. He was spotted a few hours ago sixty miles or so north of Peshawar."

"That's a hellish area. Mardan, Islamabad, the roads are rough but they exist," I remembered.

"We are finding DNA with familial matches to Bin Laden in that area," Deuce confided.

"What kind of people: are they transients, refugees, locals?" I inquired.

"Some as long as twenty years, others appear new to the area."

A smile crept across my face. *We've got them.* "We can't wait once we have an address this time. That was my biggest mistake."

"We're not waiting," Director Goode assured.

"Once we have them, both of them, of course," Deuce turned his steely eyes to mine, "and everything is settled, this task force will disband. We have the option to turn you over to the US Marshalls for them to hide you away as though you were a mob informant." He paused and I sensed that there was another possibility he preferred. "The information in your head is valuable, but so is the operating system it is running on. What would you like to do after all this is settled?"

The question stumped me. "I suppose I'll be a mom. Raise my son. I'm going to need some parenting books or something because I have no idea how to be a mother."

Director Goode smiled maternally, "I think you'll figure it out."

"Now is a good time for you to start thinking about the next year. I assume you don't want to live downstairs forever. Whatever you choose, know that you will be protected."

Guarded, I mentally translated.

"Well, Director," Deuce stood up and Goode followed suit, "Don't get up, Beauty. Elsa, I will see you next year. Merry Christmas, Beauty."

Muscles followed Deuce out the door and closed it to leave me with Director Goode.

"Belle, would you like the good news or the bad news first?" she asked tentatively.

"Bad."

"I had intended to ask if you wanted to call anyone for Christmas, a family member, but I'm afraid you don't-,"

I interrupted, "When?"

"2006. Your father drove into a tree one June evening. His blood alcohol was almost three times the limit. I'm sorry."

"I knew he was dead, I just had a feeling. Really it's better...if anyone ever figured out who I really am, or was."

"Five or six people know that name. We try to keep track of who knows that we have Belle Jones, but the information is loose. Israel, Great Britain, even France recently placed an inquiry."

"DGSE or DRM?"

"DCRI, actually. Why?"

"What would the *direction centrale du renseignement intérieur*, their internal intelligence agency, have to do with me? I expected the military intelligence or military external security to handle problems like me."

"I'll look into it without revealing your location. That is unusual," she agreed. "On to the good news: I have a present for you."

"Is it a way for my bladder to not be squished, because that's what I want most right now," I admitted. She went to her desk and retrieved a pink wrapped box.

"It's a really lame present, but," she handed it to me and I unwrapped it happily.

"Catalogs?" I opened the box to find three baby furniture catalogs, two baby clothing catalogs, and a book of popular baby names by origin and gender. Muscles came in as I leafed through the little blue onesies and pressed my fingers to my nose to stop the tears. "Thank you," I squeaked and she handed me a tissue. I asked to use her restroom and toddled off for respite.

I paused for a few minutes before flushing and listened at the door out of habit.

"...happy to arrange a temporary companion for her if you would like to take some leave," Director Goode spoke quietly.

"They're all gone, director."

"Oh, I'm sorry, I had the impression that your sister,"

"Ma'am," Muscles warned.

"I'm sorry."

I stopped eavesdropping and finished up to wash my hands. I had been in that bathroom thirty-six times during my stay on the base. I caught my balance briefly on the door frame. *How do women do this and WHY would anyone choose to do it again?* I wondered as Muscles closed the distance to me. "Will I be able to access my old funds to help purchase the clothes and furniture?" I inquired. By that point the CIA had consolidated most of my various accounts into one rather large one. Some of my jobs paid well and some of the money was stolen. I still had various 'banks', mostly in lockers and other hiding places with cash of several denominations. US dollars are good almost everywhere. I could live for many years off of my ill-gotten gains if I was allowed to.

"I'll let you know," she replied; since Deuce's arrival Director Goode responded with that phrase more often than not.

"Thank you. Merry Christmas, Director," I offered.

"Thank you Belle. Let's make it the task force's last Christmas together."

"Agreed."

Twenty minutes later I was in my own bathroom stuffing myself into a bathing suit. We used the pool for most of my exercise these days: I was allowed to splash around for a while but then Muscles made me walk in the water for several laps. It was boring as hell but it did help my back pain.

"Are you okay in there?" Muscles asked.

"Yes, just feeling like a sausage. There's nowhere for me to fall. There, done. I don't think this pouch is going to put up with me much longer." The front panel of the maternity bathing suit was fully stretched.

"The two-piece still fits," Muscles replied and I came out to see him tugging at the back of his shirt subtly; I recognized the signal of stress.

"So I guess you're stuck spending Christmas with me," I pulled on the loose swimsuit cover.

"No, I get to spend Christmas with you," Muscles replied without a smile. "I'm like you, Alexis. No family left."

"Did you have brothers or sisters?"

"A sister. She was special needs; that's where I learned how to control the human body. We fought for her to have a normal life for thirty years and then she and my grandfather were both killed in a tornado. He was trying to get her into the shelter and she had a fit," Muscles had turned his back to me.

Tears came to my eyes. "Jack, I am so sorry. That is the saddest thing,"

"When I was gone for three days," he referred.

"You only took three days? Jack, you need to take some time when death happens!"

"You're an expert on grief?" he asked bitterly.

"No, but I am overly familiar with death. I have lost and I have killed. No one innocent, but I have more or less murdered twenty-four people, Jack." The number seemed staggering. It adds up to one body for every year of my life.

"We leave for the gym in five minutes," Jack said and exited the cell. We stood there awkwardly as they opened the door for him, his back still to me, me feeling his pain. They closed it again and I sank onto the futon.

Well done, Beauty. You just had to know, didn't you? Like the holiday wasn't hard enough for everyone. God, that was just a month or so ago. He took three days to…arrange the funerals? Settle the affairs? I never considered what I was leaving behind for those families, if they had families. Alexis, you cannot do this to yourself. This is a new life, a new name, a new role and you cannot dwell on what you've done for the rest of your life.

God, sometimes I just want to forget. Forget everything, Ari, Luc, Abba, the whole lot. Go back to when I only felt a daughter's grief, not a thirst for revenge. Not fatal fury rampaging across the Middle East. Like a tornado. Poor Jack! Poor Jack's family! The old man, just desperate to get the woman to safety, the tears came after the first sob escaped; it almost sounded like a hiccup. Every breath became dedicated to the ripple, the rhythm of sound escaping and air disappearing from lungs as they became increasingly desperate for oxygen. The injustice of an innocent death, one, two, three thousand. There have been tornados that killed as many as I have: the sudden thought just confused me. *But storms disintegrate when they've finished; they don't have to live with their results. This air, this air right here was once a part of a storm, or many. Every air molecule has been around for eons, they've ripped thousands of lives apart. Once a storm, now a pleasant breeze; what is this universe around us?* The sobs slipped away and I caught my breath. The baby pushing against my lungs made his presence known. *You're just a storm waiting to happen. Please, please don't be an angel like me, an angel of death. Be a nice boy, a mild child, loving and kind and not at all like your mother. I should really give this kid up for adoption. I'm in no way fit to be a mother.*

"Belle?" Officer Morgan asked as she opened the door for me. "Hormones again?" she saw my state.

"I'm no mom. I can't be a mom. I should give this kid up, let him have good parents. I'm not, how could I, I can't," I started crying again.

"Belle, your body is full of hormones. You're going to be a great mom. Wait and see, okay? I have a feeling that once you're holding your precious bundle, you're just going to click into place. If not, if you try it and really truly can't do it, you can always make that decision. Trust me. You will love him so much that everything will just fall into place."

The gray matter finally fired up and the hysterics stopped. It was a welcome change from my perspective: outside of fury I haven't known much in the way of emotions for the last decade.

"That's brilliant, you're right! I can always try it and then after a year, he'll be weaned: surely I can be a cow for a year!"

Officer Morgan failed to completely stifle her laugh.

"Right, well, we'll see you later, water walking time!" I hoisted myself up and carefully crossed the cell. Jack was waiting with my coat and we avoided eye contact and conversation masterfully until I was actually in the water. We stuck to neutral business and each pretended that nothing had happened.

"Sir," I heard a familiar voice and saw a military uniform out of the corner of my eye. I learned as a child that if you pretend you're not paying attention, people will accept the premise. I couldn't make out the words and keep walking at the same time so I chose walking. Nothing that peon had to say would impress me. When I turned for the lap I recognized the soldier; he had been in the hospital room with the big-ass gun.

Sergeant...Walker? Wilks? Something with a W. Big gun, small bullets, I smirked to myself but avoided eye contact as Jack turned and walked toward the door out of sight. I finished the lap and turned again, unwilling to engage.

"No smart ass comments or complaining about marching underwater?" the peon inquired. "Last time I was on watch while you were on pool patrol you wouldn't shut up." He started walking alongside. "So, did you have a nice Hanukkah? CIA give you lots of presents?"

"I'm not Jewish, and no." I edged away from him closer to the dividers.

"Good lord you're fat now."

"I'm making a human."

"Next generation of psychos," he muttered to himself. I rotated mid-lap and started toward the end of the pool closest to where I last saw Muscles.

There was a time I could have fought with him, even like this, unarmed, in a pool, he's fully armed and loaded. I can barely walk on land. I don't know where Muscles went or when he'll be back. Please don't tell me this bastard is in charge of me.

"How many more laps, Jones?"

Don't get out. "We were just starting, Sergeant."

"Then why have you slowed down?" he reprimanded, "Keep it moving, don't stop on the end." He touched his belt and I saw the yellow flash of a Taser device. I turned quickly and moved out into the water. I was three meters into the lane when I heard a welcome bark.

"Sergeant! Dismissed!" Muscles growled. "Belle, come post. Hang out."

I crossed immediately to the pool ladder and put both hands on the top rung; our agreed-upon response to an order to 'post'. We had run the drill before and this was the third time he had ever requested me to post. Muscles followed the asshole out and I stayed put with curious amusement at his anger.

"Okay, Belle, I need you to get out now," Muscles called and I carefully hoisted myself up the steps and took his extended hand. "Come sit on the bench," he directed and draped a towel around my shoulders. "Can you sit here for me for a few minutes?" he asked and I nodded. The pool room was warm but I felt a shiver coming on

"Captain? Jack: I need a female officer at the pool please," Muscles listened for a few seconds. "Thank you." Muscles hung up the phone on the wall behind me. "Let's go to the showers, get you dry and warm again," he suggested and I wrapped the towel around me. The lockers are clear on the other end of the pool near the weights and treadmills room and I looked curiously through the tinted glass to see what I could make out. "Male personnel coming in!" he called warning and we heard no objections from the locker room so he came in with me.

"I'll be fast," I offered quietly, still receiving the vibes of a brewing storm.

"I'll be nearby," Jack stated, "a female officer will be here soon." He set a bag with a change of clothing on the bench in the stall and was still right outside when I turned the water on.

By the time I came out of the shower Officer Belot had arrived. She must have been sweating in her outdoor uniform with the coat fully zipped.

"I'll just put my shoes on. Is Jack outside?" I inquired and wrangled shoes on around my belly.

"Belle, I'd like you to tell me exactly what happened while your companion wasn't in the pool area," Belot stated with gentle firmness.

"Typical guy crap; he called me fat, said something rude about my baby," I relayed the brief conversation verbatim when she expressed interest. "I honestly think he's just pissed that he's working over Christmas."

"Alright, thank you for your assistance. Are you ready to go?" she inquired politely and I led her out into the main rooms where Muscles and Captain Stover were waiting.

"Can we go home now? I'd like to take a nap," I announced and they all seemed agreeable to the request. Muscles didn't say much but he did pull the hood of my coat up over my head when we stepped outside. *If he keeps this up I'll forget how to take care of myself. Like I was an expert on that,* I scoffed mentally.

Muscles didn't stick around once I was back in the cell. I ate cereal and curled up in my dolphin blanket but didn't immediately fall asleep.

"Thanks for dropping in, Tom," I heard Captain Stover say quietly; his voice slipped through the open food slot. "I want this repeated to every shift. Jack and the big guy have absolute authority here, anything he asks you do. I want it to be crystal clear. They will not tolerate any threats to the asset or threatening behavior including unnecessary roughness or threats. Wirt went cocky and overstepped his bounds out of some dumbass power trip. The video shows everything and the minute his finger touched his stun gun Jack came down on him."

"The Sergeant is trained in four different martial arts and went through full Ranger training; he's been doing specialized work for the top brass for the last several years," Sergeant Moore said.

"We also don't have Shirley Temple in there," someone else pointed out.

"Decent segue, thank you," Stover took over again, "she's only getting bigger folks."

Thank you for the reminder!

"It will become harder for her to pose a threat unarmed and we need to respond to any violence with her baby in mind. Wrists and elbows. If you don't have to, don't. Let Jack handle it or do anything he asks. If there isn't a dire threat of death...use your brains. Do not put yourself in a position where you have to explain why you did something to a woman in her condition."

Trust me; it's no picnic in here. I wonder which four? How can I possibly survive getting any bigger?! Getting shot was SO MUCH EASIER than this. Recovery time was faster too. Granted, getting to this point was a lot more pleasant. Oh Luc. You're having a son! He'd probably be thrilled. What does he do again? Mayor? I should Google™ him sometime, figure out if he's still in office.

Luc and I first met in a Montmartre café; both in town on business. I needed fresh gear and was sucking down the terrible coffee France is famous for to stay awake to meet the dealer. I ran into him again the next day at the train station; he was heading home to the Reims area and I was heading toward Berlin. My cover was that I was a translator for a wealthy businessman doing business across the EU. Luc was kind and goofy and offered to put me up for a night when my train got delayed. I have never enjoyed a man's company more. The next day I was off to Berlin to prep for my next mission and Luc was a memory.

Back in France earlier this year searching for the decryption specialist I ran into Luc again. His step-children were with his separated wife for the summer and I ended up back at his place. It was quiet and peaceful and I felt like a real human being for the first time in ages.

I didn't jump right into bed with him; I'm almost a lady. One thing did lead to another and two weeks into my month-long stay we embraced *l'amour*. Anyone who has that much sex is bound to get pregnant. I hit Africa and Israel again and started feeling sick so I holed up in the French countryside for a break from the constant pace of an operative. When it got worse rather than better and when my period stubbornly refused to visit again I took the test.

I have only had genuine lusty sex with a handful of people; I've screwed lots of men and then taken what I needed. They would figure out later that I had truly screwed them. I made them all wear condoms, even brought my own and I can be very persuasive in my lingerie. If a man's option is to wear a condom or not get sex, he'll almost always choose the condom. In fact, only one man has ever walked out and by that point I had already planted the bug.

Dire threat of death, I mentally returned to the conversation outside my cell.

"Ask 'em now," Stover said.

"Is Sergeant Wirt okay?"

"He's running external fence patrol and has been removed from the detail. I have no wiggle room here, ladies and gentlemen. I know this isn't anyone's dream job but you are here and not out there. Read the reports; psychology of a pregnant woman is very different from our usual guests here. Don't attack her baby and don't piss off her handler."

The thought was comforting as I finally fell asleep. My dreams were wild again, with Muscles helping me escape while all the guards were at a Christmas party talking about how much they hate the CIA. My pregnant belly kept getting in the way so I squatted down and popped out the kid and was normal sized and shaped again. Then the kid was actually an egg, so we picked it up and ran out into the woods that surround the compound. It was only getting weirder as I woke up with the impression that I was actually part bird and going to birth an egg. The door was preparing to open as I woke.

Thank god, someone to watch me pee! I thought sarcastically and rolled onto my feet before closing the door on the entrant. *Oh yeah, pregnancy is just charming. The kid is squishing my lungs and my bladder and my nose hasn't stopped running yet this week. Who's out there?*

"Tell me what you'll be doing today," Muscles requested.

"Weights and measures: we'll be tracking the uterus' movement upward using this tape measure and this, and taking her weight and other diameters: breast size changes, the pelvis and waist; I'll check her heart and the boy's heart. Everything is very standard. If she has any complaints we'll try to address them too," Commander Susan's voice was welcome; after Sergeant Power-Trip my skin crawled at the thought of a man touching my belly.

"I'd like to complain about my tenant here, he's kicking me in the bladder," I joined them after washing my hands.

"Commander, could you look at her nose? She hasn't stopped sniffling all week and I'm concerned about a possible sinus infection," Muscles requested.

"Pregnant rhinitis is very common, but I'll check it out. Okay, Belle, if I could get you to step onto the scale here," she requested and I did. "Hmm," she didn't look pleased.

"Yes, I know, I'm huge!" I grumbled.

"No, you're a little underweight. I know you may feel big, but you're not weighing what you should be, even assuming you were underweight to begin with. Try to get in lots of small meals; that may be easier for you to handle. Now, Mr. Tape Measure," she went to work with the tape measure and I stood patiently holding my top up to let her work around my knit pants. "That's coming nicely. Could you take a seat for me? I need to get your heart rate, blood pressure, and then the baby's heart rate."

She ultimately concluded that I needed to eat more and stress less. We wished her a Merry Christmas and soon it was just us and the eye camera.

"Can we talk?" Jack asked. I had expected it; too much had disturbed the status quo.

"Of course. Gentlemen, can we lower the flap please?" I requested out the food slot and the cork board was lowered. "Let's talk."

"I want to talk to Alexis."

"Okay," I exhaled and took in the deepest breath I could manage.

"We called her Sissy because after I was born, it was the only thing she would call herself. She had physical and mental handicaps: we constantly had to keep an eye on her and she needed help doing everything. Her arms worked; they were strong. They were Army strong, that's really how she got around: with braces or the chair. Our grandparents raised us: mom was into drugs and dad died shortly after she did. Is this too much for you?"

Oh Jack, I slid my hand flat against the table, "If you knew Belle Jones you'd never ask that question." I was honest and sincere and it shook me a little.

"Anyway, Nana died four years ago so it was just Pops and me for Sissy. One day a man in a suit and an ascot caught me in an elevator on base. My mentor back then sort of shoved me toward him so I listened to what he had to say. He knew about Sissy and Nana and Pops, he said that he could arrange for 24/7 home care for my sister and grandfather if I was open to a looser job description. And he did it! Pops calls me two nights later saying that this service had contacted him, they were all paid through the end of the month; he didn't know what to make of it. We spoke three days later and he just raved about how great the nurses were, how someone came and cleaned the house, they were going to tend the lawn and Sissy loved this one nurse."

"You would do anything for your family," I understood.

"I told him then that it was for Sissy's birthday, it fell on the same month. Sissy was incredibly challenging; mood swings, violent spells, she couldn't chase you but she could beat the tar out of you if you came in reach. That night I found a blank business card with a cell phone number hand-written on it."

"What, under your pillow?"

"Basically."

"I left home after Keith was killed by the bastards. Went to Canada, then to Israel and sold Kabbalah threads to Americans and Canadians. There was a suicide bomber and I just…it happened so fast and I put a bullet in his forehead. I just wanted to stop him; there were so many people and I had already walked through the results of a suicide blast. That shit haunts you."

"I've walked through towns blown away by tornados and through post-blast areas. I've never decided which was worse. Blood versus memories, familiar versus strange," Jack sighed.

"Well, we're still kicking," I comforted. "I'll be twenty-five in a few weeks. That's really not too young to be a mother."

"Was Christmas a big thing in your house?" Jack asked.

"It was a thing, but not a mega decorate-the-neighborhood-non-stop-carols-at-Thanksgiving thing," I replied, "What about you?"

"Sissy kept a small artificial tree in her room year-round. All the little ornaments had to be in the right place and there was never a topper. She could throw a fit and destroy everything in her room except that tree."

I watched his eyes as the storm swirled around in his brain. His emotions rarely showed; someone who didn't know him would never see the way he processed pain, joy, or surprise. I felt a little privileged to be in on the secret.

"I am so sorry," I finally said.

"For what?"

"Your loss. Your losses; I'm sorry that your sister suffered whatever conditions she had. I'm sorry you and your family got beat up just trying to help her. I'm sorry you did whatever you had to do to keep Sissy and Pops safe and happy. I wish I was that noble. I wasn't trying to help Keith, he was already gone. I wasn't honoring my mother; I was trying to avenge her. Everything I did was ultimately selfish."

"Bullshit. I read your file: the children, the families, entire communities that are safe now, or were at least safe for a period of time, who knew peace solely due to your effort." Those stormy green eyes fixed on mine and I wondered briefly what he could see behind my orbs. Jack slid a hand out flat next to mine without touching. "I'm sorry I left you with him."

"You had no way to expect that. It wasn't that bad, he just made me a little nervous." I forced my eyes to his again, "Unless you saw something I didn't."

"Did you see him reaching around the stun gun? His fingers smoothed across its handle with disquieting confidence. He had no need, he had no orders of caution; he just couldn't keep his cock down."

"I'm not familiar with the expression."

"When a person just can't stop thinking with their balls, they have to push the envelope, be reckless, to dominate without cause. You find it in soldiers and cops but also in lawyers. Lots of lawyers and businessmen too," Jack replied.

"He pissed you off," I recognized.

"Call it my mama bear instincts," Jack joked with his version of a broad grin. If both sides of his mouth moved it was a grin. Anything less was a smile or blank. I had never seen him smirk sincerely. "You are going to have the world's most terrifying mama bear complex when your son is born."

"We'll see. I'm trying to decide whether I should keep him or give him up for adoption. Officer Morgan pointed out that I could give him up as a toddler if things don't work out."

My stomach growled and Jack pushed up to stand. It was back to work for the badass butler.

I don't know why I was excited when I realized that it was Christmas morning. Maybe it was the knowledge that next year I would have a child to have Christmas with. I woke to the smell of cinnamon rolls and chocolate and eased up to stand.

Huge cinnamon rolls with thick white frosting filled most of a plate on the food tray. Next to it was a cup of hot chocolate and a small mountain of napkins.

"Sweet!" I shared my elation loudly and set my table. I put one of the rolls in a plastic food container and the other one in my stomach. It was epic. The sugar buzz was extremely pleasant. I got dressed and ready to go out even though I suspected that everyone who worked with me would be out for the day.

I was leafing through the baby crib magazine happily when I heard movements in the hallway. The door beeped and opened and John dressed as Santa Claus stepped through the portal.

"Ho, Ho, Ho!" he greeted.

"I should have known Santa was CIA," I grinned and greeted.

"We know who is naughty and nice. Have you picked out a crib yet?"

"This bassinet is kind of cute. I'm trying to keep size in mind; I can always replace it when he outgrows it."

John sighed in a very un-Santa like manner and straddled my desk chair. His eyes were so tired: they looked at least a decade older than he was. "We're going to get this bastard."

"We gotta get them together somehow. Take out the whole damn compound."

"No, too close to martyrdom. Blaze of glory," he shook his head, "We're close; I can feel it. We are so close. We've got a red circle on a map."

"Yes, but it's the circle of hell. Have you seen a monitor lizard?"

"You can find those suckers all over the place."

"I shot one once and I swear it just pissed it off," I briefly remembered.

"We're going to get these bastards and then you're getting out of here. We'll change your name, treat your scars, maybe fix your deviated septum, set you up in a safe place. He'll grow up in a small town, a peaceful place in the middle of nowhere with a yard and a few choice neighbors. He won't know anything about this place."

I looked around at the walls and the massive door: that was the biggest reminder that I was in a cell. It looked like a bank safe door. "Then we need to get this over with before he's old enough to remember."

"You have another fourteen weeks before his due date."

"God, don't remind me," I rubbed my belly ruefully. "Least pleasant experience of my life. I am never doing this again. Add that to the surgery list." I glanced at my face in the mirror, "I wouldn't mind the nose job though. Something thinner."

"A nose can change a whole face. Anyway, we have a little surprise for you upstairs. Let me see if he's here yet," John stood and checked the hall. Muscles was there and we went upstairs to find a small but warm-hearted Christmas party. We drank virgin eggnog and ate homemade sugar cookies that Natalie had brought while listening to seasonal music. Someone started a classic Christmas movie on the big screen of the conference room we were in and most of us stayed to watch. I'll admit I was enrapt by the second flick, an animated story shown while we ate a catered turkey dinner. I didn't notice when Director Goode stepped out and barely noted when Agent Won left to follow her.

If I was going to choose someone to crash a Christmas party to a halt, I wouldn't have chosen Natalie. Her earrings were still flashing red and green lights when she flipped the lights all the way on.

"Sorry, maybe we can continue this later. Sir,"

While I was staring at Natalie I felt Muscles' posture change and knew he was hearing through his earwig. He got some message that jived with Natalie's and I was called out of the room and escorted down the hall to the director's office.

"Authentication complete. He sent it from Islamabad from a restaurant," Agent Won stated from behind the Director's desk while tapping at the keyboard.

"Close the door, please," Director Goode requested and the guard with me did so, leaving himself on the outside at her indication. "Belle, you have mail from The Canadian."

I turned my attention to the large television and Agent Won transferred the screen. "Dear Liberty, A Christmas present. If still alive, contact. In neighborhood. Could be a happy New Year. Cheers," I read aloud and noted that there was a video file attached. "Is it clean?"

"We're screening it right now," Agent Won stated. "Belle, he sent this from a wireless port in Islamabad. We've never seen him do that before, maybe once or twice."

"I think we'll find the answers in the video. If he did it, he did it on purpose," I reported.

"Do you two know each other?" Director Goode asked.

"Not intimately, but yes. We're basically on the same team; I saved his life once and then he spent a few months trying to track me down to return the favor. That was annoying so I left him a note in his hotel room with a drawing of the Liberty Bell. I haven't heard from him directly in two years now."

"Belle, go down to Cyber and work on the video with them. I may need to make some decisions here in short order," Director Goode requested and the three of us left her.

Thirty minutes later I was sucking on a candy cane when the video feed was played for me. At first it was dark; men spoke rapidly and I listened in on their conversations. At first it was Arabic and then it switched to Pashtu. I don't speak Pashtu beyond basic phrases.

"We'll replay it for the dialogue. Let's keep watching," Agent Won said quietly. The video was short, maybe ten minutes of footage. Most of it was dimly lit but there were outdoor scenes as well, vehicle shots, a few people, and then from a distance a very good shot of a man I would recognize from any distance.

"It's him," I said and stopped talking when I saw a brief shot at a number written on a piece of paper. That was the end of the film. "That's his phone number. He wants me to call him."

"That's Omar Al-Zahrani. He took this footage near Omar's current location," Agent Won realized.

"Let's get the dialogue translated, I don't speak Pashtu," I recommended

"I do. Play it again please," Muscles required and Agent Won clicked the button. "They're talking, niceties. The first man is offering a prospect for a suitor for the other man's daughter. He knows a man who knows many powerful men in the way of God. He'll put in a good word for the first man if he can help him find someone gifted in…" Muscles listened for a few minutes, "something with technology, wires, I don't know that phrase." The dialogue ended and the visual section began.

The phone rang once and Agent Won picked it up. "Ma'am," she listened. "Yes, we can do a frame by frame but," there was a pause. "Yes, of course. Would you like it upstairs or, right away. I'll tell her." Agent Won hung up and turned to me. "We're going to call him. I'll bring you a ghost phone and get it set up upstairs. She wants you to talk to him. Mr. Deuce is on the phone with her right now; he can't come but he'll be hooked in to the call."

It took an hour before I was sitting in Director Goode's office with an earpiece hooked into my head. I was sipping eggnog again and trying to keep calm as the phone on the other end rang three times.

"*Salam*?" a man trying to sound like an old woman answered the phone.

"You really are terrible with impressions," I replied.

"How do I know who I'm speaking to?" the Canadian replied in his natural voice.

"I'm not at Liberty to say," I guessed the best response, "Merry Christmas, by the way."

"You got my present."

"What do you want?"

"Him. Captured, please. I need an expert and I understand we share a cause. Are you available?"

"Maybe," I lied calmly. "Suppose you save my computer some time and tell me where you took that shot."

"I'll give you GPS coordinates if you agree to meet me in person after the job."

"That's not my style."

"I know. Give me time to convince you, I'm sure we can find a set of circumstances when," his voice stopped and changed. "Someone's close; seventeen clicks north-northwest of Mardan, no rats in sight," he spoke with quiet urgency and we all listened tensely. "Get him, promise me, come right away," We all heard crashing and the sound of things falling.

"Hands!" I heard an American voice demand.

"Shit! I've got to go now, darling, the Americans are here. Not the best present," the Canadian said calmly from a short distance and I imagined him holding the phone in his raised hands. There was a strange sound and all of the noises became quieter. We all waited and did nothing more than put our phone on mute.

"Who is this?" a new man's voice demanded.

Muscles stepped up to the phone and hit the mute button. "Martha Stewart. Call it in," he stated and hung up.

"What will they do to him?"

"They're Special Forces, they'd have to be. They'll detain him for questioning. If they weren't ours then they'll figure out pretty quick that we want him," Muscles stated.

"Thank you, Jack," Deuce's voice came from the Director's phone. "Agent Won, go through the screen by screen with your team. Urgent priority, my apologies and additional funds will compensate for this overtime."

"Right away sir; we'll start calling people in."

"Let's get some IMINT on the location he identified," Deuce added.

"CIA is all over it. We'll see if those guys were ours or yours," John replied.

"Alright. Everyone back on your heads. We'll redo Christmas once we have the bastard."

"Best Christmas present ever," I responded and we all broke up.

Chapter Five: Bacon

A week later I knew more about the Canadian, including his name. Ryan Rogers was now at a black site somewhere and his information regarding our targets was a gold mine. January 1, 2011 they let me talk to him over the phone again.

"Hello," I greeted in my calmest voice.

"Do I know you?"

"You knew me once, but I never knew your name, Ryan."

"Even, 'The Canadian' sounds better than that," he replied. "Where are you?"

"Where are you?" I returned the question.

"Were you working for them all that time?"

"We did what we did. Motives rarely matter in the big picture. Are you okay?"

"They haven't tortured me, if that's the question. Pretty shitty for you to send in the boys in black."

"Wasn't my decision, trust me."

"Should I?"

"Don't you want to?" I posed. "Tell me, Ryan, who have you been working for?"

"Not Canada, eh?" he replied. "You know my story; you know why I did what I do. Not having weapons makes a different, less deadly war. Plus I love to blow shit up."

"I've no objection," I replied honestly. In the last year the name, "The Canadian" had been bandied around as much as mine among the less civilized communities.

"I always thought we'd get along, but you do enjoy running away."

"I'm a busy girl. Do you have those coordinates?"

"Those numbers are up for trade. My freedom for his capture, no strings attached. You let me go; I'll send you a note with everything I know about him."

"How do I know that you won't decide to get pissed off and start blowing up Americans?"

"I'm talking to you, ergo you're alive, ergo, anyone coming after Yanks would be insane," he laid down the logic for me.

You got that right, bub. I thought to myself and glanced up at the screen before me. "Why were you there?" I asked per the directions before me.

"El-Amin. One of his men requested four metric tons of heavy weaponry on the market. I followed it in to see where it went."

"I'm glad you're okay," I said honestly. I didn't love the rake but I didn't hate him.

"Hey, do you suppose you guys can go after some of the dealers? I'm happy to hand out names and addresses. Sketch artist?" His voice was forced casual with just a hint of the nasal indicating that he likely came from a francophone family.

"You know my priorities," I replied after a silent pause. The baby kicked and I remembered my real priorities.

"People change, Libby."

"People never change. Priorities change, personalities may be tweaked, but in real life people don't change. Plus it's a little creepy that you're calling me by your sister's name." I was guessing on that detail, but I strongly suspected he knew someone named Libby because I heard him say the name in his sleep. From Jack's face I gathered that I had made an error. "That place, was it El-Amin's house or did it belong to Al-Zahrani?"

"I dunno," he replied with a heavy sigh. "I Don't Know!" he protested more energetically a second later.

Please don't hurt him.

"Not the hood again, guys!" The Canadian whined slightly and I heard movement on the other end. "Liberty?!"

I lurched forward as though proximity to the phone would help him. "Where are you?" I demanded with more urgency.

"Interview terminated," a rough man's voice stated quietly and there was a short beep.

"Son of a bitch!" I exclaimed and looked for something to throw. We were in the director's office; just Muscles, Won, Goode and I. Guards were outside. "Who was that?"

"Belle, we'll look into it," Director Goode stated. "That's enough for now," Director Goode said and spun in her chair to face her screen directly.

"Enough from me or from him? Where the hell is he?" I demanded with a temper stoked by her nonchalance.

Jack lightly rubbed my back over my left shoulder. For a brief second there I thought it might be a caring caress but then I remembered who he really was and why he was there. *Is this a kind act or just a way to remind me of his physical proximity? Would he pinch the nerve there, make my left arm useless and seize my right elbow to wrist? Where is his other hand, is it touching a restraint? Back and forth, back and forth, nearer to the pressure point, down into useless territory. Scratching? Oh, scratching, oh that feels so good.* My senses bailed on my paranoia to wade into the waters of pleasure. I even closed my eyes for several seconds to revel in the animalistic sensation, dropping my guard entirely.

"Come on, let's go home," Jack tempted quietly and calmly.

Yeah, that sounds nice. Bacon can handle himself. "Okay," I pushed against the table to smoothly stand up. "Bacon can handle it."

"Bacon?" Goode said.

"The Canadian."

"He goes by Bacon?" Jack inquired.

"Come on, Canadian bacon?" I protested with a smirk, "That's what I've been calling him privately for the last four years."

"What is 'Bacon' in Arabic?" Agent Won asked and I told her. "What about French?"

"Bacon?"

"Keep going, the common languages."

"*Hilib doofaar*," Director Goode replied from her screen, "That's Somali, *domuz pastirmasi* in Turkish, Russian *bekon*, *behkon* in Azerbaijani: what is the point, Agent Won?"

"If she called him "Bacon" and someone heard that, we could have been missing a code key," Agent Won explained.

"Who cares? He's not the real target here, no one really wants him!" I pointed out and took Jack's arm.

"There's been chatter. If Al-Zahrani was interested in you, he might have been interested in some other parties. Parties which may include Mr. Bacon," Jack pointed out.

"Was he interested in me?" I asked Agent Won point-blank. She looked over to the Director.

"Current intelligence suggests that he did not take you seriously. He looked into you only because one of his lieutenants insisted," Director Goode divulged.

"You can ask him yourself when we get the guy," Jack promised. "Come on, let's go watch a movie. Do you want to go to the pool?"

I turned with him without objection or a glance backward. I mentally noted that the guards outside were a little jumpier than usual but no one acted on an impulse.

"You don't have to coddle me, Jack," I informed as we returned to the cell.

"You weren't about to throw things up in the office?" Jack replied knowingly.

"Of course I was," I said lightly. "Bacon -- Rogers, he's not a terrorist."

"He makes his living by blowing things up," Jack pointed out as I waddled to the futon. "How does one make a living destroying things? The money is in acquiring and selling them, isn't it?"

"Normally, yes. I doubt he has much in the way of money. If he does what I think I heard once; that he sells duds or sells and then blows up, then it is shocking that he is alive this late in the game." The thought dug around in my brain: the hormones or the time spent in captivity had developed a sense of empathy I was unused to. *Who has him; how did they find him or know to track him? If he walked out of there today, would he be dead tomorrow?*

We know the cost, the price. We know the realities of risking lives, limbs, health, money, he and I have so much in common. Two rogue people on a mission, missions against that world, those worlds. Against death, oppression, crimes we don't personally agree with. To do what? He lost someone he loved too. He chose to attack the weapons, I the people. I ran a hand through my hair and started braiding it out of habit. *He's smart, not my kind of smart, but definitely aware of the consequences of pissing off one warlord, much less ALL of them. God, I need to see him. To see him. My eyes on his, my hands...*

Rogers and I met for the first time right after most of the damage in one of my hands had occurred. It was wrapped in bandages for the burns and he helped me open a door in the Iraqi hotel I was staying at. The Canadian attempted to strike up a conversation in the worst Farsi I have ever heard.

"You should stick to English," I informed him quietly and shoved him into a closet with me.

His hand had dashed to the small of his back and my revolver poked him in his liver.

"You move, you die. I might just want to talk," I offered.

"Likewise, except we'd both die," he replied with his accent.

I sniffed his jacket and recognized a faint scent of explosives. "Nice. Then I'd say it's to our mutual advantage to talk first, as you'll end up dead if either of us acts."

"Oh dear lord, you're her, aren't you?" His eyes had seemed genuinely elated. "Come on, you must be. They don't make many women like you."

"You're into blowing shit up?" I returned a question, "I might have use for you."

"*Belle furieuse,*" he accused me quietly. "I'm a big fan." The man's hand slowly withdrew from his back, moving while holding eye contact with me. "Now either we both have seconds to live, or only I do. I know you'll kill me but I have no interest in killing you."

"The hell does that mean?"

"You're the underworld's nightmare. I like that. I like it a lot. I'm a thorn in their side but you, lady, you're the black plague for terrorists. That's fucking awesome. I had no idea you were in the area."

"That's kind of the point."

"So, if you're not going to kill me immediately, we should probably leave the city."

"Any innocents at risk?"

"No, no, but we are white and there's going to be a bit of a nuisance in about an hour down the block."

"The garage?"

"Yeah, it's more than a garage."

I sighed in inconvenience. "Fine. Where's your stuff?"

"Packed in a jeep outside."

"Let's go," I directed. I kept my gun in hand until we were outside and I had him walking a few steps ahead of me. I remember thinking that what I was doing was incredibly insane but if anything was true I was better off away from an explosion. My poor eardrums had been through enough that week.

The crazy man shouting in Arabic was a bonus to the day; he was rapidly approaching the Canadian with a huge knife in his hand. No one needed a translator for that message.

"What do you want me to do?" The Canadian asked without turning toward me.

"Um," I looked around the alley. A giant rotting bag of fruit had presented itself as a candidate and I seized the soon-to-be projectile. "Duck!" I directed and as the man cringed the bag flew over and beamed the trouble maker. He fell down and we sprinted to the escape vehicle and got out of there. "So, you're the Canadian?" I had inquired once we were out of the city limits and had passed the first village.

"That's what they call me."

"Well I'm going to call you Bacon," I had announced with a smirk.

"Where can I drop you off?" he had replied.

He really wanted to spend more time together that night. I remembered as I mentally returned to the buttercream yellow cell.

"Unless he's not who we think he is. Maybe he's an arms dealer and throws off the scent by linking himself to weapon cache explosions," Jack considered.

No way. Well, hmm. "Anything is possible." Right on cue my little soldier kicked twice. *Yup.*

"What do you know about Mr. Rogers?" Jack inquired as he straddled a chair and handed me a bottle of water.

"Six foot two with shoes on, carried a few extra pounds. Black hair, brown eyes, but pale as hell. He has one of those faces; I thought he was young in that first encounter in Iraq but I get the impression that he's old. You know, like forty."

"What else?"

"He knew his explosives. I mean, really an expert on everything that might make stuff go boom. If I had been researching him I'd have looked into Canadian military or police EOD personnel who went missing in the early 2000's.

Obviously we already know all about him now. He has always professed to be a fan of mine."

"Was he one of your partners?"

"Only in the field," I replied with a light note of salaciousness. "I never needed to sleep with him, so no. We did once pretend to have sex to cover ourselves; poor security guard ran like we were ghosts!"

"I meant in the field, I didn't mean to imply…"

"Oh," I felt a little silly. "Is Tom McEwen back from vacation?"

"I'll check. Do you want to talk to a therapist?"

I feel like there's something swirling around in my head that I can't quite get a hold of… Someone is eating an orange. I like oranges. Can I have the peel? I love orange peels. What? Jack was talking.

"…not on base yet, but he can talk over the phone. He's thrilled you were willing to talk."

"I feel like there's something stuck in my brain; he usually just probes around in there. I'm scared, okay? The last time one of my outside associates was caught and brought to help us, something horrible happened to him."

"Yeah?"

"Yeah. I think he's in a hospital somewhere." I leaned my head back to touch the wall and look at the ceiling. "Ari…he was a geek, a tech god writing something for us when he sort of snapped, did something stupid and almost got himself killed. I….well, I sort of…happened to him." I struggled to explain while keeping tears out of my eyes. "That's when I hurt my ankle. They'll show you the tape if you ask."

"I've seen the tape. I also saw the tape from week 1. It's hard to believe that person and you are the same person. There's even a change between the two incidents."

"Yeah, the whole baby thing really softened me up," I replied spitefully.

"It happens to soldiers too, you know," Jack said softly. "In the field we all snap into a persona, it's how we survive. Then we come home, where it's safe and we don't know what to do about it but we change. It's not a snap thing either; it takes time and we lapse and relapse because what we know feels better. We know we're supermen and trying to be normal again feels like a disappointment. We miss the high."

I lowered my chin to look at him directly. "I did. But people got kinder, more understanding and I didn't want to harm them; I, uh, I don't know. Time passed and these people became my people and I chose them over," I stopped and my voice and lip trembled. Jack left his seat and brought back a box of tissues.

"Ari might be in a hospital or something, but he is alive. You gave him years and years of life, Alexis. The soldiers would have killed him."

"They do, you know. There was a kid here once, got too aggressive and…I knew he was dead when I saw him in the medical center afterwards. Seventeen."

"How old were you when you first had to kill?"

"Sixteen. Israel. I stopped a suicide bomber the usual way."

"I'm sorry that happened to you," Jack offered. "I was eighteen, the usual way."

"I'm sorry you have those memories. They never really go away."

"They haven't yet," he admitted. "So, you're afraid that we'll kill Bacon too."

I smirked at the nickname but reality hit me. "He is somewhere and he has to be scared. Bags over heads and that voice didn't sound warm and fuzzy to me. He is not a threat to us; I don't even know why we picked him up. Yes, okay, technically he blows things up on a regular basis but its only stuff for terrorists! Hell, you guys should hire him! And now it looks like he found Al-Zahrani!"

That fact sunk in fully for the first time.

"I need to step out for a few minutes. You want someone?"

"No, I'm just going to clear my head." I moved over to my bed and stretched out while he left and the door resealed.

I was about to go to bed at 10 that night when the door unexpectedly unsealed.

"Leave it!" I heard Jack call in the hall outside as the port swung open. "Belle?"

"Yeah?" I was still sitting on the edge of my bed, not about to lie back if they were going to get me up again. Jack entered and went straight to my wardrobe.

"We need you upstairs. There's been a development." He tossed me a sweatshirt and came around with socks and the clogs. I was dressed instantly and we were on our way. Several people had gathered in the IT conference/war room, including Deuce and the Director.

"Okay, go," Deuce ordered and the screens came back up from screensaver.

"That's El-Amin and that might be Almasi; that doesn't make sense though unless they're having a conference or something," I pointed out. "Is this IMINT? I'm impressed."

"They come outside to smoke," Agent Won said.

"Yes, he doesn't allow it in his house," I replied instantly. "If you're planning to spy on him, don't plan to do it for long. He's smart; he'll catch on to pretty much anything."

"It won't be for long," Deuce assured me.

"A drone strike would destroy any chance of intelligence gathering, sir," Jack pointed out.

"How do we take him alive?"

I buried my head in my hands and the world was silent for a moment. *I'm TIRED! Okay. Think. Think hard. Most important thing ever. Think. Nothing. Seriously? Nothing! You're a fucking genius, think of something! Sleeping, sleeping beauty, snipers, poison, sleeping powder, wait, is that real? No. um. Something, give me something. Guards. Look at the guards. Where are the guards? Food. Water supply? Double agent? Traitor? Inside man. Inside woman. Oh, a child! No one suspects a child! Trick a kid...shit. That's a shit idea. Shut up, would you?*

Sleeeeeeeeeeeep. What the hell is Almasi doing there? That's not his territory. Why did they gather? Do they know about the Canadian? Do they all know? No, that's not his style. People don't change. People don't change. Same thing, habits everywhere. Can we hack him? "Can we hack him?" I opened my eyes and asked the room.

"Maybe," Agent Won replied, "Big emphasis on the maybe."

"The minions, can we hack his lieutenants? Ozzie's paranoid, he'll have disabled his cameras but," I proposed and the idea took life.

"The CIA should have the workup by now on the facial rec," Deuce stated.

"It would be awesome if we got into the security system," Director Goode reflected aloud.

"Hacking takes time. I don't like this, we don't have time. We can't lose him again, I'm running out of friends to find him for us," I blurted and Jack snorted softly. "Seriously, let's talk to Bacon again, nicely. He doesn't deserve the black bag crap!" I faced Deuce directly for that one. "Bacon, what's his real name again? Ryan? The Canadian knows some of these people and their associates. He offered to sit with a sketch artist earlier, maybe he can tap into the people the CIA have photos of, see who he recognizes. Where does the estate get their food?"

"Good questions," Deuce recognized. "What else? No such thing as bad ideas."

"I once gave someone's bodyguard salmonella so I could get to the mark. These guys are tough but they won't stand watch and shit their pants. I'm sure you have all kinds of nasty little bugs we could infect them with. An inside person would be great. We need to consider," I added, thinking of something Bacon had said earlier, "that Waldo isn't in the direct area. The Canadian told me that there were no rats in sight; that was a Bin Laden reference. Is there a way to put the entire camp to sleep?"

Dead silence followed.

"The best hackers I know who are probably still alive are in Israel," I offered. "Too bad we can't strap a camera onto a monitor lizard.

Nobody messes with those things. Nasty little bastards," I added under my breath. *Worst possible surprise to wake up to. Dragon O'Death, surprise! Death.* An idea hit me hard, so hard I stood up and the room paused again. "Surprise. Biggest, craziest surprise ever."

"Such as?" Deuce asked.

"Me. People are wired against hurting a pregnant woman, the time that it would take to override that would buy me the normality segment I need. I'll just walk right through the doors; no guns, no tanks, no bombs. Me and soldier boy here," I pointed to my belly. "Maybe they kill me, maybe they don't but it will definitely catch their attention. They all know my face by now, especially with Almasi there. Dude hates my guts harder than anyone in the world."

As though the universe supported my idea, one of the cameras on one of the screens zoomed in on a large poster placed on the interior wall there. My face was one of the items on the poster along with a helicopter, the Canadian, and something that looked like little cameras. "Things to watch out for," I couldn't make out the brief text on the poster but the point was clear. "Cannot ask for better publicity."

"Young woman, you let yourself be captured without incident because you couldn't bring yourself to potentially kill an embryo. Your child is almost viable, how is this any better?" John from the CIA was first to point out.

"How many thousands have these three men alone killed?" I replied quickly. "How many, John? Anyone have that figure? How about the potential numbers from their next attack in this stupid war? Are we up to a million yet? Every day he is plotting, planning, executing; put me on a plane tomorrow, let's end this. I walk into their compound and I will get the attention of every man there."

"You will just trigger a higher alert, make the attack more difficult," Deuce replied.

"What about Bacon: he could contact them, serve as middle man, pretend to trade me for their good graces. We go in for the trade; they're partying for their victory."

"They'll put a bullet in your head before they party," someone pointed out.

"No," Jack finally spoke and his words were like granite. "No, end of discussion," he was face to face with me and there was a spark in his emerald eyes that almost made me nervous. He wrapped his left hand around my right wrist and firmly escorted me out of the room.

"Jack," I said quietly when I realized that he was pulling me the wrong way down the hall, away from the elevators. This was wild and unexpected and he didn't say a word until we were in a three-station office and he had closed the door.

"Sit down!" he pointed to a chair and I obeyed. "You are going nowhere, Alexis. You are my asset and I will keep you safe, alive, and healthy. What are you trying to do to me, Alexis?"

Wait, what? "You don't have to do this crap anymore, Jack!" I went on the offensive because it felt natural. "Your family is gone, there's no one to serve or protect for your, "looser job description." You're free if you let yourself be."

"Well you're not!" he pointed and slammed into a chair facing mine. "There is no way in hell you are going back to Pakistan to waltz into his compound. You're a brilliant mind, Alexis, how do you really think that's going to turn out? Do you know what they might do to you? As a woman, have you never considered the kind of danger you put yourself in?"

"You think I'm new or something?" I pointed out. "I have been tortured, Jack. I hold out pretty well, as it turns out."

"Are you listening?" he demanded.

"Yes,"

"Yes?"

"Yes...sir?" I guessed. This was a whole explosion of one aspect of his personality and I was no longer sure of what kind of ground we stood on.

"You know things you did not know before and these men, one of those men is able to make you talk."

"Not if you come in behind me hot and fast," I stuck to my guns on this idea because the more I thought about it the better it seemed as a plan.

"No. Maybe the Canadian, but we have far too much to lose from you. You are my responsibility."

Awwww, Muscles cares about me! I glanced through his smoke and mirrors anger façade. "Jack, I am an assignment."

"Bullshit!" he almost interrupted the word. "You need to start thinking really carefully as to why you are so willing to throw yourself away. Because until you,"

This time I interrupted him. "This is MY WAR!" The blurted words were soaked in unfiltered truth. "We can finish this thing, Jack!" My glare matched his and we held it for a few seconds. "Maybe they put a bullet in my head. You guys come in right then, you can pull him out. There's like, a few hours or something before he would die. Twenty-six weeks is viable; it's not great but it's possible."

"No."

"You are the top in your field for what you do," I pointed out, "And so am I."

"Once. This discussion is over. You are going nowhere. Now come on," He leapt up from his chair and seized both of my wrists to pull me to my feet.

The irony at his word choices would have made me laugh but there was something distinctly unfunny about his hands on my wrist and shoulder/neck as he marched me through the halls back toward the elevators. *God this is embarrassing*, I thought as we passed the conference room. *Just go with it. And maybe stop arguing with someone who plays with zip-ties and straightjackets for a living. I wish he would talk.* I almost opened my mouth but thought better of it when we were in the elevator with two other soldiers who had joined in along the way.

The first door between the cell and the elevator opened for us with a key card swipe by one of the soldiers. *Who is on deck?* I glanced around to the guards around my cell. *Benzion, Williams, and Steele. At least Benzion will be cool about this. Come on, Muscles, you're embarrassing me!*

"Good evening. Code purple with this, leave her open for a minute," Jack greeted the guards cryptically as the cell door opened. Williams went into the cell and I waited in silence, his hands still on me. Williams carried a few things out with him.

Did he just refer to me as a 'this'? Okay they're taking my razor, code purple, that's…what is that again? It ain't good. How pissed off is he? What will he do next? I wondered if he could feel my pulse from his grip on my wrist and suspected that he could when he stopped holding my neck and started rubbing my shoulders instead. Jack told me to get what I needed and go get ready for bed in the bathroom. Suspiciously, he told me not to open the door of the bathroom until he told me to.

I waited five minutes, seven minutes, ten minutes in relative silence and sat on the closed toilet seat. *Oh my god, bastard put me in time-out,* I concluded and checked the soft-band watch I was permitted to have back when they put me on an hourly schedule and started making me take breaks. The band was almost rubbery and slid on without a clasp. The casing was wafer-thin; someone had put a great amount of thought into making a harmless watch. *Twelve minutes. Screw this,* I stood up and stepped up to the door.

"Belle?" Jack called and I froze with my hand just inches from the knob.

"Yes?" *Do I really want to cross him?*

"Thank you for your patience. You may come out if you would like to."

A hundred smarmy, snarky, and rude comments swirled in my head but my tongue rejected all of them. *Why, why is he doing this?* I opened the door and peeked out. The door was sealed, the room looked about normal but there was an extra pillow on the futon and Muscles, Jack, no, Muscles stood in a tight t-shirt and what appeared to be sweatpants and...*socks. No shoes, nothing, no equipment. What the hell? Screw it all, I'm exhausted.* I climbed into bed and covered myself up.

I woke up around four and waddled to the bathroom and back without needing to turn on a light. I could barely see a movement of Jack's head as he lay on the futon backlit from the food tray's opening into the hall.

Think really carefully about why I am so eager to throw myself away, I remembered his words and closed my eyes again. *Baby is viable. She's only getting bigger, folks. Wrists and elbows. Don't have to explain why you did something to a woman in her third trimester. That poster was real; they're looking for me, watching for me, almost like they expect me to show up. No rats in sight. Poor Bacon. "Have to go now, darling, the Americans are here." So hilarious.*

The poster...something about that poster...rats. Put a camera on a rat? Rat robot? Dragons? No...god, there's something really important I'm just not remembering...

My bladder woke me up again at nine and I didn't realize that Jack was gone until I came out of the bathroom. *That was real though, right? He slept here? Oh yeah, throwing the life away. That crap. Oy. Something about rats? I should get dressed.*

I went about my day; dressed, ate breakfast and cleaned the cell. Jack returned while I was making my bed; his pillow and blanket had disappeared.

"Tom or Cyndy?" Jack greeted me.

"Tom," I chose my psychologist. *Never did talk to Tom yesterday. Topic number one, Jack! Good grief, I'm not your child!*

"Belle, I need you to think out loud please," Jack requested and the door sealed us in again.

"Alright, fine. There's something about that poster that is tickling my brain and it's not quite...out yet."

"The poster with you and Rogers and the cameras?"

"Yes. Things they would need to watch out for. A silent helicopter, hidden cameras, someone they knew was in the area and someone...me. The girl who would take them on; a big fat enemy force, a warning against my...the damage I could do, would do. Should be doing," I reflected. *Don't piss him off again!* "Jack," I looked into his eyes, "I cannot stand to lose him again. It would kill me."

He didn't have time to answer; the door opened and Tom came in with a small smile and apprehension in his eyes.

"Happy New Year!" I greeted him.

"Hello Belle, good to see you," Tom greeted back. "This is warmer than the offices upstairs; I vote we meet here."

"She's going nowhere," Jack mentioned briefly.

"Okay. Let's drop the flap then," Tom pushed past it and handed Jack a giant pair of earphones, the kind that cancel out everything. I propped myself up to sit in the bed, Tom brought a chair over and Jack sat on the other side of the room near the food tray.

"Dude's gone crazy," I started, "I proposed a simple tactic with approaching the target,"

"Such as?"

"Me, hugely pregnant, walking right through the front gate," I replied. The words did sound a little crazy.

"It would get their attention, but it would also get you killed."

"But we would have Omar! Why does nobody see this!?" I protested emphatically.

"It would kill little you too."

"Don't call it that," I glared. "Besides, he's viable. Hell, we could do a caesarian on the plane if you like that idea better than a post-mortem extraction."

"How do you feel about being pregnant when you probably want a baby least?" Tom asked pointedly and waited in silence.

"Seriously?" I whined and flopped over on my side over the pillows. Out of the corner of my eye I saw Muscles jolt up slightly before he slacked back into his chair. "Omar Al-Zahrani is almost in our crosshairs and you want to go on about…," I sought the word briefly, "details!"

"How are you and your entourage doing? Everything good with Muscles? Not so much?"

"He got super possessive last night. Dragged me out of the conference room and told me in no uncertain terms that I'm his responsibility and he's in charge of me and my life. Then he was all, "you need to think about why you're so willing to throw your life away," followed by storming me back to my room and putting me in the bathroom for twenty minutes while he apparently changed into sleeping clothes, disarmed, and set up a make-shift bed on my futon so he could sleep in here with me."

"Wow."

"We were in there and…Deuce said there were no stupid, no wrong suggestions. Tom, stop thinking about me as a person. Think about me as a tactic, a tool. We have the opportunity, a golden opportunity to stop the deaths of every man, woman, and child that bastard and his friends. That camp, my god, that camp is full of psychopaths, and I just want," I took a breath and swung around to lie across the bed so I could stare at the ceiling.

"Belle, we're going to get him. He is literally in our crosshairs," Tom assured.

"Unless he isn't," I considered, "No, we did get a video shot of him at that camp, but we haven't seen him since. This entire thing could be made up by him. And if Waldo isn't there or too close nearby, then where is he?"

"How do you know he isn't there?"

"No rats in sight. Bacon said that before he was arrested, when he had seconds left of his life. You know, living it is terrifying but revisiting it from a point of safety...that was rough!" I confessed.

"Ah, Bacon; did he trigger a reminder of how your captivity began?"

God I hate psychologists. "Look, we can talk Bacon, Ozzie, or Muscles."

"But we really need to talk about the baby. Have you thought of a name?" Tom pressed.

"Yes, I'm going to call him, "Death to Ozzie." It's catchy, isn't it?" My voice dripped with sarcasm.

"I suppose it's better than "Kill Waldo," but not by much. You don't even want him dead." Tom surmised.

"Who, Waldo? Nah, go ahead and kill Waldo. World is better with him dead."

"I know you like to be in charge. I know you're naturally going to want to push for things to go the way you think they should."

I'd like to push this baby out, how about that?

"Look, I'm not going to get any more pleasant or complacent about the Ozzie thing. Fine, don't send me. Let Bacon get himself killed if he's into it. I still don't know exactly what his motivations were in Pakistan or with that scum. Granted, he's done more dangerous things for less lucrative causes. Can we talk about the jaguar in the room please?"

"Interesting, jaguar?"

Oh my god is he going to read into this? Of course he is. Fucking shrinks! Gaaaaaaaaah. Not really a cat. If anything he's more like...a bear? A python? Wrapping me up tightly against my freedom? Like a straightjacket? You will not kill yourself. You will sit in that bathroom until you can come out. You are going nowhere. She is going nowhere. You are mine, mine, mine, mine, mine. Mr. Boss Man, the ceiling couldn't see me roll my eyes but Tom probably did.

"Belle; do you want me to ask him to step out?" Tom inquired.

"He has the headphones on, he's fine," I decided and pushed myself up to sit. "Hold on a minute, Tom, I'm hungry again. Let me get some milk."

"Are you still underweight?"

"Only for a hippo," I wiggled out of the bed and onto my feet. Jack stood up, waiting receptively until I pointed to my stomach. He pulled out water and milk and let me choose before handing it to me.

"Didn't you used to call him your badass butler?" Tom inquired, "When you say he spent the night here,"

"Just on the futon. It wasn't like that."

"Not even a little?"

"He just slept on the couch," I restated.

"All night."

"I saw him when I went to the bathroom at four, so yeah, I assume so."

"So he trusts you not to hurt him when he's prone."

Not really, I mean, I think he's a really light sleeper. He was awake when I returned from the bathroom.

Tom took my silence for consensus and started talking about building healthy relationships in the real world. I drank my milk and ignored him. When he got up and started strolling around the room I started silently mocking him behind his back to Muscles, who quickly got the point. Tom spun around once and caught Muscles and I slapping on angelic attentive expressions.

"You didn't hear any of that, did you?" Tom accused without passion.

"He didn't, I did. Yeah. Blah-blah relationships, blah-blah people, blah-blah trust. Blah-blah normal, healthy stuff. It's cute and all, but, Tom, I'm not normal!" I leaned against the back of one of the table's chairs. "I. Am. Not. Normal. I never will be. It is a fact."

"Well you still need normal relationships. Healthy relationships; you need to learn them and pass them on to your son."

"Am I going to be the only one he knows? I cannot possibly raise him alone; I need help. I have hundreds of thousands of dollars in my names; you have to find me some kind of top-secret nanny or something."

"I don't know the circumstances of your situation post-release. You won't be alone though, Belle," Tom said and I noticed Jack sat a little straighter and knew he was receiving something in his semi-permanent earwig.

Jack's hand shot up less than a minute later and Tom stopped talking. "Pause!" Jack requested and then removed his cans. "I didn't want to compromise the therapy confidentiality but I needed to interrupt," Jack explained.

How considerate. You know it actually was kind of sweet for him to stay over; my thoughts were interrupted by the dialogue.

"Agent Won needs you to look at some frames. She's bringing them down."

Because I'm going nowhere, I added mentally and Jack put the headphones back on.

"I'm going to give you some literature to read, maybe some videos to watch. I know you were normal once; you were an outstanding student, you had friends and a brother."

"You know I hate psychology," I complained.

"I know. You'll never enjoy people poking around in your brain. It's one of those things you either love or hate; like Jane Austen or quinoa."

"Mmmm, quinoa. Yum. With lamb and pine nuts…" I remembered. "There's this place in Algiers," I almost told a story but stopped myself. "Wait, when did we switch gears from focusing on my violent tendencies to a preschool friendship class? Oh my god, do you think that just because of this," I pointed to my protrusion, "that I'm not a…me anymore?" I felt my blood rush through my stiff and burdened body. "You listen up, Tom," I shook my finger at him angrily, "I am still Belle Fucking Jones. Those men over there, they're scared of me and they haven't heard from me in half a year now! Those men are evil, murdering bastards and I scare the shit out of them. Terrorists, grown men with stockpiles of weapons, they play with RPGs for fun and they put my picture and name on their walls with "Belle Dangereuse" on the front in big red letters," I punctuated each word after my

155

one-time name. "No matter how Pygmalion you go on me, nothing will change what happened. That version of me is still right here, the scars run deep, far too deep for you to buff them out. You can't have Belle Jones."

"You can't be Belle Jones!" Tom replied with animation. "In fact, you're not Belle Jones," he added.

"I'm not X128 either, Javert!" I tossed the reference from another famous prisoner's story at him.

"I'd really like it if you both calmed down," Jack said and I realized that he was on his feet and had moved around the table. I mimed it and he took off his headphones.

"We're done," I informed Jack.

"Okay," Jack pushed the flap out until someone from the outside lifted it away and the door popped open a few seconds later. "Dr. McEwen, thank you for coming," Jack shook Tom's hand and Tom left with an expression that told me this conversation was not over.

"Agent Won sir," a man in the hall announced and Jack brought Lisa in. She had about thirty large prints, freeze frames from Bacon's video and pics that appeared to be from IMINT. We three sat around the bed and worked through the images with the help of magnifying glasses she brought with her.

"This one bugs me," Agent Won admitted about ten minutes in. "It's VID-001-A12 at 08:01:23."

"Yes, there's something, a reflection there but no telling what it is reflecting," Jack agreed and passed it to me.

"Too bad we can't just talk to him and ask him where he was standing and how he got the video filmed," I muttered, yesterday's abruptly ended interview still fresh in my mind. "This part of the video, we've already seen Al-Zahrani," I remembered.

"He's featured in the six-minute range," Agent Won reported.

"We're assuming that the feed is continuous. What if it isn't?" Jack pointed out.

"I don't think it is. The experts on lighting could tell us, but there are definitely some gaps," I recommended. "Agent Won, please talk to the guys upstairs. Get an interview with Ryan Rogers; even if he's secretly a weapons warlord or some other trader, we have a bigger fish to catch. Besides, we can let him go. I can hunt him down no matter where he goes."

"Sweetie," Agent Won approached and I instantly knew she was going to tell me that my hunting days are over.

"I know," I sighed. "It's just going to take a while to get out of the habit."

"You know, regular life is pretty awesome. You don't have to worry about being chased or attacked, you can watch TV and movies, go shopping,"

"With a protective detail," Jack added.

"That will definitely help me fit right in to wherever you plant me," I muttered.

"You'd be surprised," Agent Won replied and picked up another photo.

My eyes wandered to my fake window, which was set on a rolling countryside with puffy white clouds in the distance. *Not here; that's where I'd be. Will he come?* I glanced at Jack briefly, *He has no home to return to unless he rebuilt it. I wonder if any of these people will visit me: I kind of want to meet Starr's child. I wonder what Natalie is going to look like in a few years? She'd never come visit; I still terrify her.* I smiled as I remembered Natalie when I met her: she shook like a rat-dog. She was maybe 22 and I was an alien to her. *I'll be the alien out there. Alien plus spawn.* I must have heaved a more audible sigh than I realized because when I glanced over again Agent Won and Jack were moving in unspoken agreement to stack up the photos to go. I let her leave without argument, choosing instead to use the bathroom before facing Muscles again.

"They're really going to release me?"

"It would be pretty hard to raise a child in here."

"The good news is that I haven't set foot on U.S. soil in so long, no one here should know my face. John said they might do a little surgery, hide some scars, maybe fix my nose," I studied his face for subtle signals. I don't even know what I was looking for.

"You said last night that you have been tortured before."

"Yes. Twice. Well, one and a half times. The second time got interrupted fairly quickly as my backup arrived."

"I thought you worked alone."

"I do, did, mostly did," we both sat at the table, "I worked in conjunction with others at various points in my career; Israel taught me most of my tricks and I ran several missions with their operatives. I came across an asset here and there and utilized them to mutual advantage when possible. With one or two exceptions that turned out very well." I pulled my hair aside to show him the scar on the back of my head. "Curling irons, with a few simple modifications, make excellent torture devices. That spot on my foot? Cigar. They were just messing with me. You know how in the movies, the hero always uses the chair they're bound to as a weapon and then breaks it easily? That so never works."

"What did work?" he asked with a small smile.

"Lies. Deception, manipulation, and concealed weapons in strange places," I smiled as I remembered a bamboo hair ornament turned dagger getting me out of the kind of zip-ties he liked to use. "I didn't just hurt a lot of bad people; I also saved a lot of downtrodden victims. Fed them, warded off their oppressors, gave them days or weeks of peace, time to recover, renew, and strengthen. They still have to fight their daily wars, but for a while…"

"You know, almost everything I learn from you matches perfectly against the person presented in your files," Jack said and I wondered if I heard approval.

"Almost?"

"Alexis doesn't show up."

"Ah. Now you sound like a psychologist."

"I hate shrinks," Jack confided honestly.

"I just got into an argument with Tom. It was pretty stupid but I felt like he was trying to wash away the last decade of my life; everything I've done out there. Don't get me wrong, I don't want to remember some of that stuff. A lot of that stuff," I corrected, "And maybe I shouldn't be, but I'm proud of Belle Jones. We have Omar Al-Zahrani and his henchmen in the crosshairs now because of her, and my next act is the rat himself."

"Belle Jones is pretty amazing, but Alexis is the magician behind the act, the person inside the persona. If you can go from schoolgirl to operative, what can you do from here? Besides motherhood; I mean, I keep hearing wild rumors that you're pregnant or something," Jack joked and I couldn't help but laugh.

"Motherhood? Oy. Civilian life," I nodded slowly, "I can't retire! I haven't hit twenty-five yet!"

Jack had his full lopsided grin on and I couldn't help but laugh.

162

Chapter Six: Deception

The first forty-eight hours after the point where we knew we had the compound in our crosshairs were the most tense for me. I thought it was insane that they would know where a long-sought target was and do nothing serious about it. I also spent both of those days in my cell.

Jack did not sleep on my couch after that first night: I guess he thought I was safe enough, or at least sane enough. He never did explain what metrics or terms he made that decision on. I like to have criteria or thresholds to measure things by and he never shared what the rules were.

By the third day I was getting cabin fever. When he joined me for cereal that morning I let him sit and we ate together for a few minutes before I pressed suit.

"Jack, can we go upstairs today?"

"No."

"Please?"

"No."

"Please??"

"Yes."

"Really?" I was overly excited.

"No," Jack replied in the same monotone, "Maybe the pool."

"What are they doing up there? Do we have the bastards or not?"

"Director is on her way down," one of the guards called through the food window. I glanced down to check that I was in proper clothes: yesterday I hadn't changed out of pajamas. I pulled a brush through my very curly hair: the result of one of my activities in captivity. I had pulled my hair into seven tight braids while wet; it looked ridiculous while they were in but the result was delightful.

Maybe I'll get a perm when I'm out of here. I considered and Jack stood up to greet the incoming guards, Benzion and Belot, with the Director.

"I wish I was coming to tell you," Director Goode said and stopped herself. "Belle, it's about Rogers."

"Why, did you kill him?" I asked with disillusioned bluntness. That was a real possibility; one that had worn out its welcome in my mind.

"No, no, he's alive. It was decided that we may take up his offer. He is offering to do almost exactly what you said; to contact them and offer your trade. His conditions are a little controversial," she mouthed the last word like it was the most important word in the world.

"Controversial?"

"He wants to meet you in person before he goes. We will make arrangements for the remainder of the plan; I will need you to sit for a makeover of sorts so he has a picture of you allegedly under his captivity. I have techs building the background and finding the clothes now. We will hide the pregnancy from the camera and from Rogers; he'll never see below your chest."

"They will kill him," I stated. "If he walks into that camp, they will treat him no better than me and even if they don't, the resulting forces will."

"He is currently traveling under sedation; when he wakes up he won't know where he is. We intend for him to think you are in Guantanamo Bay," Director Goode continued. "We will run rehearsals tomorrow; the event happens tomorrow night. Then we sedate him again, put him on a plane and dump him in Pakistan with what he needs for the mission. Bear with me, Belle. This is an excellent opportunity,"

"I'll do it," I cut her off. "But I will tell him that he is going to die."

"I think he already knows that," Jack offered and I knew he was right. If Rogers' primary condition was to see me first, then he knew perfectly well what he was walking into.

Maybe he's ready. Maybe he's more than ready. A year ago I would have done it. A week ago I would have done it.

"Makeup will need her around noon," Director Goode said to Jack. "We will need her to look like she has been out in the field, not safe and warm here. I'll bring her booking photos as a reference."

"Excuse me; I was a very clean person 90% of the time!" I objected.

"You've been captured in the general area of Afghanistan and been held by Rogers for at least three days. You can take a shower tonight when they're done with the photo shoot," she responded and then returned her focus to Jack. "Please let my office know if there are any problems." She turned her back to me and headed for the door.

"Hey!" I said loudly and Benzion put his dad face on for me. "You going to meet him, or are you just going to throw him away? Is he below your notice, just some Canadian bait?"

"That's enough, Belle," Benzion stated firmly. He was closer to me than Muscles was but I didn't care. Benzion wasn't about to hurt me and even if he wanted to Jack would fly in to rescue me. Director Goode exited while we were busy reading each other's vibes and the moment passed.

They took me upstairs into an interrogation room for makeup application. There I met an old man and a very young woman and the table was full of makeup and kits.

"This is your costume," the old man said and handed me a pile of clothes. "The purpose is to make you look like a Pakistani woman who has been roughed up but not beaten severely. You are cold and alone and a little frightened and you have not bathed in a week. Please change." He turned back to his table and I stood there awkwardly for a moment until the girl noticed.

"I think she is modest," the girl said to the old man. He grunted and took a large water jar with him into the hall. "Do you need help, miss?" the girl asked me but Jack waved her off and pulled a chair over so I could sit in the corner to shuck my pants and pull on the clothing I would have worn in Islamabad to blend in. My breasts are perfect, aside from the scars, and I have no shame in them. Besides, women in Pakistan wear brassieres.

"She better be ready," the old man returned with a full water jar, "I'm losing daylight."

"Metaphorically," Jack muttered: we were deep in the interior and I wasn't even sure we were above ground.

"Metaphorical daylight!" the old man ran with it and I almost laughed. They sat me in a chair and the girl started with my feet while the man pulled my hair back and held various discs up on my face. I watched as my feet got 'dirty' with a light brown powder over some strategically placed liquid dabs and smudges. I closed my eyes after a while because the old man was doing something disgusting just above my right eyebrow.

"Okay, open eyes," the old man instructed and stared at me for a few minutes in silence. "I don't like it."

"Too Hollywood," the girl agreed and got up from the floor to hand him a baby wipe.

"Okay, that's okay. Hey, boyfriend," the old man addressed Jack, who was watching the whole scene. "How would you hit her?"

"He doesn't hit me," I protested.

"From the side or the back; I wouldn't face her and swing," Jack offered.

"I would have turned at a noise, it would catch my ear," I added and the odd couple started pointing and chattering, followed by painting and gluing and application of various things to my ear and face.

"Here, chew one of these," the girl gave me a small brownish-orange tablet. "Don't swallow, just squish it around and then spit it out. You can swish with chocolate milk afterwards."

They did other things, leaving my hair until last. The girl worked something slick and wet through my once-gorgeous tresses while I drank a protein shake through a straw courtesy of my badass butler.

"Why does she smell like a smoothie?" Jack asked a question I had considered.

"There are several natural ingredients in our dyes and compounds in the mixture on her hair," the girl explained.

"Where's the set?" I asked as the old man started packing up. Just then, Belot walked through the door and her facial reaction was all I needed to know about my appearance.

They walked me down to another interrogation room and it had been transformed into an almost-third world slum. I could easily see the scenario in that setting.

"Yeah, I've been here before," I joked and stepped into the scene. Everything was as authentic as we could make it: a bare incandescent light bulb here, a gas lamp there, we used a common camera for the shots and took a few with an old school Polaroid. I was posed handcuffed in various ways and with different expressions. I was starving by the time we had finished.

It was easier to hide the baby than I would have thought: angles and poses really do compensate nicely. I was so hungry that I ate while still in my makeup and costume: someone had brought in a homemade couscous dish.

"If you will hold still, I will remove the prosthetics," the girl came in while the guys started to break down the set. I sat for her while the harsh chemicals were dabbed until the glue gave way. I used baby wipes on my hands while she chipped away on my head. Finally she stepped back and put the solvent away. "I will wipe your feet off and then you may want to take a shower. We'll give you the soap you'll need to use."

"Thank you. It's really amazing how much a person's appearance can be changed, isn't it?" I replied and we had a pleasant conversation walking down the hall as we returned to the original makeup room. A very nasty surprise was waiting for me there.

"X128," the bitch greeted me coolly.

Where the hell did she come from? Good god, I am not dealing with her.

"Get out," she ordered the girl. "I moved your stuff across the hall." The bewildered girl left and Belot came in with us. Williams was already there and I decided that I definitely did not like this situation.

"She was getting me soap for the makeup," I stated in a neutral tone.

"Take off your clothes," Jessica replied, deigning to speak to me through a very small smirk. "This woman has been around dangerous goods and makeup which could be used during an escape," she said to the guards.

"She will be appropriately searched inside her quarters, ma'am," Jack said with a clip in his tone.

"Now," Jessica said firmly, "Standard protocol. X128, take off your clothes and place them on the table. Do it now or they will call the others in to help you."

Jack stepped up to her until they were inches away nose-to-nose. "This is not in keeping with protocol for this case and you know full well that your superior officer will not approve."

"Approve of searching a dangerous woman? Careful, Jack, you seem swayed by her charms."

Yep, I'm going to murder her. Twenty-five is a good number to stop at, and the world could live without her. My son shouldn't live in a world with her in it.

"Help her," the ice-queen demanded and Williams shot me an empathetic look pleading for a rescue.

I'll kill her naked. I decided and pulled my shirt off over my head, tossing it onto the table. I tucked my thumb into my pants and jerked them down to fall in a pool of thin fabric around my ankles.

"Hold on," Jack said and stepped back onto my side of the room before pulling at his own shirt.

What the hell, is he getting naked too? That's so awesome. Oh! I should moon her while I have an opportunity! I carefully stepped out of my pants and picked them up with my toes until they were within my hand's reach. They joined the top and scarf: I hadn't been wearing shoes. *What is he doing?*

Jack had removed his tight black shirt, revealing an olive drab t-shirt which highlighted his every rib and ripple. The olive shirt came off quickly and I thought I saw a spark of desire in the bitch's eye. "Officer Belot," Jack handed her his green shirt; "I believe you are an expert in clothing inspection, would you clear this shirt please?"

My watching was noted by Jessica and she barked at me to carry on. I turned my back and unfastened my bra before throwing it over my shoulder with a brief side glance. "No music?" I asked playfully. She meant me to be shamed and humiliated and I refused to let the bitch win. *I'm going to kill you naked, Jessica.* "I think they used to put tassels on these things. Are you enjoying the view? I'll admit that I've gained a few pounds," While I was talking, I heard Belot say something briefly and Jack thanked her politely. I crossed my arms over my chest when I saw Jack in my peripherals coming around to face me. His black shirt was back on his chest and Jack was carrying his green shirt pinched between a finger and a thumb. I got the idea instantly and pulled on the offered item. It hung well past my butt.

I turned and winked at Jessica before hiking up the hem in the back, bending forward slightly, and letting my butt tell her what I thought about her. The panties fell after I let the shirt drop again and turned to face her. My feet were planted at shoulder width with my hands on my hips in victory.

"That's a full search," Belot stated.

"I will be discussing this with our superior officer," Jack stated firmly.

"If you're done with me, I need to shower now. You're not invited," I told Jessica.

"I had full cause; an application tool was counted missing from the makeup set," Jessica announced.

"Was it five inches long, a pencil's width, with a plastic tip?" I inquired of the guards and Williams nodded. "Try the inside of her left boot," I suggested. The expression on Belot's face was priceless once again as Jessica flushed red. "The clothes were from costuming; mine don't seem to be around anymore. Tell you what, you can keep those panties, Jessie, I don't want anything you've touched that close to my skin.

I've had a lovely time, goodnight," my sarcastic wit was dangerously close to making Jack laugh. "Oh, Officer Belot, could you make sure that girl gets her scraper back?" I added as a final touch and Williams held the door open for me.

"Belle, we can duck into a room until someone fetches some clothes for you," Jack offered in the hall as people started to notice us. There were at least a dozen people in the hallway and only two were female.

"Everyone good?" I asked jovially and loudly, "Let them see me, Sergeant. I want them to know about a forced strip search under false pretenses which she was kind enough to manufacture herself. I just hope that darling girl gets her property out of the bitch's boot," the girl appeared in an open doorway and handed me a small zip-top plastic bag with three small bottles in it.

"Thank you for your patience today, miss," the girl said and I gave her a warm smile which she rapidly reflected. I thanked her and Jack handed the bag to a guard. We walked back to the cell like that, with me wearing nothing but a t-shirt.

I took my time in the shower: my hair took a great deal of scrubbing and I also wanted to wash away the horror of Jessica. Jack asked if I was okay twice before I turned off the water.

"I'm fine!" I protested grumpily. *Okay, she got to me. Literally, physically, mentally, emotionally, just knowing that she's out there with that kind of power combined with that level of CRAZY!!! I am not doing this. I am not dealing with that psychotic bitch, she ought to be arrested.*

My thoughts were interrupted by voices in the main part of my room.

"Explain again to me how this woman is a high ranking official?" Director Goode sounded incensed. "So she took a tool, hid it in her boot in what was apparently clear sight if Belle detected it, and then...this is the most outrageous abuse of power I have ever heard of. She forced her to," Director Goode stopped again, probably because she couldn't form words.

Something stirred in me as I finished getting dressed and hung up my towel to dry. *She cannot possibly blame him. He did everything; he gave me the shirt off his back.* I opened the door and there was a small crowd in my room including Tom near the door, Officer Morgan, Goode and Jack. Everyone was staring at me and I froze like a bunny. A wave of emotions ripped through me and I could only stand there until I finally stepped backwards and closed the door behind me again.

I sat on the closed toilet lid and stared blankly forward. I have no idea how much time passed, nor did I track the conversations outside. I know that someone, probably Jack, handed me my pink dolphin because when I came back I was crushing her. There were no voices from my room so I opened the door and peeked. The door was open but no one was staring so I crossed from the bathroom directly to my bed and crawled in, covering my entire being with a hole between pillows for fresh air.

I must have fallen asleep because I woke up and briefly wondered why I was in a tent before remembering the situation. I was hungry but also on high alert for people. "Jack?" I asked quietly.

"He's nearby," an old and gravelly voice said.

OH GOD, DEUCE! It better not be her. She better not be here. It's no good; I'm going to have to kill her.

I sat up after summoning my courage and flopped the covers down to my waist. The portal was still open and Captain Stover was standing vigil in the doorway.

"Captain," I greeted quietly. My voice was cloudy and my face was a little damp; it seems I was crying at some point. "Please be aware that if I see that horrible woman again I will attack only her but with intent to kill." *Fair enough to give them a heads-up; they have been kind to me.*

"Noted," Stover said quietly. He took me seriously because he knew me.

"You will not cross paths with her again," Deuce stated. "She is currently in a holding cell pending investigation of her theft and conduct. She will remain in holding until after we have completed Operation Flapjack; I find that I'm too busy to address her presently."

I gained the impression that the words "too busy" could have had finger quotes on them. "Where is Jack?"

"He went to go abuse a punching bag at the gym. He'll be back soon; I can call him if you would like."

"Let him get it out. I must be taxing on him." I flopped backwards onto the pillows again. "Is it tomorrow?"

"No, it's around 2200," Deuce replied.

Jack is both smarter and kinder than I had given him credit for, figuring out a way around a strip search like that. I propped myself up on my elbows again and looked at Deuce directly. "We're still doing the Canadian tomorrow night?"

"Yes. They will have a costume for you again; we decided that for the scene you will be a normal prisoner at Gitmo. They are finishing his cell's details now; we will bring you up to the window. It's a medical-style cell with a large window. Everything will be planned and controlled."

Everything in me felt numb and heavy. I would have gone back to sleep but my stomach growled.

"What will you eat?" Deuce asked. "Jack said that you have to be reminded to eat on a regular basis."

"I kept myself alive out there, but no, I've never been great at self-care. Are there leftovers from dinner? That was delicious."

Deuce picked up the radio on the external food tray and spoke with someone briefly. By the time I had finished in the bathroom there was a bowl of couscous on the tray.

"Thank you," I said with genuine gratitude for this enormously powerful and busy man sitting calmly babysitting me. I ate half the bowl and started crying again for reasons I couldn't explain. I didn't have the energy to run to the bathroom so I just folded my arms and nested my head in them on the table. I cried until the urge passed and caught my breath. *She's gone, she's in a cell somewhere, she can't hurt me.*

As if he could read my mind, Captain Stover cleared his throat. "We put her in cell X128."

I almost smiled but didn't have it in me.

"Under a security quarantine pending investigation," Deuce added, "no rights, no phone calls, nothing."

I returned to my bed and realized that Jack's t-shirt was mixed in the sheets. It still smelled like him and I slid it on over my shirt before climbing back into the bed. "I will do what we need done tomorrow with Bacon." I pulled the sheets over my head. "Show him whatever circus you want, let him throw his life away. Take down the terrorists; wake me when it's over."

I closed my eyes and took a deep breath and immediately fell asleep. When the baby woke me up I realized that I had been asleep and got up to go to the bathroom. *What time is it? It was a little after ten, now it's three. Is that a nightlight? Jack? Ooh, okay, bathroom!* I got to the bathroom just in time as the baby kicked again directly to my bladder. When I came out Jack had sat up a bit from his bed on the futon.

"Jack?"

"Hi," he said quietly. "Do you want me to leave?"

"No. Do you want your shirt back?" I was sweating in the extra layer so I peeled it off.

"Does it help?"

"I really, really appreciate what you did. It was brilliant." I could either be honest or look at him so I faced my bed.

"I almost high-fived you when you mooned her," he admitted quietly as I settled back into bed.

"That was one of many ideas that happened during those minutes. The others revolved around killing her."

"Deuce can do worse than killing her."

"Yeah, he made her X128 under quarantine."

"I'm sorry that happened to you," Jack offered quietly.

"You make it a lot less bad. I'm still…I'm not okay with it," I admitted softly. He didn't reply and I wondered whether or not he heard the words. I closed my eyes and waited impatiently for dreams.

Chapter Seven: Ozzie

"Run through it for me again," Director Goode requested as we sat together in her office the following afternoon.

"Prison jump suit, extra baggy to help hide the baby just in case. We walk up to the fake cell in the staging area, the window shows from my upper chest upwards. I stand on the premise that we are at Gitmo, that I am an inmate there working a deal with the US. We talk about whatever he wants to talk about; obviously he wants to see me in person for some sentimental reason. Or he wants confirmation that I'm alive and well, regardless; we go until you guys pull me. I behave with veiled resentment and contempt for the guards and they treat me like an inmate until we have totally cleared the scene," I recited for her while chomping on a giant pretzel stick.

"What do you do if you have an emergency?" Jack asked.

"I lift my foot up."

"We have to do this in one go, so let's do everything we can to avoid any issues," Director Goode directed.

"Cameras will be everywhere," Agent Won added. "We'll hear and see everything."

"You do what we have to do and I'll give you anything you want that I can give you," Goode promised.

"I want Al-Zahrani, Almasi, and El-Amin captured and I'd prefer to keep the Canadian alive," I admitted.

"We'll do what we can," she replied. "They're waking him up now; two hours to show time."

Two hours later I was standing in a hallway one floor up from the staged room. "Orange is definitely not my color," I joked with Benzion and Agent Starr.

"Benzion is going to hold your left elbow, I'm on your right," Jack said, newly decked out in a military uniform like Benzion.

"Check it out, you outrank yourself," I kidded with Jack and he smiled.

"Reel it in, Belle. You're not supposed to be that happy," Jack replied.

I started laughing and couldn't stop myself. It was preferable to the crying but still wildly inappropriate. We had to wait another ten minutes for me to sober up so we could head downstairs. Once faced with the door I needed to walk through, everything clicked into place for me and we were able to proceed. Jack and Benzion moved me into place in front of the window and we exchanged all the silent conversations of a prisoner against their guards. It was all for nothing: Rogers had his back to us.

"So, Ryan, huh?" I greeted him and he turned slowly. He looked like he had lost ten pounds since the pictures from Pakistan. His eyes were hollow and dead but he did smile when he saw me.

"Liberty," he greeted me. "You're okay?" he stepped toward me and the window while squinting.

"Yes, well," I gave Benzion side-eye, "Okay enough. I didn't send the soldiers after you, please believe that."

"I do. You had no idea where I was." Rogers continued talking about where he had been and what he had done over the last year since I saw him.

"So, what did you do with the uranium?" I asked in the course of conversation.

"It's fine. I left it with Simon Pierre Gastrad; we have a no questions asked policy where I give him radioactive stuff and he makes sure it stays on the legal side of things."

"That's convenient," I admitted.

"So, what do you think my odds of coming out of this alive are?" Rogers asked bluntly.

"Really, really slim," I told him honestly. "But...I volunteered to do the same thing."

"No!" he replied quickly, too quickly and with too much urgency. "Liberty, you do whatever you can, whatever you need to in order to live your life well and fully. You're so young, god; you look even younger now without makeup."

"My name is Isabelle," I said gently.

"Of course it is, Isabelle. It fits you so well. Could you," he paused, "could you take your hair down?" He looked a little craven and I pulled it down out of its ponytail.

"You specifically asked to see me in person; why?"

"Libby. Do you remember the night in Lebanon, the hotel room with the balcony?"

"I watched you sleep while I was investigating you, but,"

"I wasn't asleep the entire time. Just before you left, I woke up. I saw you jump off; knew it was you. It was February 18th, 2007, around two in the morning."

I was stunned by the impact one little incident in my life had on him. "That was the night I heard you call her name."

"Libby was the kindest, sweetest, most angelic person who ever lived and she was killed by an errant RPG doing charity work in Africa. She was my next door neighbor growing up, like my sister but never a lover. An angel if there ever was one," he reminisced. "No, I never got you two mixed up, but that night I saw you and knew what you were."

"You knew what I was the day we met," I smiled.

"Not really, I knew your reputation, but, look, you showed me that I wasn't alone out there. Someone wasn't trying to kill me, someone had my back. That kept me functioning out there. It was perfect: I never knew where you were so I could always pretend you were around."

His logic was unimpeachable; almost a Schrodinger's cat scenario. "Sometimes I was," I admitted, "But I won't be this time. I've gone through the whole cycle here, I fought them, I accepted it, I fought them again and frankly I'm tired of the consequences. I can't escape from here on my own and if I ever get out it will be because they let me go."

"Don't fight them, Isabelle, work with them. Throw me under the bus if it helps, I'm ready to face my death. Just be okay. Your life has been too dark, too crazy. I've left my craters-"

"Is that all it was? That one night?"

"That, and you were the one who offed the people responsible for Libby's death," he shrugged. "I've come full circle now, plus I've been exposed to so much radioactive material it's kind of a miracle I'm alive."

"You did some good work. You really did," I offered sincerely.

"Yeah, well," he was choking up a little and looked away.

"They're telling me to wrap it up. You have a plane to catch," I distracted.

"I...okay. Well, thank you. For the rescues, for the protection, for Libby."

"That one job in Kenya, 2008, was that you?"

"Yes, it was a small job but it seemed important."

"It may have saved my life," I grinned and he smiled back at me despite the tear running down his face.

"Good," he whispered and cleared his throat. "If you get out, could you look up my niece Susan? I want her to know who I was."

"I'll do my best."

"Thirty seconds," someone down the hall called.

"Okay, well, go get 'em. That bastard killed my mother and Almasi and El-Amin have so much blood on their hands it's a miracle they haven't burst into hellfire," I offered with a lump in my throat.

"There's a thought. You know, two weeks ago I could have made that happen," he joked but instantly sobered. I reached in and he stepped forward so my hand graced his face.

"No touching!" a man down the hall ordered us and I withdrew my hand, stretching out the fingers to prove it was empty. Jack took the wrist and pulled it gently but believably behind me to click on handcuffs in front of Rogers' witness.

"Lib—Isabelle," Rogers lurched against the opening and Benzion stepped in front of me while I stepped back. Two other guards jumped into the lurch, one with a little neon yellow can in his hand. He pointed it toward Rogers and shouted that he would get peppered if he didn't comply. Benzion gave us the clear to move and he covered my six while Jack walked me out.

Out in the hall, once the door was closed behind us, Jack removed the cuffs quickly. I didn't hear the screams that inevitably accompany a mace application so I assume Rogers did what they wanted.

"This way," Agent Starr called quietly and we followed her up the staircase and back to the prep room. They gave me back my clothes and let me change in a bathroom. I caught a glimpse of myself in the mirror and thought about what he had said about being young.

I never really realized how much older he was than me; Rogers is fifty this year, or he would have been. He's probably right about the radiation, he's constantly been around the stuff and nothing about our lives was sterile or safe. I'm glad they tested me for all that stuff as well. My head hurts. I hope they let me go home now. All these rooms remind me of Jessica. I washed my hands thoroughly just in case there was something foreign on his skin. I doubted it, but it wasn't worth the risk. I returned to the prep room and looked around for a cue.

"We may as well focus on the hunt for Bin Laden at this point," Director Goode walked in, "It's going to be at least thirty hours before any action. They're drugging him for transport now; flying back to Afghanistan will take time."

I knew she was right: I had crossed the Atlantic from France and it was already a long enough flight. Most of us moved on to the cyber conference room and I watched the enemy compound under the brightening light of dawn. There wasn't a lot of action and the screen flipped from the green of night-vision enhancements to the yellow tone for brightening the details.

"We got into one of the henchmen's phones. It's not much but it is something," Agent Won reported.

"My people are in perimeter positions," John added.

"Now we wait," Director Goode said what we were all thinking.

Now we wait, she said at least thirty hours. It is nine p.m.; six a.m. there. It's at least 16 hours to fly there from here, plus adjustments and onsite preparations, rehearsals, so, if he leaves at 2200 tonight, he'll get there at 2300 tomorrow local time.

"What time is the transaction?"

"1830 local time; the sun will be setting. We give a wide perimeter between initial contact and the actual take-down."

"I think that's around 32 hours," I thought aloud. *This is going to be hell.*

I was wide awake at six the next morning. *Twenty seven hours. Where is he? He's still in the air. He'll be in the air until this afternoon. I should go back to sleep. Has it only been nine hours? Forget about him, just forget about him. Go back to sleep. Sleep will help the time pass.* I stared at the ceiling until hunger hit and then resigned myself to cereal. I tried to do everything extra slowly but still ended up bored out of my mind before I would have normally woken up.

Okay, so, pretend we have them, all of them. What happens next? Bin Laden. Probably in Pakistan. It's a big country with lots of nooks and crannies. What's next? What's next? Don't want to count chickens but we could be very close to getting Ozzie and friends. So close. Dead or alive, no matter the cost. No matter the cost…the cost has been high. Without the satellite time and the non-stop surveillance, hundreds have died looking for two men, one man by most accounts. Thousands have died at these two's hands. What goes on inside of their heads? What drives them and why do thousands of strangers need to die for them to call it success?

Will they go to Gitmo? Here? Somewhere else? Will anyone be alive after the shooting is over? Will we be able to recover enough data? Any data? Please, just let us get him. Let this be over with. If they have to kill Rogers, make it a clean quick death, no torture or anything. I think we've both seen enough of that world.

"Miss, are you awake?" a female officer called from the hall.

"Up, dressed, showered, fed, and bored!" I replied.

"Someone named Fred requested your assistance in the lab," she added.

"Beam me up, Scotty!" I pulled my jacket on and waited for them to open the door.

Twenty minutes later I plopped down next to Fred's workstation and he explained that he was trying to guess what kind of encryption the bad guys would use. This kept me entertained for most of the morning until they made me take a break.

When my mandatory break was over, we went up for weekly inspection with Director Goode. We were all delightfully distracted when a very large box arrived: the bassinet was delivered to a swing office and we all went to check it out.

"Of course it's blue," I silently rolled my eyes as Benzion opened the package with a box cutter and we all pulled the various pieces out of their Styrofoam homes.

"Part A, four each," Jack muttered as we laid things out in surgical preparation.

"This can't be G, there are like twenty of these things and G only has 12," I reflected and compared pictures to packets. We carried on like this for quite some time until Jack stepped away to listen to his earwig for a minute in the far corner. I started screwing the Fs to the C21s with the included screwdriver until I could get the legs under the basket part. I was tightening those when I glimpsed a uniform in the doorway.

"Hi Officer Morgan," I greeted casually and straightened.

"Code," she said quickly and pulled her gun out of her holster while moving through the doorway and skirting the side of the room. Williams came in behind her and aimed for my head.

"Stand down!" Jack said from behind.

"Do not move," Williams ordered and I froze in place, temporarily baffled.

"Belle, please drop the weapon," Morgan's gun was aimed on my leg. I opened my left hand and the screwdriver dropped to the ground.

"Step backwards," Williams directed and I backed away until Jack's open hands stopped me.

"There are two screwdrivers in the set," Jack told them as the guards put their guns away. Williams climbed into the worksite and quickly retrieved both tools. I was still in shock but Jack held me safely.

"Clear her," Williams asked Morgan and she approached me. Jack led my wrists to the back of my head and held them there so gently while Morgan worked from my feet upwards to check me for additional tools/weapons. My baby kicked her hard when she was passing over my stomach.

"Code four," Morgan said quietly and stepped away from me. Jack released my wrists but I didn't really move for a minute. My hands floated over my face and stayed there as if my fingers could dam up the flood of emotions at this sudden turn.

"Home," I mumbled into my hands and felt his hands on my elbow and back helping me maneuver through the room and out into the hall. I didn't look around until we were in the elevator. Morgan and Williams were still with us but no one tried to talk to me. I went straight to my bathroom and then into bed to hide from the world.

"Hey, are you awake?" Agent Won's voice was calling so I pushed the covers down. The room was empty; she was using the speaker.

"Why?"

"It's dinnertime. Want to come eat with us, come share the nervous energy?" she suggested and I had to grin.

"Sure, let me grab Jack."

"Jack's in a meeting but I cleared it with him. Captain Stover and I will fill in for him," she explained. "What do you say, ten minutes?"

I agreed and cleaned myself up before the door unsealed. Lisa Won was dressed like she might be a bodyguard and Captain Stover had rearranged his usual accessories; I mentally connected the changes to Jack and briefly wondered what kind of restraints they were each concealing.

Up in Cyber, I surveyed the group: there were about eight people there, most were already at the tables they had moved together to make one large surface. As we sat and ate spaghetti I realized that only some of the people knew the time of our intended attack. They were the ones who kept looking at their watches or the clock on the wall.

That silent section of the group looked around at each other knowingly at the half-hour. *Fifteen hours.*

We forcibly distracted ourselves, telling holiday and vacation stories from our pasts, trying to explain some game with cards and dice to non-players, (so you build cities on the board and then try to knock them down?) and that all led to an animated cross-table discussion about a specific popular board game that comes out with a new version every year or so in what must be an attempt to stay globally relevant. I never knew how much it mattered to people which piece they got to play.

"What kind of game did you play as a child?" Agent Won asked me.

"We played chess. A lot of it," I admitted.

"I keep a set in my desk," the Hispanic man sitting next to Kmetz responded and I struggled to remember his name. I knew his face, or at least the back of his head.

"Me too," a man and a woman said at the same time.

"Oh my god, we're all stereotyped geeks!" Kmetz cracked a joke and people laughed. "Okay, does anyone in Cyber not know how to play chess?"

Silence pressed and one or two of the people hesitantly admitted to ignorance. The conversation moved on to checkers and I caught a glimpse of Jack across the room. By around eight p.m., most of the people had either left or returned to work. CIA HQ was doing most of the monitoring for Operation Flapjack, so boredom and impatience were rampant in the lab.

I was tired, but knew there would be no sleeping waiting for the most important moment of my life to happen. I lingered in the lab until nine and it became obvious I was stalling.

"Belle," Captain Stover approached quietly.

"I know. I have to go back now," I sighed.

"Do you want to play some chess, or are you ready for bed?" he asked and my face must have lit up because his reflected the expression.

"You play?"

"I may have played a little," he was downplaying it and I loved him for it. "There's already a set downstairs."

We said goodnight to everyone and Jack, Stover and I returned to my cell. Jack sat in the opposite corner on a laptop and Captain Stover and I set up a game on the dining table and started a marathon. He stayed until I was incredibly drowsy and Jack interrupted the matches several times with step-by-step instructions designed to eventually get me into bed.

During a bathroom break I peeked at the clock. *Seven hours. I can do this; I can stay awake…no. No I can't. It's two a.m. and I'm fried. Come on, suck it up,* I reprimanded myself and returned to the game to find that Captain Stover had transferred the game to the food tray.

"It would be unsporting to continue against a half-asleep opponent. You can kick my ass tomorrow, Belle," Stover greeted me quietly. "We'll wake you up when it's time, just get a little sleep."

Those conditions worked for me and between the two of them I was in bed within minutes. I tried to keep myself awake but utterly failed. I slept hard until about five, when I got up for a bathroom break and quietly cursed my bladder before groggily schlepping back to bed.

"Alexis," someone whispered my name and I considered opening my eyes. "Alexis, are you going to sleep all day?"

"How late was she up?" a man asked quietly.

"Zero two-thirty, sir," Jack replied. That woke me up and I looked around.

"Hi?" I greeted Director Goode, Deuce, and Jack. "What time is it?!" I remembered urgently and tried to bolt up but my belly slowed me down. *Oh my god I need to pee.*

"Beauty, it's around eleven," Deuce told me. "We just got these pictures we wanted to share with you."

"Almasi is deceased. El-Amin is in critical condition and Al-Zahrani," Director Goode listed and I flew through the photographs looking for the things that really matter.

"Is he dead? He doesn't look dead, is that a helicopter?" I asked rapidly while my bladder screamed at me.

"We got him, okay Belle? Ozzie's alive and in custody," Jack cut to the chase as my feet swung to the floor. I ran to the bathroom without another word and continued the conversation through the door.

"What about the others in the compound?" I asked.

"Some alive, some dead," Goode answered me, "the baby sits directly on her bladder and I'm guessing she's been asleep for a long time," she explained and I blushed and wondered if they could hear me pee. "We're pending final details."

"We were able to use Rogers as a camera feed into most of the compound," Deuce added, "He even made up some flash grenades for us."

I washed my hands and couldn't wait any longer for the final question. "And Rogers?"

"We're investigating exactly what transpired in those twenty-eight minutes but current evidence suggests that he was initially lightly wounded and may have taken his own life." Deuce was very calm, very serious and I mentally ran through his words in my head while joining them in the main room.

He was suicidal to begin with. It makes sense. It checks the boxes. Twenty-eight minutes is an eternity. Landing, fighting, infiltration, explosions, more fighting, "Is there any onsite video?"

"There should be. We'll figure out exactly what happened, Beauty," Deuce consoled.

"Shouldn't you be dancing?" Director Goode asked a valid question but I didn't feel like bursting into song or dance. I felt numb and breathless and my head was funny and my hips were suddenly so heavy. Then everything in my chest felt like I was falling asleep and then…

Hey, Muscles. Why…I'm on the floor. Fuck. Fuck. Oooooooh fuck. I'm okay. I feel…fine actually. I looked around a little and realized that I had been laid out on the floor like a rug and my feet were up on the futon seat, pink socks in my direct line of vision. Jack had my left wrist in his hand taking my pulse.

"Where is the medic?" Deuce asked with quiet urgency.

"Belle, hi, how are you feeling?" Director Goode knelt down on my other side.

"Don't move please," Jack requested. "You fainted."

"Oh God, look, this does NOT get out," I demanded, "So embarrassing! Look, I feel fine."

"Then you won't mind us getting you checked out at the medical center," Deuce replied quickly and I knew it was useless to argue with him.

"I'm fine," I groaned but Jack refused to release me or move.

The gurney came and took me away to the medical center where I almost died of embarrassment for seven hours before they agreed to let me go back to my cell on bed rest as a precaution.

"I don't want to talk about it!" I called to Dr. McEwen when he came to visit me around seven that night. Stover joined us and Jack left my side for the first time all day after telling Stover to keep me in bed. They had put this stupid triangle pillow under my feet to keep them up.

"Okay. Open mic night; you pick any topic and we'll talk about it," Tom replied and pulled a chair around.

"Baby names and my son's future," I chose and we discussed thoughts, whims, and possibilities. Jack came back with his pillow and blanket and set up camp on the futon again.

Three days passed after the worlds collided and the shooting had stopped and I found myself in a tech booth getting ready to give a well-rehearsed speech to the man whose blood I wanted. I held Starr's hand and nodded to Kmetz to make my microphone live so I could talk to my lifetime's nemesis. "Hello," I kept my voice ice-cold and calm. "Oh come now, you know my voice, or you should. Everyone you have encountered thus far has wanted something from you, but I don't really care about your smoke-screen friend," Kmetz cut the microphone for a second and Jack handed me an open bottle of water. "I'm switching to Arabic," I told the Americans in our little room and we went live again. "They call me Beauty," I continued in Arabic, "They should have called me Fury. You should have called me Death." I sounded like a psychopath and was immensely pleased at my vocal training and rehearsals. "They all want your boyfriend; I just wanted you. I wanted to look into your eyes and watch you wet your pants."

"You were never more than a silly little girl," Al-Zahrani informed me with condescending patronization.

"I was a little girl, but not silly so much as fatal. You stole something from me and I knew I could not retrieve it but I could definitely make you pay." I glanced over and a tech was making a wrap-it-up signal. "The problem with being a secretive mastermind behind the scenes is that no one knows you exist; not in the proper world. You have hidden yourself so delightfully that I will now have no trouble making you disappear entirely. Goodbye, dishonorable bastard; you should never have started with me."

Kmetz cut the feed and gave us the all-clear but I didn't talk until we left the room entirely. Jack wrapped arms around my torso and I realized that my hands were shaking and my knees were made of rubber. Someone sat me down right there in a chair.

"Belle, he's hundreds of miles away," Starr reminded me and I nodded mutely.

I was basically useless for the rest of the day. Agent Won refused to let me help in Cyber and I could barely form sentences to talk to the Director or Tom. I went back to putting the puzzles together on my cell's table and leafing through the baby names book to decide what to do with my little soccer star.

Upstairs, every minute was being devoted to analyzing the materials we had been able to gather from the compound. On the fifth day, John from the CIA came to visit me and explained what they knew about Ryan Rogers. The Canadian probably knew that he was dying

201

of cancer; he had demonstrated some subtle signs of illness in custody. He had walked into the lion's den, played his role like a hero. He took discreet cameras and microphones with him, giving the team the eyes and ears they needed for a successful strike. A microphone recorded his last moments as he picked up a handgun from somewhere, pointed it at Almasi and said two incredibly meaningful words: "last one," before pulling the trigger. Then he had a short monologue directly into the mic on his body. They let me listen to that section of the recording.

"I don't know that you can hear me," Rogers had said, "but I think you can. Please understand two things; you are an angel, you are my angel and you have a good heart. Believe it. Second, I'm done now. My choice, my way, my option. We did it our way. My name is The Canadian. Go Canada."

John clicked the recording off as soon as he said, "Canada," and I suspected it was to cover the final shot. I thanked him for the information and tried desperately to compartmentalize everything in a way that my mind could work with. I cried, I chucked dolphins at the walls, I told stories about him and I cried again.

I was in my cell for the majority of the next several weeks. I spent vast amounts of time watching seasons of a variety of television shows and funny movies. I discovered distaste for 'spy' and action/adventure movies because I spent half the time mentally yelling about inaccuracies. It may have been the hormones, but I began to like reading Jane Austen for the first time in my life.

Day after day I killed time. Natalie was the biggest surprise when she started visiting regularly with activities and ideas. Two weeks after my birthday and the day before the anniversary of my brother's death she threw me a 25th birthday party upstairs with what must have been mandatory attendance because that room was packed. There was cake and ice cream and everything that should be at a birthday party (except alcohol). I hadn't celebrated a birthday since I turned 16 and I even received a handful of presents from nursery wall stickers and onesies for the baby to cocoa butter lotion to fight the stretch marks. I managed to go the entire party without crying and I was so proud of myself.

Whether or not they intended to inundate me with action the following day, I was flooded from the minute I woke up until I went to bed. It prevented me from dwelling on Keith's death and my vigilante style revenge turned lifestyle.

Jack took me swimming and/or water walking four or five times a week. We went to the medical center or saw Susan in my cell every week as we hit the 30-week mark and I breezed through three different books on birth and motherhood. Jack took prenatal yoga with me via DVD and Starr joined us for those stupid breathing exercises.

"You know," I huffed during a session in late February, "this pregnancy thing is pretty disgusting but birth just sounds horrible!"

"The part about squishing a human out of a small opening or the part with the skin tearing and poop?" Jack asked.

"Our babies are covered in slime and floating around in their own pee. Yes, the whole thing's gross if you think about it. I don't recommend thinking about it," Starr added. "Just focus on the end result."

"Yikes," I said aloud. *The more I think about it, the scarier it is. They don't sleep through the night. I've never changed a diaper in my life, much less a boy, and apparently that makes everything more complicated. How the hell am I going to do this? Oh for fuck's sake, stop kicking me every two minutes.* I swung slightly from side to side, a motion I would only previously have used if my arms were around a machine gun. The kid liked swinging, or at least he stopped punching when he was being swung. *Should I get him circumcised? What age should I start getting him into a martial art? What if he doesn't like fighting? What if he likes reading? Then I'll get him books, duh. Where is he going to go to school? Should I put him in private school? Would that be safer? Will we have bodyguards? We could get him a female guard and make her look like a nanny. People are so sexist like that; they'll assume she's a nanny.*

"Um, hello?" Agent Starr was waving her hand in front of my face.

"Circumcision," I explained in one word. "If you have a boy," I asked Starr.

"If I have a boy, his dad is Jewish so...we haven't even had a thought about not doing it," Starr replied. "Sergeant, do you have any thoughts?"

"If you don't do it as an infant, he may choose to as an adult and from what I've heard it is extremely unpleasant for an adult. One hand, you can't be un-circumcised, on the other, there's a load of stuff out right now about foreskin pleasure reception."

Sounds like he got snipped as a kid. If I ever needed to hide out in Israel for any reason, it would be best if he was circumcised. Then again, his father wasn't. Can't say that I was a fan. On or off, should I get him baptized? That can definitely wait. I looked around and the open door caught my eye. *Is the door going to hit the crib? Maybe, if it's fully open. Then again, the noise would wake the kid up anyway. To get out of here and into a real home I need to get Bin*

Laden. I need a nap; I yawned and tried to swallow it.

"Okay, guys, we gotta get Waldo now. Take him, kill him, don't care."

"And we're back to killing Waldo," John from the CIA knocked on the open door.

"Unless you expect him to be crushed under my weight, you guys will have to do the actual killing," I teased. "How's it going down south?"

"Profilers concurred with your evaluation and we chose to keep him in solitary without questioning him beyond the basics. I actually came to tell you that he's starting to twist his beard."

"Wait until he starts skipping prayers; then introduce a valve," I advised. "Then again, you guys have broken more men than I have," I admitted.

"One or two," John quipped dryly. "So, I hate to bring it up, but how are you doing?"

"I'm fine. We're down to the last eight weeks or so," I patted my belly.

"I wish we had a due-date on Waldo," John admitted.

"We've at least partially disarmed him; the loss of Al-Zahrani will be a major hit to him mentally, emotionally, and in terms of resources. That raid was incredibly successful!"

"Yes it was, Belle. You done good, kid," he joked.

"Yeah, almost good enough," I replied wistfully.

Chapter Eight: Pax

Sunday, March 27, 2011 was a big day for the base. Things got insane sometime around Wednesday prior to that and I was all over the place that weekend, analyzing input and running through audio recordings in the lab and in my cell. Agent Starr had come to say goodbye on Friday as she prepared for maternity leave and lighter duty at another location. She told me that she had passed on the sealed file where she kept my drawings away from prying judgmental eyes to Jack.

I guess I was still emotionally dealing with her departure; I kept seeing her in every head of blond hair and making star-related comments.

Anyway, Sunday was a huge day. Sunday we realized that the biological materials we had retrieved from vaccination operations were leading closer and closer to pinpointing Bin Laden's location by the DNA trends. When we cross-matched those trends against a few other factors we had been looking at, we found several concurrent locations.

I'll never forget the moment: Fred and John from the CIA, Agents Won and Kmetz from the DIA, and Leona Hampshire from Homeland Security were in the Cyber conference room with

Jack and me eating red beans and rice for lunch. Director Goode walked in, still on her phone to someone but she caught our attention. Seconds later she hung up and informed us that Al-Zahrani was giving out real information to an Army Interrogator.

The room erupted in sounds of joy and triumph; I let out a whoop and I was not alone. I wanted to jump up and down but could barely stand up. These days I was visiting the doctor at least once a week if not twice and my belly got places ten minutes before I did.

Just twenty minutes after Goode broke the news she took another call in the hallway and almost immediately returned to wave me into the hall. I waddled out carefully past my colleagues and Jack closed the door behind him once we were all out. Susan rounded the corner with a wheelchair and before anyone issued a word of explanation, I sat down in it because I was tired from the ten steps.

"Hello again Belle, you seem happy," Susan greeted casually and started to push me toward the elevators. "Sorry to interrupt the party but we need you again in the clinic."

"I'll get backup," Jack said and seized his radio.

"They're already waiting for us," Susan replied and there was no discussion in the elevator. A gurney was waiting for us on the main level and

Susan and Jack helped me onto it before they spirited me away.

A pee test, thorough sonogram, and a few other tests and I was finally told that my blood pressure was causing complications and the best option at that point was for me to be on strict bed rest for at least a week before a possible extraction.

"Commonly known as birth, right?" I asked crankily.

"You're at 37 weeks; unless the baby is in more immediate danger or your health worsens, we'd like to keep him in there as long as we can safely," the visiting doctor replied before turning to the guards. "Please avoid any unnecessary fetters if possible; walking may be a challenge on its own and any attempt to escape would immediately be terminated by her body's birthing processes."

Moron, but hey, thanks very much, man who just looked at my vagina and now thinks he knows me. I mentally cursed at the physician as he left the room. Susan and her clipboard returned.

"Dr. Gloria Morales is going to come visit and check on you next week. We'll see what she thinks is best for you and him," Susan gave me the wonderful news. "In the meantime, you should stay in bed as much as humanly possible and try not to get stressed out. If anything changes, let us know; you might see traces of blood in your discharge or start feeling frequent contractions."

Jack and I thanked her and soon I was back on the gurney being spirited back to my cell horizontally. I was bored in minutes and greatly resented that they had brought me back on the gurney instead of the limited dignity of a wheelchair. Adding to the humiliation, I had a thing about being strapped down on a table – a remnant of the second torture session I had suffered in the field.

Susan came around to check on me that evening and I'll admit I was in a less than chipper mood. With Starr gone, there was no one to commiserate with and I went to bed grumpy.

I woke up facing the bassinet and felt like it had gotten six feet closer to me overnight. It was still in its nook next to the wall but the mobile-covered baby holder had never seemed so real. *We're talking days now, not weeks,* I remembered and felt a surge of panic. *On the bright side, C-section means no pushing, right? No pooping and screaming and hoo-ha tearing....oooooooh my god I can't do this. I can't do this. Just, someone, do something here. Tell me what to do, tell me it's going to be okay. There's going to be a tiny human in my life in, like, days! No, no, calm down. Calm down. Breathe...hey, I can breathe! Like, a real breath! Uh-oh, is that a good thing? What did that video say about it: I remember something. Damn it, woman, focus. Ozzie's spilling information and I can't help them do anything about it because I'm playing the role of "Rolled-up rug"! Gaaaaah!!!*

What do women do just before their baby arrives? Pick a name? Decorate the nursery, which in my case is known as that area over there, I stared at the bassinet and hoped that it was big enough. *I had another three weeks and then…I didn't. Don't. Stay in, stay in, stay in, you need to gain like another two pounds and get bigger and stuff. Would it help if I ate more? I guess…I guess that makes sense. Am I still underweight? Did they say? I don't feel underweight, I feel like a hippo. A hungry, hungry hip –.*

My thoughts were interrupted by a loud bang in the hallway, which prompted Jack to leap completely over the table from his spot on the futon and dance his way over to my side. He pulled something out of the inside of his boots with one hand and signaled me to get in the bathroom. I tried to return to my field instincts and immediately realized that rolling and the army crawl were completely out of the question.

"Code 4, code 4, standby for confirmation," someone in the hall stated and a minute later someone called some incomprehensible series of letters and numbers. By then I had crawled to the bathroom. Jack waited for me and then helped me walk carefully back to the bed as if the added grace would magically erase the near-tumble and frantic crawl moments before.

"What the hell was that?" I bellowed once back in bed.

"A box fell," Benzion called through the slot.

Box fell? Good grief.

The first 24 hours were the best and the worst as I weighed the prospect of lying there for the next week or so day after endlessly boring day. Deuce came to visit morning and night for three days and then disappeared for two days. Natalie came and fretted about finishing her baby craft project before the kid came out.

We started a series of superhero movies with egregious abuses of a certain male actor's bared body parts. For whatever reason, action sequences predicated upon mutant powers slipped past my wall of experience-driven cynicism.

Medics had me pee in a cup every 48 hours to monitor my progress. On Friday afternoon, Jack and I were watching a "Pirates of the Caribbean" movie when the wheelchair arrived to whisk me away.

"Gloria!" I greeted with joy as I caught a glimpse of the kind doctor. Dr. Morales was slipping on a paper apron over her green scrubs. *Oh God, am I doing this today? What about a NICU unit? I'm not ready! He's still premature!*

"Hello Jane, how are you feeling?" the doctor greeted. "Let's take a look at what we're working with."

Jack helped me out of the chair and almost lifted me onto the table.

"We should probably have removed her pants first," Gloria said gently and Jack had a brief "duh," expression. Gloria handed me a large white sheet. "Hang on just a moment; I'll get the Commander to come help you undress. You can keep your brassiere on; there's a modesty top there. It should open in the back." She stepped out of the room and left Jack and I alone.

Jack pulled the curtain around us and I flung the sheet open like a sail. By mutual silent agreement we moved our hands under the sheet so he could ease off my clothing. Jack kept eye contact with me from the moment his fingers hooked into my pants at my love handles until I was covered completely from the top of my mountain to the tips of my toes. I caught a brief glimpse of pink inside the leggings as he folded them and set them on the counter. Then he came around and almost lovingly helped me out of my jacket. Then Susan walked in and stormed through our curtain.

"What's going on here?" the Commander demanded.

"Preparation for examination?" I offered and watched her mind leap to conclusions. "Okay, first of all, he's my doula so yes, it is appropriate. Second, everything has been covered by the sheet. No funny business."

"Fine. Would you like to just roll up your top? I'll let the doctor know we're ready for her." Susan reopened the curtain partially as she left and I got the vibe that she didn't approve of Jack helping me.

Yeah, because I'm definitely in seduction mode here, I thought sarcastically. *This is quite possibly the least attractive I have ever been. Overweight, massive belly, wider hips, disproportionately big boobs and bloated damn near everywhere. Granted, the examination table does seem ideal for a little coitus. Not sure about the stirrups.*

As if she read my thoughts, Dr. Morales came in and popped out the stirrups. Jack turned his back on her to face my head directly; he had come to stand at the line where my clothing stopped. Gloria was talking about speculums and my cervix but I found I preferred to hold Jack's hand and make silly small talk about all the places we'd rather be. When she and CDR Susan finished with my lady bits they pulled the sheet down to expose my belly and cover my legs.

"Would you like to see?" Gloria inquired as the sonogram started to show on the screen. I looked in the opposite direction, toward the door and Jack. "Well, baby looks good. I'd be much more comfortable with the equipment here; a neonatal unit," she explained to me. "Mom's holding up."

"I will make my recommendation that we extract as soon as," Susan started and I angrily interrupted.

"Birth! It's birth, not extraction. If I'm doing this like this then we're calling it birth!" I huffed and became very hot. "You had your shot at extraction weeks ago!"

"So we're waiting for the NICU to be set up here?" Jack intervened rapidly and loudly.

"Yes. I recommend a caesarean section and I'm happy to go over the procedure and your options after you get dressed," Gloria smiled and I calmed down as Susan grabbed a wad of paper towels to remove the gel from my stomach. Baby wipes came into it and the doctor walked out.

Ten minutes later I was dressed again but acutely uncomfortable in the outer office. I had been duly reminded that Dr. Morales was not read-in on Operation Waldo and Dr. Morales had set out a series of drawings showing the state of my uterus at this stage in the pregnancy.

"Your body is displaying a number of signs that you are ready to give birth. One of the benefits of the C-section is that it takes out a number of uncertainties and shortens the birth process. The day of the procedure," Gloria explained calmly and slowly and walked me through the process. She showed me pictures of the unit they were waiting for and explained the most likely scenarios for the baby's condition upon birth.

"I was thinking Tuesday," Susan proposed.

"That should be good. Hold out for a few more days of bed rest, Jane," Gloria encouraged.

Just a few more days, I sighed to myself and leaned back wearily. *I'm fucking terrified.*

I started throwing up on Sunday. This was a whole new experience: I was basically bent at the waist and holding on to the toilet rim to steady myself. I couldn't manage the hunch-and-hurl position I had known since childhood with a small mountain attached to my front. Jack came in to that scene late Sunday morning: I had made plans to tease him about being so late that day when urge to purge hit.

"I gotcha," he rubbed my back gently in between rounds. "How long have you been doing this?"

"Couple of minutes, I think," I caught my breath and he flushed the toilet for me.

"Okay, you're okay, you'll be fine," Jack assured but I could see him go for his radio out of the corner of my eye. "Jackson Delta four-one-oh," he called into it and waited a second for recognition.

JD 410, what the hell does that mean? Oh, I think I'm going to die. Another round started and the dry heaves followed.

"Immediate medical backup requested," Jack followed.

"I'm okay," I choked on the words but managed to stand up and lean back against the wall and tried to catch my breath. "God, my head hurts."

"Vomiting and headache," Jack reported and the radio squawked something back.

"Medic!" someone called from the other room and Jack bent his knees to pick me up and carry me out of the bathroom and onto the gurney waiting there. We rushed down the halls and into the elevators; the men around me were talking in urgent tones but I was so tired and weak and heavy and blurred that I couldn't keep up with what was happening.

"Unit better be ready," Jolly Medic said in a very businesslike tone. "Oxygen on," he slipped the nose hook on me.

"Scissors," someone said and my top was cut off; it probably had vomit on it.

"Scrubbing now," a woman said.

"Hey there Ali," Jack spoke directly into my ear and it was very reassuring. "I have to go scrub. They're going to keep prepping you and I'll be right back." Jack stood and turned to the people around, "keep her company and shout if it gets crazy."

"Jack!" I cried as he started to walk away. "I'm scared," I admitted and heard a waver in my voice.

"We're going to be fine. Your son is ready to come, his bed is ready for him, and when we're all done here, we'll play card games and watch that movie you love and you'll be able to see your feet again," he joked and calmed me. Jolly Medic looked pretty strange with his face half-hidden in a mask but at least he kept talking to me while he worked.

Here I go, my thoughts wandered, *I always thought I'd have someone with me when I had a child; Keith, mom, someone. Luc…what was I thinking about him? I know I was thinking about something, something important but I can't quite remember…* Several people entered the room in full masks, caps, and gowns and I gathered that two of them were Gloria and Susan.

"First things first, when did you last vomit?" Gloria inquired.

"10:42!" Jack called from somewhere.

"It was dry heaves; I should be safe," I answered.

"Excellent. Well if you start feeling like you need to do it again, Branson is going to have a spit tray ready for you."

Lucky Branson, I thought to myself and realized that Jolly Medic was Branson.

"So, ready to sing the birthday song?" Gloria kept making casual conversation.

"Now I want cupcakes," I admitted.

"Yeah, what flavor?" she kept the dialogue going as she drew on my tummy. "I love strawberry flavored cupcakes, but they're hard to find sometimes."

"Great, now I want cupcakes," Jack entered. We ended up talking about cupcakes and desserts for several minutes and Jack played with my fingers until we got into a debate about donut types (everyone knows cream beats jelly!). We were pulling the kid out when I looked that direction to see the grossest, most fascinating sight I have ever seen.

"Is he okay?" I asked when I didn't hear the crying I expected. The baby immediately started wailing bloody murder and he was handed off to someone waiting there. "Go watch," I requested Jack while the doctors stitched my stuff back where they found it. The baby kept shrieking and I started laughing until they had to caution me about moving my diaphragm for a minute. It took some time, but soon I was in a hospital gown and able to hold my son for the first time.

"He's a healthy baby boy. We'll need to observe him for a day or two, but you'll be able to go home in just a few days with him." Gloria beamed.

"He's so small!" I cooed.

"He's a healthy size, seven pounds six ounces and eighteen inches long." Gloria replied.

"Hello Pax," I whispered to my baby.

"Who wants cupcakes?" a familiar and gravelly voice called through the door and Jack snapped up to his feet. I could feel my silly grin but couldn't hide it. I felt like sunshine was pouring out of my face. "Happy birthday, little guy!"

Pax stopped crying and wiggled his arm up and down.

"No cupcakes for you until you're a little older," I joked and he punched me in the boob. "Am I going to have to rename him when I'm released?"

"Yes, so if you haven't yet, keep the name you want in mind," Deuce replied.

"For now, we should call him Phil," I decided.

"Phil? Oh, like the French word for son. Brilliant," Deuce agreed.

"When can I get back to work?" I asked as he opened the box and showcased the sugary treats.

A nurse came around to take Pax away to the unit down the hall and I felt a distinct distrust of him being out of my sight.

You're going to have to get used to it; he's not going to be with you all the time. They have every incentive to keep him with me; to keep me happy until they can nail Bin Laden. But...then what?

Chapter Nine: The Ides of April

I recovered quickly from my surgery, and on Wednesday I introduced Pax to his new home. I soon discovered that breast feeding was not pleasant, that the bras made for feeding are ridiculous, annoying, and uncomfortable, and that the most comfortable way to carry Pax was in a sling carrier strapped across my chest.

Director Goode and Deuce allowed me great leeway on who was permitted to touch Pax. In case my own paranoia wasn't enough, I was also wary after reading about infant immune systems. I wouldn't even let Natalie hold him, preferring to keep Pax on my left breast as he followed me around my day. Agent Won never reached for him but I would have let her hold him. She probably sensed my mommy instinct combined with my globally-developed reflexes.

I felt a sense of normality when I sat down for the weekly status update meeting in Director Goode's office. Pax was snoozing peacefully and we had all established that he wasn't the least bit sensitive to noises.

"We just got our hands on a copy of the software, it's on its way here now under tight control," Agent Won stated.

"There's no guarantee on when the CIA or NSA's software will attain compatibility capability," John added.

"Was Natasha configured for it?" It occurred to me that my former colleague's supercomputer, lovingly named Natasha, was probably full of programming which correlated to his cyber genius and skills.

"We are having issues getting around inside Ari's computer," Agent Won admitted quietly. "It freezes us out to the point where we're afraid it's going to burn itself."

"This may or may not still be accurate, but I once installed a kind of secret trap door into the hard drive. It was when I installed the fail-secure protocol." I had the rapt attention of everyone in the room so I continued. "I put it in and linked it to a second machine so that if I ever needed to, I could shut down Ari remotely."

"Your laptop?" Director inquired.

I shook my head, "I'm trying to remember where I left that machine. Where were we," I dove into a long-ago memory. *How long is two years? A blink or an eternity, I suppose. Where were we? When was this?* I drew a total blank in my mind to the point of panicking. *Remember, remember, remember!*

I didn't realize my eyes were closed until someone set a hand on my shoulder. I knew the touch; it was Jack. Pax was squirming himself awake and something in my shirt felt damp. *I don't know if I should pray that's milk or urine. They're all staring at me again,* I realized upon opening my eyes. "If I can find the machine, we might be able to use it to get into his machine which probably has the software configured to use this program. Would you excuse me? I'll let you know as soon as I can remember." I pushed a hand on the table to support standing and Pax started his pre-shriek vocalizations. *Hmm, is he hungry? My boobs feel like he's hungry. Hmm, actually, I'm pretty hungry. And tired. Maybe I can feed him and get him to take a nap and then I can nap! Yup, that's a plan!* I glanced back at the table to see Deuce about to speak.

"Beauty; any idea when or where you were at the time: can you give us any kind of window?" Deuce inquired.

"After 2008, I remember Ari was so excited about Natasha. She was new then and he talked about her like she was his daughter or girlfriend. We were…" I shook my head. I couldn't remember.

"It's okay Beauty. We'll find it or we'll do without," Deuce reassured and Jack escorted me out to where Benzion was waiting.

In my cell I cradled my son to my right breast and immediately felt the latch. I hooked him into my right arm and got comfortable on the futon. *Where were we, where did I hide the computer? Briefcase; it was in that brown briefcase, I put it somewhere normal, where it wouldn't be noticed, like a bookshop or library, or an office building, or an attic. Gaaaah why can't I remember? It's only been two or three years. Stop trying to remember and you will.*

"Milk?" Jack asked.

"Yes please."

"Drink the white and I'll give you the chocolate Ensure®," Jack tempted and I agreed. I drank them both and waited while Pax kept on suckling to satisfaction. My left boob complained but waited as I burped my happy son and rocked him to drowsiness. Thank God he slept well and enjoyed going to sleep.

"Can I have the piggy?" I asked as I headed toward the restroom. Jack produced the breast pump we had nick-named 'the piggy' because of its suckling function. I couldn't bring myself to use the term 'expressed' in reference to my boobs so instead I 'used the piggy'. We set aside a bottle for later before I collapsed into bed for a much needed nap.

I woke up cranky even though Pax was still happily snoozing away. I went to the bathroom to clean up and came out when I heard the door unseal.

If they wake him up, I mentally grumbled and looked to see who it was. "You have a hell of a lot of nerve strolling in here!" I growled at the man who walked in. He deserved it; his hair was a little longer and he had gained a few pounds but FBI Agent George Tomopolis had balls showing up out of nowhere after months of silence.

"Hello Alexis," George greeted.

"Don't, "Hello Alexis," me! Get away from my son." I warned.

"Reel it in," George replied. "How are you doing?"

"I had surgery to pluck a kid from my womb, found and helped capture Ozzie, and now I'm taking down Bin Laden. Seriously, get away from my son." I warned him a second time as he stepped toward the cradle again. "Jack?" I called loudly. My stomach was incredibly tender, my heart was racing and I wondered briefly if this was a dream because it didn't feel real.

"Who's Jack?" George asked but did move away from the crib. "Look, I just wanted to come see you, see how you were doing. I heard about the birth and,"

Jack came in and I exhaled. My left hand rested over my incision location and everything was far more upsetting than it should have been.

"You're okay, hold on a second," Jack greeted me. "Sir, I need you to leave."

"I have full authority to be in here, this is my case," George tried to explain.

Benzion poked his head into the doorway and I could tell he was waiting on Jack.

"Do you need help walking?" Jack asked in a quiet menacing way that totally impressed me. Jack was younger and almost certainly stronger than the FBI agent who was pissing me off.

Just get out, George. You may have balls but I have Muscles. Did you really think you could just run off into the night and then reappear?

While I fumed silently my body's pain reached crescendo and I knew I needed to lay down stat. George stalked out and I noticed Benzion's arm extending as a natural guard reflex behind the unwanted visitor.

"You're okay," Jack returned to my side and walked me back to the bed like he knew my condition. "How bad is the pain on the scale?"

"Just a six, maybe a seven," I gasped and my attempt to control the pain through breathing exercises backfired on me horribly. "Definitely seven," I added. Jack got on the radio to request a medical visit and I stretched out across the bed and prayed that Pax would stay asleep. The angles of the hallway put me in the perfect spot to overhear a hallway conversation.

"Who is Jack?" George muttered.

"He's in charge here, Agent Tomopolis. Sir, let's leave the sector," Benzion proposed and we lost the rest of the conversation.

"What happened to him?" I wondered aloud. "He's FBI, the man I originally sent materials to; the man I chose to capture me. He was on the team until he left, right around the hospital incident. He read my mail so I used him as an information inlet. I didn't even realize how angry I was until he was here and way too close to my baby. I swear he was doing it to piss me off!" I realized I was rambling and stopped. We were mutually silent when Nurse Branson arrived.

"Hello," Nurse Branson arrived with his usual jolly demeanor.

"Hi, it hurts," I greeted him. My head was twisted to face him but the rest of my body stayed flat. He started asking embarrassing questions and examined my stomach and incision.

"You've been overdoing it. You also ripped a stitch and might have a small infection. I'll need some blood work, and the commander should confirm. In the meantime, let me give you some pain medication." He went about his work, drew the blood and gave me something that made me care a lot less about the pain. Soon something was taped over the incision area and I was

231

staring up at the ceiling with a mixture of disdain and bemusement.

Blah-blah-blah abdominal surgery, blah-blah stitches, blah-blah taking it easy; apparently in the real world people have to listen to their doctors. Huh. Well you're not immortal. Holy crap, what would happen to Pax if something happened to me? This isn't serious, is it? "How bad is it?"

"Your incision site looks angry. I should never have let you out of that hospital gown. You should have been resting with minor strolls, not," Jack started ruminating and I cut him off.

"Oh relax. It's no big deal," I dismissed and felt uneasy about the words as they flew away.

"Really?" Jack pulled up a chair and sat at my side. "Then tell me how I endorse your continued participation in this project."

I stared at him for a moment, trying to fully comprehend what he had just said. *They can't pull me, I got them Ozzie! I got them Ozzie! I...what would that mean anyway? Without the Waldo project I'm just a resident. Just a...* the portal was in my line of sight and I could hear the guards outside. *Just a prisoner. Ask him what he means.* "What are you saying, Jack?"

He stared at me with hollowness behind his eyes and I waited with mild disbelief at what he might say. "You are twenty-five years old, Alexis, and you're a mother now. We all know how bad you are at taking care of yourself, but it's time to learn. How do you think you can take care of him if you can't be trusted to take care of yourself? That means you need to learn to recognize when you are hungry and ask for food. It means recognizing when you're in pain before it turns unbearable. Go to sleep when you're tired. These are things most people learn in their early teens and for a variety of reasons you either never learned them or have forgotten. It really addles my brain to think that with your mind, which apparently holds multiple languages and knowledge of things the NSA envies, you're wildly irresponsible to your own body!"

"Hey! Am I drunk all the time?" I defended calmly. "Yes, I forget to eat sometimes, but I've never gotten sick from it. Yes, maybe my natural life skills are quite rusty, but," the rest of my argument died in my mouth when I looked at Jack's face. One of the first lessons I learned in the field is when to shut up.

As if my baby hated the silence, he squealed in cranky protest and started his disgruntled cry. I tried rolling on my side in an attempt to roll out of the bed but Jack stopped me with a gesture and went to him.

"Hey buddy," Jack said quietly and I watched as he gently picked Pax up and held him. "Hey, buddy," Jack cooed and something in me wanted to laugh.

The ruthless caretaker, I mentally noted but stayed put. "Jack?"

"Someone needs a diaper change," Jack announced. "I got it. You just...rest."

I waited as he changed Pax and then eventually set him next to me in the bed. On my side I could at least see and touch my cranky baby. I remembered the hollowness in my stomach and paired it mentally with Jack's lecture. "Jack, I'm hungry. Is it time for dinner?"

Pax must have understood what I said because he immediately waved his arm toward my boob. "You hungry too, baby boy?" Pax made that face and I mentally tried to negotiate how to feed him, trying to remember the sideways feeding position.

"Sir, message from medical," Lt. Branch announced and held a radio through the food slot. The medics were calling ahead to warn that they would start me on antibiotics and someone was coming to evaluate my incision site. Immediately after the radio was returned, Jack's back straightened for his earpiece.

"Yes sir. No," Jack started his odd conversation and I unbuttoned my new top to feed my son. They had added a uniform top that was easier to open after the birth; a simple button-down blouse in the same gray that did nothing against milk stains. "Yes sir. I will find a surrogate."

The words alarmed me more than any death threat or explosive caution and Jack reassured me briefly with his body language. He finished his conversation with Deuce and returned to me.

"Surrogate for you, not for him. I need to be somewhere and you cannot be left alone while unable to care for Buddy. Do you still want to have the chef salad for dinner?"

By the time my food arrived, Pax was either full or bored of eating. Jack put Pax in the crib for a moment before basically picking me up and standing me like a tent pole. I ate quickly while standing: my stomach disapproved of sitting.

Susan, Officer Morgan, and Captain Stover came in together. Jack gave Susan details on my condition and listed instructions for the guards during his absence. I think the rudest thing he said was, "she's doing alright on the food conditions, but ask her anyway."

Susan helped me back to the bed and Captain Stover played with Pax while I was examined and given medication. She warned me not to do anything that caused me pain and injected a painkiller. "Now, Belle, all of this will go in your chart for Jack to read but you're a grown woman so I'll be wild and talk to you directly." Her words were delightfully frank and carried the air of a woman who is tired of men. "We sliced you open and yanked a kid out, so your uterus and a half dozen other things are extremely irritated right now. Not only are you going through normal after-birth issues like the womb shrinking back to normal size and the rest of the baby-making gear shedding, there are also surgical complications. You need to take it easy. Give the stitches a chance to put you back together. They're here to help out with the baby and with whatever you need. No carrying the baby or anything else; no lifting; be careful sitting, and if something hurts don't do it. I'd like you in this position as much as possible for the next day or so. I'll be back in the morning to check on you and Jack might check your temperature a few times. I'm leaving pain medication for him to give you and it should help you sleep. Let someone help you walk to the bathroom because the medicine may make you dizzy. You'll be able to breastfeed on your side, but consider using formula."

I thanked her sincerely and let her help me to the bathroom before she left. Officer Morgan was standing ready as soon as I opened the glass door. Our friendship, if that's what it was, had never fully recovered from the crib incident. I found it insulting that I was still deemed a dangerous threat after all of my time in complacent captivity. *I'm definitely no threat now; I can barely walk. Neither of them is armed, not even a Taser. Stover looks so cute with Pax; I bet he has children of his own.*

The Morgan-Stover tag team stayed with me until after the drugs sent me to sleep. Drug-enhanced sleep is the best: all those reflexes and worries just take a vacation from my lines of thought. Even in my cell, where I normally felt quite safe, there were PTSD-like symptoms on top of a mother's panic most of the time. I hadn't slept so well in weeks and had barely slept since I held Pax in my arms.

I stirred but didn't open my eyes. There were strange sounds, strange but not alarming noises. Pax was grunting, there were suckling noises and a slight, almost distant hiss of pressure. *Coffee*, I realized. *No, not coffee. Pax…is fine.* I felt the pull again and sunk back into sleep.

I woke to find Commander Susan standing at the foot of my bed.

"Hi," she greeted quietly. "I take it you slept well?"

"What time is it? I was just…out," I excused and felt the need to feed or pump. Susan helped me get my day started and soon I was back in bed for breakfast. She surprised me by sticking around, even helping me get the piggy started.

Pax was asleep again and Susan peeked in on him before she left.

Jack showed up right on time to help clean up the pump and bottles. He was quieter than usual and I worried about what was going on in his mind.

"I think I slept for twelve or fourteen hours," I offered on a false bright note. "Did you stay the night?"

"We broke it into shifts. Pax is right on the normal schedule rates for sleeping and diapers," Jack informed.

"He's so small," I admitted. "Do you want to talk about anything?"

"No, I'm fine. Just trying to make some decisions," Jack admitted. "Do you want to watch a movie?"

"Go with your gut. I found that the biggest decisions I have ever made were never decisions at all. Leave home, kill a man, investigate deeper, choose to love, come to America, have a baby; none of them were deeply thought out or debated. I had options, of course, but not really."

"Yeah," he seemed to understand that on a deep level.

"Coffee," I recognized the scent and it awoke a memory. "Ireland! It's in Dublin, Ireland. There's an old shop there," I gave him the address and the names of the owner and co-conspirator for hiding the equipment which once hacked Ari.

"What were you doing in Ireland?"

"IRA research," I replied without pause. "They'd disbanded but that kind of know-how was still highly relevant to me. Many of their members shared enemies with me: some were quite willing to help my cause once they knew of my hit list."

"Delightful."

"I'm sorry I'm irritating you," I offered sincerely.

"What? No, you're not the," Jack cut himself off and waited a minute before talking again. "So, what exactly about that agent set you off?"

"George," I sighed and assessed my anger. "He just abandoned me. No goodbye, nothing. He was here and then he was gone. I know that all of my relationships here are temporary to some extent, but to just disappear...I worried. I had to wonder what I did, if anything. Then he just kept coming closer to the baby, like he was...daring me or something. Testing me, mocking me while I'm not fully operational." The words out of my mouth struck me. "Oh my god, I have been through way too much therapy!"

Jack almost smiled before he turned away. "I will relay the information on Ireland. Thank you."

For the next three days, I behaved exactly like Jack wanted me to and he began to send side glances of disbelief my way. I became very conscious of when I was hungry and tired and discovered that asking for help got easier each time. It took a week of rest and medical attention, but I was able to return to the cyber unit the day after my once-familiar suitcase containing the laptop was flown in from Ireland.

On my few trips outside I could see some cherry blossoms scattered across the horizon. The simple beauty among all of my cold hard gray facts made me smile.

We all kept working, knitting together the bits and pieces of intelligence, conjectures and facts. I saw George one more time mid-April on my own terms, in an interview room.

"Well?" I asked him as we faced each other over the table.

"I'm a federal agent, Alexis. I don't need to explain myself to a prisoner." George had emotionally distanced himself; I recognized the signs of emotional compartmentalization.

"No, you owe me no explanation. You're free to walk right back out that door. But I will say it was a shitty thing to do. I accepted that the timing may not have been in your control; I can deal with that. It should bother you, George. It should bother you that you worked so hard at a relationship and then dumped it so easily. Obviously something changed, or maybe my intel was never quite as good as I thought."

"A professional opportunity came and I took it."

"Yeah, me too," I replied and leaned back. "So, why are you here? Shouldn't you be in California?"

"Whatever you think, I did start this thing. Even if I'm not on the team, I want to see it through. Plus, I wanted to see your child. He looks like his father."

I never told anyone about Luc. He's messing with me. "Not really."

"Sure he does. Luc, right? Luc Antoine Mercier. No, no one has told him about his son," George reassured calmly.

"How the hell did you find him?

George pursed his lips like he was trying to decide what to disclose. "French intelligence."

"They were investigating him?"

"Um," George replied. "No?"

Of course, they were investigating me and he showed up. We were probably seen together. I remembered and relaxed slightly. *Poor Luc, I hope they didn't harass him!*

"I can't really give any details. The man in charge will share what he can when he wants to." George supplied and I understood. "Don't worry; no one can take your son away."

"Thank you," I exhaled.

"I'm leaving soon," George added, "I look forward to hearing about how you take down Waldo. Take care of yourself, Alexis," George stood and Jack stepped in from the hall. I stood and shook George's hand like we were civilized coworkers.

"Are you alright?" Jack asked after closing the door behind George.

"Yes. It's right about tax day, isn't it?"

"Around it, yes," Jack replied.

"Well," I said in high spirits, "Caesar was warned about the ides of March; perhaps Bin Laden should beware the ides of April. Let's get him."

Chapter Ten: Child of Death

"We could have Bin Laden within seventy-two hours."

Director Goode's words were dizzying as they sunk in. I glanced around the table in her office where Deuce, Won, John, Leona and I sat. Jack was nearby and the guards were outside. It was the last Wednesday in April and a special staff meeting had been called.

"Al-Zahrani is offering us the last known address for Bin Laden and his four most likely alternatives," Deuce announced in a slow, measured voice. "He wants a deal; better conditions of captivity and a few other things. I need to speak to Beauty before we continue."

A consensus was reached without words and everyone left until only Deuce and Jack remained with me in Goode's office. Jack joined us at the table and Deuce continued.

"Don't you dare let him go," I cautioned.

"It will never be considered as an option for as long as I am alive," Deuce assured me. "The bastard does have terms. He wants to meet you. He'll give us two locations up front and two after the interview."

"So, they'll fly me down to Gitmo?" I inquired.

"If you agree. You do not have to do this, Beauty. The IMINT program is up and running thanks to the Irish briefcase program."

"Am I well enough to travel? Who will take care of my son?"

"We will travel in comfort. Agent Won and Officer Morgan will be responsible for the child's care until we return."

"What time do we leave?" I checked the clock; it was 9 a.m.

"Sir, this is not," Jack started to say.

"Jack!" I interrupted solemnly. "No. There is nothing I would not do for the ability to take down the head of Al-Qaida. There's nothing any of us wouldn't do."

"We will use a GPS device to further your security and Captain Stover will travel with us. Wheels up in an hour," Deuce walked to the door as he spoke, opening it to let the others back in. Everyone at the table had some reservations, but it didn't stop me from passing Pax into Officer Morgan's loving arms and getting into the golf cart.

Kmetz attached the GPS device to my ankle and Stover inspected it before we left. Everyone must have had their bags packed because we left the building ten minutes after the meeting disbanded. The golf cart took us to a helipad and men with large guns ensured that I walked a

244

straight line into the new vehicle. There were no windows near my seat so there was no need to blindfold me during flight. The helicopter took us to a small airport and we climbed into a Gulf Stream where Service Members in their dress mess greeted us with polite stiffness.

It's not for you, ego maniac, I reminded myself. *It's still impressive. It's a really big deal for them to interact with Deuce. I wonder how long it will take to get there. Oh my god, is that a television? This is nice!* I nested in a small couch and Jack sat next to me. *This is not going to be pleasant. At least its Jack; Stover and Belot are fine and Deuce is always fun. I wonder what he did to Jessica. This isn't really a heavy guard; then again the plane and Gitmo will be crawling with security. This should be just fantastic.* I thought sarcastically as we took off. Stress sent my head spinning from thoughts to dreams.

"Belle," Officer Belot called and I snorted myself awake. "We're preparing to land."

"We're doing it today, right?" I asked.

"We can, or we can wait until tomorrow. Today is preferable," Deuce replied and we rattled through our descent.

"The asset's clothing options are available as requested, sir," a sharp-looking man reported.

I'll admit that I prefer asset to prisoner. What the hell am I going to say to this guy? The door opened and stairs descended but I had never felt more trapped.

An hour later I waited in an observation room while Ozzie was brought into an interrogation cell. I was comfortable in the cargo pants and t-shirt that I had chosen from my options; it felt familiar and strange at the same time. Two strange guards were inside with an older and slightly bedraggled version of my life's nemesis. Chains bound his hands and feet and the bright red jumpsuit did nothing for him.

Omar Al-Zahrani looked bored more than anything else; bored and a little tired. It was 1800 and I would have been hungry if my stomach hadn't been full of butterflies.

"He gave us the first two alleged sites," an Army interrogator reported to Deuce.

"Beauty," Deuce spoke directly to my ear, "Do anything you want. We'd like the site locations, but you can find them without him. The software is already zeroing in on the first two sites."

"It's been months; Ozzie may not even know where Bin Laden is by now," Jack added.

"Alright, gentlemen, let's do this thing." I braced myself mentally and stepped into the hall. "Jack, I need you to stay out here." He shook his head and moved his lips to speak but I interrupted. "You know why. I can't be *her* if you're there. The guards have him fully contained. Stay here. It's the only way you can keep me safe from zealous security guards."

I stood for a moment in the hall, trying to clear my head, trying to be return to Belle Jones at her very worst; her very best. *Fuck it.* "Open the door."

The guard obeyed. I wanted to storm in quickly so I forced myself to walk slowly. "People often think to themselves, giving others little unofficial names in reference when they don't know or don't care for the real name." I stalked around the room, past the guards and around the table. My words were in Arabic, which was fortunate because I had to choose them specifically. "Locations," I pushed the pad of paper on the table toward him and jabbed it once with my index finger for emphasis.

"I am curious," he replied in English, "as to why you think I am doing this."

"Giving us Osama?" I mentally calculated the best possible response. "If I had someone screwing up my projects, I'd be pissed too." I tried to not watch as the first line was written out.

"I suppose you know why I did the rest of it. My hundreds of victories and a few defeats? I am truly a great man in my field."

"I will judge your greatness when your tips pay off."

"Will you personally pull the trigger? I would enjoy that. They sing your praises here, you know. Well, not praises so much as what a monster you are. It is quite a legacy. They call you Death, just as you suggested. They call you a storm, a threat," he spoke while writing.

"They are not wrong."

"But I have wondered since we spoke, how does a child, a pretty little girl, turn into the spawn of Hades? Why did you leap into a war, the greatest war, a struggle against the all-oppressing giant? We did not knock on your door; you had no need to join the war."

"You speak of your victories like they are accomplishments to adore," I replied in Arabic and switched to English. "Your 'victories' were mass murders. You maimed and murdered the innocent children of God. Your associates are the lowest sinners indulging in lives and actions no one will ever approve of. You are not a glorious general; you are a blood-soaked abomination. You ask where I came from," he had finished writing and there were three sections on the paper. I wrenched the pen and paper from his hands and briefly read the texts to confirm them before handing them to the nearest guard. "You ask who I am," I returned to the monster before me. "You ask what I am. There are two monsters in this room; and one created the other. You

248

knocked on *my* door, Omar. Have you heard of Karma? I am a simple reaction; one person, one storm; all the factors aligned perfectly. I am the child who took you down and destroyed your empire."

"Shut up and bring me my protégé!" Omar demanded with irritation.

"Get comfortable, sweetie," I fired back without thought, "I hope you like wearing jumpsuits." I felt like that was enough so I made a subtle gesture and the door clicked open for me.

The second I was outside with the door closed I slammed my back to the wall. My head and knees were blaring alarms about an imminent collapse. Jack got my arm around his neck and wrapped his arm around my ribs and we proceeded quickly to the observation room.

"Check out Kareempura and the Abbottabad area," I recommended as Deuce turned to greet me. He immediately took his phone out and started to scroll. The Army interrogator joined us in the room and obviously wanted to speak to Deuce, but he waited while the honcho made his phone call. The Army man looked like he might want to speak to me as well, but I had overheard instructions that 'no one approach the asset' and he had clearly gotten that order.

"Major!" Deuce finally greeted him and the uniform approached. They spoke quietly in a corner while Jack sat me down and held my shoulders like a strange and secret hug. In the corner of my eye I could see the guards move Al-Zahrani out of the room like the captive beast he was.

"Don't look," Jack said quietly. "It's over. You ripped him apart like a master."

The Major and Deuce returned their joint attention to the rest of us.

"The executive guest quarters have been prepared to your specifications. A dinner in your honor, sir, has been arranged if you would honor us."

"Leave us for a moment, please, Major," Deuce said and the uniformed man saluted his way out.

"I'll check the quarters," Captain Stover offered and exited.

Deuce pulled up a chair and sat so our knees were perhaps a foot apart. I looked into his eyes and found that my nose was smarting from tears I refused to shed. "You and I, Beauty, we know. We know that their silly dinner should be held in your name; that they should chant your name to our enemies and watch them likely run away. I suppose we could tell them." The idea sounded bad the second it was spoken and we all knew it.

I shook my head. "You mean to hide me, to stash me away where no one can find me or know who I am, what I did in lands they've likely never seen. In all honesty," I paused to think before I spoke, "I intend to be hidden, to take those steps to ensure our safety. Now: is there anywhere on this base where I can get a stiff drink?"

Deuce smiled. "Last I remember there was a liquor cabinet in the guest quarters. Let's roll."

We packed up and left the observation room; I walked with one arm looped through Jack's in friendly familiarity and Belot was within three inches of my free arm. Deuce himself pulled out a bucket hat and a pair of sunglasses as we approached a door and we walked through the compound with amateur anonymity.

The guest quarters looked more like a swanky condo with a living area, a small dining and kitchen area, and huge glass windows over the beach and ocean. A staircase wound up to the second floor in the open foyer and I found that I was eager to explore. Other forces were at work so I found a way to discreetly ask Jack for the piggy and he took me upstairs so I could relieve my need to nurse.

"I have coconut rum," Jack offered while I sat impatiently.

"Hell yes," I reached for it. "I think I'm going to need a shower after this."

"That's perfect. Officer Belot will need to collect your clothes," Jack informed and took the empty shot glass back. "Want another?"

"Yeah, that sounds good. Is it time for dinner?"

"It should be ready as soon as you are."

"Grand." I tilted my head back against the chair and wondered how cows did this.

An hour later I joined Captain Stover, Officer Belot, and Jack at the table for a dinner of pizza and salad. Afterwards I settled in the living room to watch television while the others did their own things around me. I noted when the blinds were drawn, when darkness fell, and I could hear people walking outside of the front door. I was watching a special on the History Channel about Puerto Rico when Captain Stover sat down on the free end of the sofa.

"Hey," he greeted softly and I muted the television.

"Is this the part where you tell me that the soldiers will shoot me if I try to escape?" I asked in amusement. *They should really know better by now.*

"I'm not really sure it would be worth it to have that conversation," Stover admitted and leaned back as I twisted to face him. "I don't think I could do what you did today."

"I was terrified," I admitted in almost a whisper.

"You are not that man's creation. He doesn't get that kind of credit," Stover spoke with a quiet and paternal conviction. "You spoke of two monsters but,"

I interrupted him. "There were two monsters in that room. Captain, I can't un-kill all those people. What's worse is that I don't think I would if I could. There have been times; of course, that I wish none of it had ever happened. I wished for years that mama had never gone to work that week; that the plane had never flown, that the shots were never fired but he knocked on my door." My murderous memories flew up from their usual compartments. "I told you once that I don't lose sleep over those I have killed, only those I have not; and that is true. I'm not his creation, I'm the reaction. I'm not sorry!" The revelation hit me more than anyone else and I looked at him with a near fear.

"What's wrong?" Stover reacted to my emotion.

"They'll ask, won't they? If I regret the things I've done, before they release me into the wild or whatever. Like the movies, before they give the prisoner parole," I tried to vocalize and cut myself off seconds before Jack would have.

"Bedtime!"

What am I, six? I wondered but pulled my legs around to stand. *How's this going to work?* Jack gestured and then followed me up the stairs into the room I had used earlier. It had one tiny window that I couldn't open or fit through, a small refrigerator and microwave like a hotel, and an attached bathroom. In the hall, I noticed a little box attached to the door's edge and a small round camera fixed on the doorway.

"Try not to look directly at it, we would like to protect your identity as much as possible," Jack said and closed the door to seal us in. "This door is now alarmed; it will sound when the door is opened. The camera is monitored externally by some lucky soldier who gets to stare at screens all night. Drinks and snacks are in the fridge, I am right through that wall," he pointed, "if you need something. Otherwise, I'll be back to get you first thing in the morning. Piggy is in the bathroom. Comments, concerns or cuss words?" he asked and the last one startled me into laughing. I shook my head and he left. The door did indeed sound a melody when he opened it and it played through the tune even after he shut it again.

Yup, no way they're not going to notice that. I noted and strolled around in my new space, enjoying the novelty until I started thinking about Pax going through the night without me. I mentally consoled myself to sleep.

I woke up early needing to pump and then fell asleep midway through. I scowled at the piggy when I jolted awake again. *These little 'joys' no one warned me about. Stupid body!* I had just fallen asleep again when Jack knocked on the wall to wake me up.

We ate breakfast in the quarters while Deuce and Belot read newspapers at the table. It was April 28th, 2011 and there was an article about the US DOD and President Obama on the front page. I could read from afar and quickly assessed that the idiot who wrote the article had never been in a war zone and would never understand what kind of choices people really have to make. My face must have given me away because Deuce smirked and gestured for me to come see what he was reading. I peeked and laughed to see him indulge on the comics and advice columns.

"I find that reading halfway-true stories only confuses me," Deuce whispered.

"Well, honestly, what are *you* going to learn about Gaza from a reporter?" I agreed.

"The opinion section is the most infuriating. I don't know what it says about me that in an entire newspaper, sometimes the only thing I can relate to is anthropomorphic and illustrated."

"My biggest accomplishment in life was hunting down and killing people," I admitted, "You're still okay."

"Beauty!" Deuce briefly reminded me of how my mother used to be horrified when I'd talk shit about myself. "You're only a quarter-way through life! It's far too soon to write your memoirs." His phone dinged with urgency and he checked it before abandoning the paper to leave the room. He was back in three minutes and announced that the plane was leaving within the hour. While I watched Belot fold the paper, I noticed Deuce pull Jack aside for a very quick word.

"I'll go pack," I offered.

"You're already packed. Good morning," Stover greeted me with a suitcase in each arm.

I barely had time to greet him before I was shuttled the hell out of there. I fell asleep on the plane and they let me sleep through the landing. I was confused, sleepy, and disoriented and Jack decided it was just easier to carry me piggy-back from the plane to the helicopter.

"I hope you got a good rest, we need you in Cyber, my dear," Deuce stated just as the helicopter landed.

"Let me see my son first," I demanded and the open door terminated the conversation. I panicked briefly at the lack of confirmation that I could see Pax but then heard Stover report in on a radio. Pax met us at Cyber and looked happy and healthy so I relaxed.

"We've been running the program over the first-round picks," Agent Kmetz briefed and Pax decided he was hungry. I did what any mother would do and fastened a very lightweight cover before feeding my baby.

"Oh get over it, I assume you've seen breasts at some point," I scolded Kmetz's expression.

"Don't bet on it," a nearby tech muttered before Agent Won resumed the briefing.

"We're sending in additional IMINT satellite time here," Won briefed in the enclosed conference room. "It's a convergence point of most of our factors."

"Where is that?" Jack asked.

"Just outside of the main town of Abbottabad, it's a relatively isolated compound which seems to experience cyclical traffic. The RNA project," she pushed a button and showed a map of dots over Pakistan, "demonstrates a familial tie in the area as well."

"Would have been a lot easier with one or two wives or children," Kmetz muttered.

"What do you want, a PSA for terrible people to have smaller families so we can find them more easily?" I shot sarcastically.

"It wouldn't have worked," Agent Kensington replied, "we needed the odds to be high in order for the project to work. Otherwise it would have been as 'needle in the haystack' as the other methods proposed."

"What about Kareempura, anything from that?" I inquired.

"Nothing conclusive. We need another 36 hours, at least," Agent Won stated and several people nodded.

"Are sombreros big in Pakistan?" A young woman staring at a computer on the other end of the table asked me.

"What are you talking about, Leslie?" Won asked and went to her screen.

"No, it's not a popular thing." I walked carefully to keep from disturbing Pax's bliss.

"It looks like," Agent Won projected the scene onto the big screen and we all stared.

"Is that a cowboy hat?"

"Chair!" I uttered while blood drained from my head. Won snapped a chair behind me and Jack helped me sit. "Rodeo," I managed and Pax wiggled which snapped me back to reality.

"Rodeo?" Jack asked.

"Transcripts!" Deuce bellowed as he caught my meaning. Several people scrambled after the transcripts from every conversation we had record of involving Al-Zahrani. I had read several of them and had a faint memory of him muttering about a rodeo king.

"Sir!" Leslie spoke again and pulled up a video file for us. Someone closed the door and she pressed play.

He looked insane; that was my first reaction as I saw the film. Omar Al-Zahrani was barefoot and wild-eyed with unkempt hair and wrinkled clothing. He was muttering in multiple languages while pacing around in an otherwise empty room. Leslie typed in a command and a transcript showed up beneath the images.

"There," Leslie pointed.

"I see in the bees and the wasps, told him to keep away from the sky. I stay indoors and he walks around like to dumb Yankee rodeo man," Omar said in the tape.

"Ms. Morrison, get the rest of the NSA team online, focus all resources on that site," Deuce told the woman called Leslie. "Audio, visual, signal, every little crumb of confirmation. Thank you."

We all looked around for a moment while Leslie Morrison got on the phone to her team to relay the order. The video started playing again and I watched entranced.

"Like that will save him. I had entire roofs, buildings, walls between me and their satellites and they still found me! How did they find me! Who betrayed me?" It seemed to drive him mad.

I am the child who took you down. I remembered and pulled Pax up to burp him. *I am the harmless little girl; I am Death for men like you. Destroyer of the empires, killer of your soldiers; they found you because I led them. I found you, I found him and now I'm going to finish the job.* A tear ran down my nose and startled me.

"Alexis," Jack whispered to me just before I was going to turn to him. "Let me carry Pax, let's go have a rest."

I handed off Pax to Jack because I wasn't sure if I was okay to carry him. I felt extremely strange; high and sad and light-headed and weepy all at the same time. My thoughts were screaming at me and it was like I was facing Ozzie all over again. *I did! I took you down. You bastards took the only people who mattered to me, you took children and old people and my damn brother and you laughed about it.* A new thought entered, *He can't live. We won't take him alive. If they do, I will find him and I will end it. He cannot be the face of the bold man unjustly imprisoned, he's far too well known. Then the lawyers, god the lawyers, no, Waldo needs to die. Good lord, even I'm calling him Waldo,*

"Beauty!" Deuce repeated my name and I snapped back to the hallway where Morgan and Shapiro were waiting alongside Deuce and Jack. Deuce's eyes showed genuine concern.

"Waldo," I uttered, "Waldo dies."

"We'll see," Jack said and handed Pax off to Officer Morgan.

"No!" I retorted demandingly, "He dies."

Deuce nodded and I calmed down a little.

"Okay," he said quietly. "But I want you on conditional lockdown until that happens."

"Done," I replied as though I had a say in the matter. Jack set a hand lightly on my back as we walked but I followed Officer Morgan peacefully. I watched Pax's face in the elevator and smirked to myself and I recognized his poop expression. *Yeah, well, I'd rather deal with his dirty diapers than the never-ending war against them. Maybe Ben-Adat really was the last one, the last terrorist I kill. I don't know if 24 should be considered high or low for a body count. High for a chick from Pennsylvania. Everybody dies,* I reasoned as we reached the door and Morgan handed Pax off to me. *Not this little guy. You're going to have a long and peaceful life, no matter what I have to do. My little Pax, my darling little prince. Hmm, little prince needs a change of clothes. What have they been feeding you!*

"Whew, that is ripe," Jack commented and I realized he was still with me.

"Maybe formula makes a difference?"

"I heard Won slept on the futon last night to stay with him."

"Does it still smell like cherry blossoms?" I made conversation while I finished re-dressing Pax.

"Lemme check," Jack crossed the room and dramatically sniffed the pads, "Maybe a little."

"She's sweet," I replied and set Pax in his bassinet before turning to Jack. "I'll never see them, will I? When I'm semi-free and relocated, I'll lose everyone, won't I?"

"I don't know. You might; if you choose to work for the government. I'm not even sure that's going to be an option. There's always a chance one of the guards is assigned to your detail. There's a definite strategic advantage to that option. These people, they weren't working together like this a year ago. The unit was formed last spring and we happened to get you in August."

Well, if you have enough sex, you get pregnant, move to America, and become part of a top-secret priority one task force dedicated to taking down the devil. My expression must have been fun because Jack asked about it. "Well, I was thinking: if I hadn't gotten pregnant, the Canadian still would have emailed me about Omar. Ozzie would be dead by now and maybe Bin Laden. Maybe Reynolds would still be alive. Maybe I would be dead."

"Except that now we have tagged hundreds of members of terrorist cells; that couldn't have happened without you on this team." Jack pointed out and I had to agree with him.

Once we settled, Jack and I went into full-blown distract-and-entertain mode. After all, we both knew we would be in lockdown for quite some time and he seemed to prefer hanging out with me to whatever he did elsewhere. Two movies led into a chess marathon which carried on into the night. I gave Pax a bath and put him to bed at the usual time but then waged war with kings and queens until Jack demanded I go to bed. The fact that he was getting his butt kicked probably had something to do with his timing.

I was up for the four a.m. feeding when I heard the voices in the hall.

"Do you think she's awake?" Agent Won asked.

"We're up!" I called back. It took a moment but they opened the door for her.

"Belle, can I sleep on your couch?" Lisa Won asked wearily.

"Come on in," I tilted my head to the futon and they closed the door to lock us in again. "What's up?"

"Everyone on the core team is under conditional lockdown," she paced to the futon and flopped on it. "We were allowed to go to our quarters and get a few things, but we have a security escort everywhere to make sure we're not talking to anyone. They set up some bunks for us but the two girls on the team are basically supposed to sleep in a closet. It's going to be like this until the operation is over."

"How many people are on the core team?" I asked while trying to burp Pax.

"Twelve of us plus the bosses. I think Elsa Goode is sleeping in her office," she yawned and I cuddled with Pax until he fell asleep. By then Won was asleep; I covered her with an extra blanket and crawled back into my own bed.

Agent Won and I stirred at roughly the same time the next morning, glancing around and noticing each other groggily.

"What time is it?" she asked softly with her face still half-into the futon cushion.

"Do you want to borrow my shower?" I offered.

"Can I borrow your coffee?" she replied and trotted into the bathroom.

We ate breakfast together. Jack didn't look surprised when he joined us with his bowl of grits and sliced almonds, but Won explained that her escort was probably outside in the hall with my guards.

"Well, I think we're all heavily incentivized to get it done," I joked as Won prepared to leave.

"Can I come back later?" she asked as the door opened.

"Sure," Jack and I agreed and we started the morning's Pilates session.

"You know," I pondered as we put Pax down for a morning nap, "one of these days is going to be a famous date in history."

"Probably the wrong one, too," Jack admitted. "The time difference is significant enough that an early morning raid would still be yesterday here. That's assuming that we tell the world the right date and time."

"We're getting close, we must be getting close or they wouldn't take all those precautions with the team," I reasoned.

"Well, we have to prevent what happened last time," Jack replied. "We have a smaller population in the core team, and I'm sure they're all perfectly trustworthy, but-,"

"I know. Cologne made it through the toughest clearance process we had. What happened to him?"

"Federal prison for a long time; he cracked like an egg."

I sat down to draw for a while to kill time before lunch. "Jack?" I asked and he stopped jumping rope in place.

"Alexis?" he replied.

"When we brought Pax home and I got sick, you were really conflicted about something. Did that turn out okay?"

He thought for a moment and then joined me at the table, nabbing two water bottles from the fridge in the process. "You know, while everyone's all hyped up right now, they should all still think about the next step. What they'll do, what their focus will be on after killing Waldo."

"Some of them will still need to play round-up with the other hundred people we've found. No one's given me a timeline for my return to the world, but I have the impression it's coming soon."

"We've been making preparations for a while now. It did help that you were extremely successful with taking yourself off of the internet. I know a lot of people who would pay enormously well to be able to do that."

"I had help. Plus, I'm sure dozens of people who just looked a lot like me were wondering where their Facebook page and pictures went. We did it in several rounds; the program is still set to run every two months automatically."

"You clever girl," Jack replied.

"Girl? Really?" I laughed at him.

"That's what you called yourself," he objected.

"Only with Ozzie," I defended. "He deserves to know that he was taken down by the unlikeliest of people, a 'pretty little girl'; that an infidel girl took him down. His ego needed that blow."

"I think that Reynolds thought of you as a girl, did you hate him for that?" Jack inquired.

"No. He meant it like a princess; he wanted to be my knight. It's funny how people get these relationships, how we play roles in set dynamics."

"Like how I couldn't be there while you ripped Al-Zahrani apart?"

Oh dear god. We're in an actual relationship! I care about how he sees me! Shit. "I couldn't bring a man in with me," I invented, "It would have ruined my character; implied that I needed a partner."

"Right. So," Jack diverted and I knew he knew I was lying. "Oh," he paused in place to receive instructions in his headphone. When no one was looking, he no longer stood at attention like a nutcracker while Deuce spoke. "Sir, copy that," he answered and turned to me. "This may be a long shot, but care to look at some photos?"

An hour later Pax was still asleep and Jack and I were studying photographs of people who were geographically near the target site. Some appeared to have been taken by a hidden camera in a store of some kind, like a pharmacy. They had little bottles in the background and a delightfully handy angle through a window.

"So, question," I asked as I noted that Jack continued to study each photograph intently. "If the exercise is to see who among these characters I recognize..."

"Patterns," Jack replied before I asked him what he was doing. "Who is with whom, how do their bodies say that they are related? The big questions. How are you doing?"

"Miserably. The photos aren't great quality, and I don't know how to say it without sounding racist, but..."

"Yup," Jack agreed. "Tan skin, dark hair, full long beard, but you can still sort by age and features."

"And battle scars," I added. "Did you see the one-eyed man?"

"Not a phrase I thought I'd hear today," Jack joked and I smiled. "Check out this one's nose," he pointed out a nose that had a ton of character, if that's what you call it.

Our study rapidly disintegrated into pure silliness from there, laughing at the weirdest characters and making up fake stories to go with the images.

"So, Uncle Ahmed the grocer," Jack invented for a man in a blue turban, "Stopped in at the pharmacy because he's just discovered that his affairs have gotten him an STD."

"Why a grocer?"

"His clothes have food stains all over them."

"In strange places; let's pull all the other photos of Uncle Ahmed," I decided and we set to work. "There, this man, he is always with someone but not the same people twice except this boy. The boy shows up with him three times, always around four p.m."

"Stock boy?" Jack joked and I glared. "Son?"

"No. The boy's eyes are blue, that's incredibly rare in that region. Sure bet that both of his parents had light eyes and this man…"

"Uncle Ahmed had brown eyes. So does the man, let's call him T1. So, T1 works for Uncle Ahmed and they are probably not grocers."

"They're putting something together, but it's not a cake recipe," I agreed. "These three are the most interesting people I've seen so far. Do you suppose anyone upstairs has a minute to try and get more on them?"

"I'll ask," Jack offered and reached for the radio. I turned to check on Pax and my son immediately started shrieking.

God! Wet? Dirty? Hungry? Cranky? What the hell is wrong? Yes, you have my attention! I thought to myself as I picked him up and started rounding the wailing bases. *God, just stop crying!*

The weekend was an utter waste of time in my cell. The only thing I accomplished was the realization that with the mystery Pakistani boy's bone structure, there was a decent chance he was half-Caucasian. Saturday night was bad but Sunday night was hell. Pax wouldn't sleep and he wouldn't stop crying, which bewildered me and half the guards.

"He's colicky," Stover finally explained as he arrived around five a.m. Monday.

"What fresh hell is this?" I asked in tears. They turned on the lights and Stover came in. He helped me firmly swaddle Pax and then held him on his shoulder to pat his back. It took a minute but my baby finally stopped screaming at us.

"He cries, he gets gassy, he cries more because he's gassy; it's a vicious cycle."

"Nothing in my life prepared me to handle a baby. Maybe a teenager, but good god!" I collapsed onto my bed. Stover shushed Pax and walked around with him for several minutes and I felt like a horrible mother as I fell asleep.

I stirred and realized that lights were on in my room. *Oh god, Pax. I fell asleep!* I heard soft singing about a kitty and the lullaby made me tired again. *No sleeping. Pax! God I'm the worst mom in the world!* I opened my eyes and darted my head around to locate him.

Natalie was pacing back and forth slowly and gracefully with my little bundle on her shoulder. "He's sleeping," she whispered when she saw me. "Why don't you get some rest; I'll wake you before I leave."

I saw Captain Stover peek in the open doorway and decided to trust him and his apparent expertise.

Natalie lied. I woke up and it was eleven o'clock; almost four hours after I had seen her last and she was gone. Jack was reading a magazine on the futon and Pax was strapped on his chest.

"Here, he's probably getting hungry," Jack greeted me and brought Pax over. He was still swaddled but went straight for lunch when I offered it. "We forgot about May Day," Jack added.

"Mayday! Mayday!" I joked. "Natalie said she'd wake me before she left."

"She stayed until about nine; I took over at 0830 and Stover read me in on how to handle colic."

I should be angry. Meh, it's not a big deal. Someone was here while I was being a terrible parent.

"Knock it off," Jack commanded quietly and I mentally jumped back to the present.

"What?"

"The 'I'm such a terrible parent boo-hoo' crap; I can feel you doing it."

"Ooh, the force is strong in this one," I muttered sarcastically.

He was about to rebut but received instructions instead. "Copy that. They need us upstairs."

"I'm in my jammies," I replied, "And feeding an infant."

It took twenty minutes instead of two and I was actually proud of making it in that time. The first thing I noticed on the floor was the absence of everyone who wasn't on the core team. There was a line of MPs in the hall like someone had parked them there and I mentally linked them to Agent Won's shadow.

"Hey," Agent Won greeted me in the large conference room where the team had been sequestered for the last few days. "They're bringing burgers in a few minutes."

"Did you sleep?" I asked.

"Sort of. I'll sleep when he's dead," Agent Won replied casually. "Where the hell is John?" she bellowed toward Leslie and Kmetz.

"Coming up," Leslie replied and I headed to the back of the room to watch over operations. An image came up on one of the four large screens that had been brought into the room.

"McLean to Task Force Neptune," an older man in a nice suit said and the camera zoomed in on him.

"Task Force Neptune, video audio check?" Leslie stood up and asked the screen.

"Audio and visual confirmed. Agent Won, what is your status?" The man asked and the zoom spread to show John's shiny head crossing the shot.

"Hi John!" I greeted with candor and he stopped.

"Hey there, beautiful!" John grinned and then returned to his tasks.

"We're green on amber," Agent Won reported and took center stage. "Stand by for night surveillance feed, full sats and echo feed. Eyes and ears in place in," she paused to look to Kmetz, who had a pair of headsets strapped on.

"Eighteen," he reported.

"Going on mute," she agreed with the CIA team and we ate burgers and fries before the real action started.

"Feeds one through five are live," Kmetz announced and several different images of the same general area popped up on the screens.

"Watson, you're on audio. Tim, Jimmy, thermals. Leslie, you make sure that we maintain this connection. We could get that call anytime and our Seals need to know everything we can tell them."

Should have gone Army, I mentally noted and checked the clock; it was close to 1 p.m. Across the top of the far right hand screen were faces like mug shots, including Bin Laden, several of his wives and a dozen close associates. Under the pictures were sets of numbers. It took a moment but I realized that each person's profile included their infrared data like height and projected weight. The data could be used to help identify individual's locations on the compound.

"Scanning initiated," Kmetz announced and I wandered to his station.

"How accurate are the projections?"

"Shaky. Clothes, locations in the house, armor, basically it tells us what's a child and what's a man. We're lucky that two of the three women in the house are small," Kmetz informed me quietly while poking at the controls.

"Belle," Agent Won called me over, "It's going to look like this for the next several hours."

"Where's Deuce?" I asked.

"On the ground," she replied quietly.

Where else would he be? I muttered to myself and Pax began to cry again. *Uh! Not now, baby! Mommy's...* "Shh," I cuddled the squalling, squirming noisemaker and caught a few people giving us side-eye from their stations. "Shh, come on buddy, not now. Mommy's trying to kill a bad guy."

Jack motioned me into the hallway and we stepped out so people could focus on their mission. Officer Morgan was out there looking well-rested and friendly and I couldn't resist handing Pax off to her when she reached for him with a maternal smile.

"Can you," I started to say as she nestled Pax against her shoulder.

"I'll take him home. Is there milk in the fridge?"

"I think so. I can't remember," I admitted. The long nights and constant crying had unraveled some part of my brain.

"Two bottles are ready in the refrigerator and there's formula. He's colicky; so good luck," Jack added to my relief.

"Thank you," I sighed with overwhelming sincerity. Officer Morgan smiled genuinely before tilting her head toward the room.

"Give 'em hell," she winked and turned away. I stayed to watch her and Pax disappear down the hall, his cries getting further away.

"I'm such a bad mommy," I said quietly so only Jack could hear.

"Morgan's brilliant with kids," Jack encouraged, "You'll see him soon. He's going to grow out of the screaming phase. I know you, lady; you will never harm or abandon him; you'll never neglect him or let anyone else hurt him. There's no option, no choice for you to make here; that's who you are."

"Promise?" I whispered.

"Yeah. So, ready to do this?"

"Neptune Spear? Who the hell named this operation?" I replied and we returned to the room.

"It's going to be in history books," Director Goode surprised me inside, "We couldn't just call it Operation Farting Cow."

The three of us swept to the back of the room and did a quick survey of the organized chaos around us.

"Alright," the CIA man in the suit said in his little window on the screen, "Start the clock."

Chapter Eleven: Zulu

"Attention all personnel," Director Goode called loudly as a clock appeared on the center screen. "We are operating on Zulu time. If you have a watch, please synchronize or remove it at this time."

Half a dozen people with wrist watches moved to either change the time up four hours from EST or, like Leslie, simply shoved the watch in their pockets.

1738 Zulu

The room was uneasy but mostly silent. I had counted a total of eighteen screens, including the four huge screens across the interior wall, and just thirteen people in the room. Kmetz and Tim were working on heat signatures and some other kind of scanning; they had two screens at their station. Watson, a bulky woman of Hawaiian descent, had a set of headphones on her ears and another on her neck. Leslie had the smallest screen on her laptop but her area had a total of three phones. Half a dozen others, all males of varied ages, were staring at their screens. Maps of Afghanistan and Pakistan as well as information and pictures of the people we expected were in the compound; internal projections of the compound derived from photos and scans, and boxes of information decorated screens in every direction.

I heard Jack's phone vibrate in his pocket; we stood so closely I almost felt it. He dug the phone out and stepped to the back of the room while answering.

"Sir?" he paused and Agent Won stared at him expectantly. "Right away sir," he hung up and turned to Director Goode. "Ma'am, we need to use your office briefly."

Director Goode declined to join us so Jack and I went upstairs with a new guard. The guard checked out the office briefly and then left us. Jack typed at a control panel on the director's desk and a VTC window came up on her big screen.

"Hello?" I stared at a strange face: a young, grim man with a buzz cut in a uniform.

"Sir!" the ginger man at the desk said. It took a moment but as Jack came to my side, Deuce walked into the shot on the other side.

What's wrong? Please tell me nothing's gone wrong, please, please, I took a deep breath.

"Beauty; I'm here with the men whose mission is to kill or capture Osama Bin Laden," Deuce greeted me. "What would you like them to know?"

"There are children in the house and in the compound. He sleeps with guns and I'd be shocked if he didn't have some idea that you were coming. I don't know what kind of firepower you can expect, but do it fast because the Pakistani military is well armed and close," I supplied to people I couldn't see. "Mostly, please, please," I took a breath, "I don't know; just, blow his brains out. No, not too much, we'll have to identify..." I looked to Jack desperately, "What do you think?"

"Keep the lines tight," Jack advised.

"Watch out for the kids, and don't assume the women will stand by."

"That's from the world's most dangerous woman, so take it to heart," Deuce told someone off-screen and I grinned at the title.

"Sir?" I added as he began to move off camera.

"I know, Beauty. Don't worry."

I nodded and I knew he knew that Waldo had to die.

1827 Zulu

"Birds are in the air; all teams deployed," John announced from CIA headquarters. Jack and I were back in the mission control room after our little chat with Deuce and the troops in Afghanistan.

"The flight will be about ninety minutes," Director Goode reported. She had slid into an open station and was working like everyone else on the team.

"Weather conditions are reasonably good, but they might get tricky," a nameless drone in a suit announced in the back.

1957 Zulu

"Secondary units are in location; primary forces are bearing down on target," John informed from CIA headquarters. He looked like an air traffic controller with his massive set of headphones on. I felt a little sick and judging by what I saw, I wasn't the only one.

"Get those engines started, I want them capable of action at a minute's notice," the cross CIA man in the suit barked.

"Copy," a drone in the room said.

"Here they come, we're picking them up on heat sensors," Kmetz announced.

2003 Zulu

"AH!" Watson winced and pulled her headphones away briefly.

"Something's gone wrong!" Kmetz announced from his station. He was now one of many who were standing at their stations instead of sitting.

"Watson, put it up," Agent Won directed and the woman flipped a few switches so we all heard the audio feed. We could hear scrambled voices and the sounds of a terrible crash or explosion.

"The chopper has," Kmetz started and was interrupted by the CIA.

"He's burying the nose to keep it from tipping. We had a situation, the mission will continue," the older CIA man declared.

"Do we have reports on casualties?" Director Goode asked.

"Medic unit with secondary forces is already in the air; hope we don't need it," Leslie chirped.

2005 Zulu

"There go the bodies," Tim announced and his infrared camera was displayed on one of the large screens so we all saw the swarm of bodies run out from the even hotter chopper.

"What's that one?" I pointed at a strangely small and faint outline moving quickly into the compound.

"Canine," he seemed to recognize the shape. "There's the second group; they zipped down from the chopper in air."

The bodies swarmed the compound and we watched the sickeningly tense dance. We couldn't really tell our bodies from their bodies once they were away from the transport vehicles and into the compound. Our audio was next to useless for the longest time; the voices sounded faint and when I did hear them, I couldn't understand the dialogue.

"Hang on," Agent Won said while typing furiously. Some of Kmetz' anonymous heat readings developed little blue flashing dots on the bodies. "Dots are us," she explained, "don't ask."

"Keep breathing," Jack touched my back.

We all heard the shots when they started. On the screen we saw the bodies take positions, pause, and then advance as others came running out to either fight or surrender; it was impossible to tell. Every once in a while a body would stop moving and stay still, but their heat signature kept showing because people stay warm for some time after death. It was somewhere between tragedy and victory for me; we didn't know exactly who was who and I sure as hell wouldn't cheer until I knew my boys were safe.

Like a fast-moving song, the action went quickly. I tried to keep up with everything but between the audio and the four shots of various forms of video, it just wasn't possible.

2027 Zulu
Pop! Pop-Pop POP BAM!

"Got it!" Won exclaimed and told Watson to hide her audio again.

"…be advised, we have a wounded UBL wife in nest, standby for confirmation on assassination," a man said over a radio.

"I connected to central command Afghanistan for audio," Agent Won told me quietly. "They don't know it yet," she winked and I realized that I was holding Jack's hand.

"Copy that, confirm identify," a woman's voice replied. "Height 76 inches,"

A moment of nothing followed until a different voice alerted them to a pending explosion. Watson managed to get her headphones away from her ears in time and we all saw and heard the crashed bird blow up.

"Couldn't risk it," Goode said quietly.

"Damn that's hot," Kmetz muttered.

"Height confirmed, identity confirmed by wife 3," the first soldier said.

"Eyes brown, weight," the woman tried.

"Dimensions confirmed; eye color cannot be determined. Let's round it up."

"Confirm status of all adult males," the woman on the radio demanded.

There was radio silence and we saw almost all of the heat forms leave the buildings and gather in the open courtyard. It was hard to tell anything in the wake of the burning helicopter, but we got the impression they were getting ready to leave.

"All adult male targets are deceased. No female residents are deceased; several are injured. All children were untouched, please inform Bravo Command," a soldier reported.

2039 Zulu

We watched in an aerial view as the first chopper kept burning and discerned that the people left behind were left immobilized in the courtyard. The second chopper lifted up and away into the night and the core team in our conference room waited with uncertain ecstasy for the all-clear.

"Task Force Neptune," the CIA man with John finally said from his dim little screen, "Be advised that the strike team has cleared the site with no U.S. fatalities. We have taken a corpse for confirmation of identity. It's a ninety minute flight. We will advise when we have final identification of Osama Bin Laden. The mission can be identified as successful. We're going on mute," he informed.

Agent Won pushed a button on a remote and a little boxed microphone came up on the CIA's screen.

"How long do you think it will take the Pakistani military to get there?" Director Goode wondered.

"Jimmy, Tim, can you lift, zoom out a little? We'll watch for arriving heat signatures," Agent Won requested and the guys set to work.

"If all male residents were killed," I reasoned, "Then, if he was there, then he's dead."

"The only person that's left was the courier," a drone in the back informed.

"Everyone, this was spectacular work," Director Goode called over the chatter that had broken out among the team, "We are pending final dismissal for this task force, but hopefully we'll all get to go home tonight."

That announcement got lots of cheers and some brief applause.

"What time is it?" someone asked despite the huge numbers on the screen declaring that it was 2057 Zulu.

"It's around five p.m.," Leslie replied from her station.

"I'll give the all-clear for dinner to be brought," Director Goode offered.

"Chinese or pizza?" Jimmy Kmetz asked in unimpressed monotone while glaring at the screen with heat signatures.

"This one's catered," A drone near the open door informed.

Jack signaled Director Goode and me and we knew he was getting a message through his earpiece. "There's a call for me," Jack announced just as Leslie looked up with a phone in her hand. She almost looked disappointed to be robbed of her announcement. The call was brief and Jack didn't say anything else until the three of us were out in the hall again. "He wants a conference call with us, Agent Won, and CIA headquarters at 2300 Zulu. That's in about two hours."

"They'll know by then," Director Goode concluded.

"I want to dash down and check on Pa — my son," I caught myself trying to say his name.

"Fair enough. Feel free to join us for dinner, we'll shut down the command center as soon as we get the all-clear, but the security quarantine should be lifted at this point," Goode replied.

Jack and I headed home and Benzion fell into step with us naturally. At some point I realized that I no longer thought of the guards as soldiers or captors, just as people I knew. They were a little like neighbors or colleagues; I knew their quirks, their personalities, even pieces of their life stories.

My baby was still squalling when I came to relieve Morgan but I picked him up and patted his back while swaying side to side like I used to when he was still in my belly. The pauses between shrieks grew longer and longer until he was finally quiet. Pax wanted to feed so I hooked him up and got comfortable on the futon.

"Why do you look so sad?" I asked Jack. He had sat at the table facing away from me, probably to respect my privacy. "You don't think it's him?"

"No, no, the facts seem to add up. I'm sure it's him, but if it is, then," Jack paused. The privacy board was down and the door was closed, so it was just the three of us there to hear and see. "That means that everything is about to change. You'll have choices to make, I'll have to make some decisions, but our lives are about to change."

"What will you do? Do you want to keep working for Deuce? Will your loose job description take you somewhere new?"

"I've been looking at places for your identity team to place you; I found a nice place in Tennessee for you and Pax. It's far enough in the country to allow for privacy and ultimately security, and there's a barn to hide a helicopter in."

The last phrase made me laugh until I realized that he wasn't joking. "Helicopter?"

"It's not yours. We're not just dumping you out somewhere in America and leaving you to your own devices."

It's weird when I think about him as 'them'. Well, he's sort of a 'them'. Deuce and Jack and I taking on the world together. What will it look like, out there? Green grass, wide open spaces? I want to get a dog. Pax should have a dog, a big one. Someone I can take as a puppy so he'll know and love us, just in case. I could use some unconditional love, plus something that works as an alarm system. Oh, he's done; I realized and pulled Pax up to burp him. *How do you poop and eat at the same time? Good grief.* I got up to change him before Jack and I had to return upstairs.

We heard the ruckus of happy people moving around to eat as soon as we stepped out of the second elevator. The food had been brought into Cyber and people were milling around the silver pans. Someone had covered the long table in the middle of the room in a cloth like a dining table and the food was served buffet-style.

"There you are!" Kmetz greeted enthusiastically. "How's Jones Junior?"

"He's fine, what is all this?" I looked around to see what seemed to be turkey, dressing, sweet potatoes, mashed potatoes and two other containers.

"I think it's the Christmas dinner we missed," Kmetz quipped.

"More like the Thanksgiving dinner we missed," another man joked dryly.

"Are we still waiting on confirmation?" someone else asked from the table.

"Yes, we are still waiting," Agent Won stepped out of her office and strolled to join us. "However," the one word captured the room's attention, "The mission we have been engaged on is complete. Whatever happened, whoever we shot, it's over now. Security should receive orders to stand down shortly and we can all go home tonight!"

This announcement was met with cheers and applause. The mood at dinner was weary but pleased with an undercurrent of adrenalin. Jack checked his watch for the fifth time and ushered Agent Won and I out of the room as discreetly as possible and we met Director Goode in her office. The strangest part was passing Susan on the way in; she was reading a magazine at Natalie's desk.

"I arranged a medic on standby," Director Goode informed and we noted that there were three chairs facing the large screen before the camera. The screen was split with side-by-side shots of a conference room showing the CIA seal and the desk and office we had seen earlier in Afghanistan. Goode took the middle seat, Won took the left and I sat on the far right while looking around for a place for Jack.

"Good evening," Deuce and a man in black fatigues entered the screen in Afghanistan. They did not look pleased and I was worried. "Give me a roll call."

The CIA dudes went first and it circled around to us.

"Special Agent Lisa Won, DIA."

"Deputy Director Elsa Goode, FBI."

"And what about the girl next to you, Director?" The man with Deuce, who had introduced himself as Colonel Stennett, squinted at us.

"The name is Belle Jones," I said clearly.

"And we already know Jack," Deuce added quickly.

"Is that," Colonel Stennett started to ask but Deuce cut him off.

"Yes. Let's get on with it. The President of the United States will make an announcement shortly that the forces under his command have executed a strike on a compound in Pakistan. This operation was led by the Central Intelligence Agency and backed by U.S. troops. The result of this strike was the death of Osama Bin Laden, leader of the terrorist group known as Al-Qaeda. His body was recovered and has been positively identified. There were no U.S.

casualties." Deuce took a deep breath. "Goode, I'll see you and your people later this week," he added, "Excellent work, everyone."

Colonel Stennett started clapping and the CIA guys joined in.

"Alright, I need to go brief Washington." Deuce announced and the screen cut out shortly thereafter. Director Goode hung up on the CIA team and the four of us were left in silence. We stared off into different directions, barely breathing.

"Why is no one cheering?" I asked in a tiny voice.

"We should. We should be bouncing off of the walls," Jack admitted quietly.

"It's over. We can move on and move up," Director Goode added.

"It's not like it's really over. Others will rise against us," Agent Won pointed. "We're attacked on a daily basis; the war isn't over for us."

Director Goode turned her head to look at me. "Congratulations, Belle. I think you may have just become a civilian."

Well, that's terrifying. "Great," I faked enthusiasm.

"Hey guys," Agent Won broke the pattern, "We just killed Osama Bin Laden."

"Someone should tell Al-Zahrani," Director Goode posited.

I shook my head without thought. "Let him find out the normal way. He doesn't deserve special treatment, not anymore. He should rot in the most miserable way possible for the rest of his life, demoted down to a normal person. Let him...let him be thrown away. What will they do with the body?"

"I don't know," Goode admitted. "This is where politics takes over. This is as far as we go."

"I fucking hate politics," Agent Won stated.

"Not fond of it myself," Jack added.

"Don't look at me, my version of diplomacy has always involved blood," I responded to Agent Won's glance. "We don't have any new orders or anything, do we?"

"Your status hasn't changed. Security," Director Goode looked at her phone, "has been ordered to stand down from the quarantine and let us go home."

"Fine," I said after a beat and I stood up. Jack closed in quickly. "I'm not going to faint!" I objected loudly as I added up the facts in my head. I stormed past Susan in the outer office and headed through my home hallways.

We went home and then Jack left us for the evening. Pax, thank god, had stopped screaming and was in a good mood from my arrival until I rocked him to sleep around ten. My brain was too busy to sleep, so I picked up a catalog and started picking out the next items to add to Pax' wardrobe until I drifted to sleep.

"Holy Cow!" Someone exclaimed and I awoke to the sounds of rapid conversation in the hall. "Belle!" someone pounded on my door and then it clanked open.

"Shh! You'll wake the baby!" Benzion reprimanded.

Pax? Good, still fast asleep.

"Calm down, calm down," I heard Captain Stover coming and waited until he was in my open doorway. "The President just announced that we killed Bin Laden."

"Yeah?" I yawned.

"Yeah," he grinned expectantly. "The whole world knows. People are dancing in Washington D.C."

"That's great. Can you turn off the light?" I turned to my side in bed and tugged the sheets up.

"Helluva job, kid," Stover added and closed the door again.

Yeah, I laughed to myself. *That's great.*

Deuce returned to base on Friday and I noted the weary satisfaction in his eyes when they called me up to the Director's office. Goode was gone; Natalie explained that our lady director had finally taken some leave for R&R and Deuce had commandeered her office.

"Natalie," Deuce called to her as he opened the door for me, "Would you be so kind as to keep the others until I open the door again, please?"

"Yes sir," Natalie agreed in a far more confident voice than she had used when I arrived here. I smiled at her and she returned a grin.

Aw, look at her all grown up. These must be what they call the 'warm fuzzies'.

"Jack," Deuce greeted Jack's sharp salute and waved his hand near his brow. "Beauty: request permission to hug?"

"Permission granted," I replied and received a warm and fatherly hug from him.

"Well, darlin', we knocked him dead. Al Qaeda's already declared that they'll seek revenge, but frankly, they plan on blowing up everything they can on principle; I fail to see how they'll distinguish one act from another by purpose."

Sounds about right.

"Come sit," Deuce gestured and we perched on the couch. "The task force's mission has been achieved; achieved and exceeded beyond our scope. Al-Zahrani will be in prisons for the rest of his life. Bin Laden was buried at sea on Tuesday. Pakistan is miffed but quiet about it and Saudi Arabia is still friends with America."

Interesting definition of the word 'friends'.

"You will be transitioned to the reintegration phase. You will be assigned a new name, your son can finally be called by his proper name, and we'll relocate you into a rural or suburban area in civilian America. There's a place in Nebraska we've had our eye on. We'll keep an eye on you, but for your security, not ours. We do ask that you play ball with us, but if you're on board, you'll have no guards, no cuffs, no shock devices, you'll be a normal, regular, free person. You will receive a monthly allowance which you'll be able to live comfortably on. If you're interested in doing some freelance work to augment that payment, we can work something out." He paused to read my face, "Not contract jobs; more like the kind of thing you've done here. No more killing people, Beauty."

"You know, I'm…I'm ready to be done with that. Belle Jones had her time, but it's time," I reflected honestly. "Think I can pass for civilized?"

"We'll teach you. You'll get used to buying things with American money and not to barter over them; we'll give you a backstory to learn for your identity. We'll check in on you regularly."

"Did anyone ever teach you how to drive?" Jack asked.

"Everything from a moped to a tank; well, I helped drive the tank," I admitted. "Can I pick my new name?"

"What did you have in mind?" Deuce inquired. "We don't want anything you've used before."

"Something simple, easy to remember and sign; I'll have to practice signing and saying it over and over again. I've used so many: Renée, Cheryl, Isabelle, Belle, Sarah, Mariam; you called me Rhonda once I think."

"Jessica? Catherine? Elizabeth?" Jack offered.

"Alexis was such a good name," I sighed. "How about Emma?"

"Alison?" Jack offered.

"Amelia," Deuce smiled.

I wandered over to the bathroom and looked at the mirror. "I think we're going to need to cut my hair off." *And lose some weight, and makeup; I need makeup.* "Are we going to change my face?"

"How do you feel about a small nose job?"

"Can I pick what I get?"

"Of course. I'll have someone bring you some selections; we should do it soon while Jack is still here to help." Deuce's phone pinged three times and we were dismissed with a wink.

They gave me a total of three days to choose my new nose from a catalog. They told me Monday evening that I was going to have a trip

Tuesday to a medical center to get my nose done. We couldn't take Pax in the helicopter, so we piled into a panel van before dawn and drove for an hour or two. Pax and I were both asleep when Jack gently woke me and helped me out of the back door of the van. Pax snoozed on, carefully tucked on my chest right up until we sat and waited in the examination room.

"Good morning, Mrs. Winchester," a tiny black man with a clipboard and a robust mustache came in accompanied by Captain Stover in full military uniform. "Let's see here: could you let your husband hold the child?"

I handed Pax off to Jack and silently assessed the doctor as he assessed us.

"You know, I have people walking in here who'd be happy to have your face," the doctor said. "My name is Walters; I'm your surgeon today. When was the last time you ate?"

"Last night; when can we get this over with?"

"Let's see," he looked up my nose for a little too long. "Deviated septum, does she snore?"

"No. Will she be able to breastfeed after the procedure?"

"We're putting her under. As a precaution, I'd recommend dumping the first round after she wakes but after that she's clear to breastfeed with no risk of harm to the child. We're going to get a set of scans, and then she's booked for OR at

eleven. Captain, you can accompany her into
surgery but you'll have to scrub."

"Not a problem."

"Can we just do this please?" I whined and the
doctor retreated.

Jack kept Pax through all three sets of scans
and I fed my son just before they started sticking
me with needles. I was hazy but I remember
laying on the table staring as the world faded
and the doctor told Jack that he could fix the
notch in his ear. I had a smart response but
passed out before I could move my tongue.

Pax...Pax is crying. Where...get open, eyes! It was
hard but I got my eyes to open. I couldn't lift my
head but Pax kept squealing for me. Then he
stopped and somehow that was worse.

"He's okay, don't move just yet." Jack said
softly but I couldn't find him. "Stover has him.
Do you want an ice chip?"

I think he kept talking but I was so groggy. I
closed my eyes again.

"Mrs. Winchester?" a woman annoyed me into
waking. I was sitting up in a chair like a dentist's
and a woman with an expression of distaste was
messing with my hand. "Would you like some
juice? The doctor will be in to talk to you in just a
moment." She had the bedside manner of a
wicked stepmother and I smiled when she left.

"I can't feel my smile!" I said; I sounded funny.

"It's just the nerves and numbing, it may take a while for you to get full feeling back," Jack read off a pamphlet and came around to feed me ice and juice.

We left the hospital under darkness in the same van we came in. Jack declared that he was spending the night because I would be too drugged to help with the baby. I didn't argue.

Eight days later they took me back to the hospital to get the cast off of my nose. I couldn't really tell if anything was different: the whole nose looked bigger and I silently prayed that the surgeon had followed directions and not given me a beak like his.

Dr. Walters was followed by a dental checkup and cleaning: I had been seven years without seeing a dentist but fortunately I had a clean bill of health. I had never seen the kind of technology they scanned me with, picturing every tooth under my swollen nose. The cleaning was miserable with the sensitivity from my nose surgery but they gave me a little extra painkiller that night and I slept it off.

The following morning, I woke first. Jack was asleep on the futon, Pax was breathing steadily and contently snoozing, and my artificial window showed night stars over the ocean.

Holy shit this is actually happening. My first thought was a doozy. *I had plastic surgery. Won is playing with simulators to see what my hair would look like with different options. Deuce and Jack are finalizing details on my next home, whether that's Tennessee or...what did he say? Utah? Yikes. That Pearson dude is coming today to start the protection program brief series. Yikes, yikes, yikes. Holy fuck.*

Hey, you're going to be free, right? Semi-free? Alone with Pax. I turned my head over to Jack, careful not to move anything else and risk waking him. *God, I'm going to miss you. Not the bossy part, just the kind, caring, nurturing parts. He doesn't want to come with me, I'm an assignment. He'll get his life back. No more impromptu sleepovers on couches because the nutcase he's in charge of might not be able to make it through the night without his personal supervision.*

No, damn it! No crying! Crying will hurt, my fucking nose still hurts and it won't help anyway. This is Tom's fault. He and that sneaky Cyndy make me all gooey inside. I was a perfectly good psychopath, I joked with myself and smirked.

"You're awake," Jack said softly and I jumped a little. He hadn't moved or suddenly changed breathing patterns but now he turned toward me. "Are you in pain?"

"Nope. Early morning freak-out session," I answered quietly. My honesty with him was absolute and unrestricted, which in and of itself was terrifying. "When do we move?"

"I don't have a date. Hopefully sometime in the next few weeks."

Yeah, you probably want to get on with your life.

"Was that a frown?" he asked with a slight hint of tease.

"No, get your eyes checked, old man." I shot back.

"I'm 29. No, wait, I'm 30."

"What's next for you?"

"Don't know. I want to travel in the U.S.: I think I've seen more foreign lands than American territory. Then I think I'll go after a degree. Use the G.I. Bill, you know."

"If they kick me out soon, you could travel over the summer and get back to school this fall."

"Maybe next year. We'll both get out of here a hell of a lot earlier than X128," he added under his breath but neither of us laughed.

Chapter Twelve: Eyes Forward

"Tell me where I'm going," I half-requested. It was the 30th of June and I had been brought to the undisclosed CIA location. It was decided that I wouldn't bring Pax on this trip, so I left him in Jack's care and went with Goode, Won, and Stover.

"We're here," Director Goode replied and waited as the door to a large conference room was opened. "This is your last debriefing with the CIA before your release and relocation. After we're done here, we'll return to base, the details will be finalized and transportation phase will begin."

"Blah, blah, blah, where am I going?"

"In here, for now," Agent Won guided gently and I walked into the door and slumped into a chair at the table.

Thirteen chairs, one broken, no windows, one-two-three cameras and probably five screens; only one is out right now. No maps, no plans, nothing to indicate intentions. Here they come, I know that one, him, him, she's new, and hey, John! I'll probably never see him again. Hmm, that might be a little bit sad. Keep breathing.

The CIA people sat on one side of the table and we sat on the other side. The meeting lasted for hours and it almost put me to sleep more than once. Leona Hampshire from Homeland Security joined us right after the coffee break at eleven. Together we reviewed my timeline in reverse order all the way to the original Bin Laden chip's acquisition and insertion into my foot. We talked about Ryan Rogers, Ari Hansen, and my Israeli contacts. The locker in Germany, the tunnels under Kandahar, and the technological breakthroughs I had made with Agent Won's team were all covered extensively.

I need to know where I am going. The thought dominated the last half-hour of the conference. The meeting broke up; most of the CIA team left without further niceties but John lingered to say goodbye.

"Do you have a moment?" I requested meaningfully and John took me into a nearby office. Stover agreed to let us close the door but he stayed pressed against it suspiciously.

"Look, this probably isn't the last I'll see of you," John tried to console.

"Will Ray have access to my location?" I asked first. That douchebag needed no assistance to push my buttons.

"No. I'm not sure I'll have the address, it's all very hush-hush. Your new nose is fabulous, by the way."

"Yeah, I'm a haircut and dye job away from being in a Bourne movie," I joked dryly and he smirked.

"Curious thing; it seems someone recently left a bag of poop on Ray's doorstep," John continued and I snorted.

"Burning?"

"No, I couldn't get the damn bag to light!" We shared a loud guffaw. "I may just miss you, Belle Jones."

"Will we be safe?"

"How could we let you be anything but safe? You'll be fine. I want to see that kid of yours in a few years. Bet he's going to be brilliant."

"We gotta make sure he doesn't have to see what I've seen. Where are they sending us?"

"All I know is that it's near a major military base. Sorry, Belle. All those interrogation skills shot to hell."

"Next time," I leaned closer, "use a paper bag and dry droppings. It'll blaze right up for you." We both snorted again and snickered away as I left. I declared that I needed to use the restroom and fortunately Agent Won decided to join me.

"So Lisa, I know you've been working on setting up my new location," I approached the subject lightly.

"Seriously?" Agent Won retorted with very minor annoyance. "You picked me as the weak link?" she accused and leaned against a stall wall to face me.

"Nonsense, but John didn't know and I knew you were the most likely to have the information. It seems to be tightly contained so I thought I'd save time," I leveled with her. "You're not a bureaucrat or a political figure; you don't have any extra motivations in this."

"We spent most of a week onsite earlier this month. It's beautiful; you'll have absolutely no reason to lay awake at night due to security fears. I mean, talk about a ring of steel."

"That good?"

"You couldn't design it better, and I'm not bullshitting you. I'd live there in peace even if everyone in the CIA was out to get me."

"At the moment, they're busy pranking each other with bags of poo," I informed her. "Far from here?"

"Far enough, but we're not sending you to Alaska or anything. I promise, when I can, I'll tell you. Right now, we need to get back to base because you have a hair appointment. You're leaving soon; you won't be allowed to show your new hair to anyone; we want to keep your new look as closely guarded as possible."

"So," I blocked the door partially in an attempt to maintain control. "This is it? My last few days of whatever the hell this is? It's over?"

"Yes, at least for now. We're not going to lose you; you may never be hands-off. Security is just too important. I kind of wish we could hire you like a normal person; your skills were just…wow, I'm going to miss you in the lab."

"Don't go crying on me," I rolled my eyes at her total lack of emotion.

"You probably won't miss the prison thing, or the hours, the unpredictability," Agent Won listed.

"At least I knew I was safe there. With you, with Jack, with Stover," I fought a small smile, "I guess if it's over, it's over. Let's go home."

"When can I take this stupid hat off?" I grumbled from the backseat of a nondescript station wagon. It was less than twelve hours after Agent Won and I said our goodbyes and Pax and I were zooming down tree-lined highways on our way south. We had changed vehicles sometime around seven a.m. after leaving the base in a classic black SUV and driving for a while.

My hair had been covered from the moment we left the salon with the exception of my time in my cell. I honestly think people believe that a haircut, like a moustache, will entirely disguise a person.

Jack turned around from the shotgun seat. "You can take it off now," he assured me and I pulled the knit cap off. Pax giggled at my funny hair but Jack kept a straight face.

"Have I mentioned that I hate my hair?"

"It did what it needed to do. You'll need to dye it from time to time, but all that's in the book," Jack replied and turned back.

The book was a spiral-bound stack of papers with chapters covering my new identity, my new background, scar care products and recommendations for explanations of my scars, my new financial information, lists of online retailers I might like to use, and basically every other detail of my new life. Maps of my new home, security system information, and step-by-step directions for how they wanted me to live my life.

"Who do I blame for my name?" I frowned.

"That would be Deputy Director Goode. What's wrong with Penny Oswald?" Jack asked.

"Just Penny; was it short for something?"

"You should probably practice signing it," Stover piped up from the driver's seat.

I sank my head back into the seat and kept my complaining silent.

This is really it. Ten months: in ten months I caught Al-Zahrani, killed Bin Laden, and popped out a beautiful, sweet little boy. My little baby boy; I bet in ten years I'll mostly think about him, not the others. Not the dead, not the locked away, not the terrorists, not the deaths, the explosions, the losses, I swallowed hard as if losing the lump in my throat would make the memories of Bacon, Ari, or Luc go away.

Right on cue, Pax looked at me and grinned with a giggle. I wiped the drool off his face and let him hold my finger possessively.

Worth it. Screw how I got here, that's not me anymore. I'm Penny Oswald, this is my son Pax, and we're going to be okay.

Chapter Thirteen: Penny Oswald

Oh my god, it's cold here! I tucked my knees up closer under the blankets and opened my eyes. It was an unseasonably cool October in my new home outside of Clarksville, Tennessee; just a hick's spit south of Kentucky. Everything about the house and the land around it screamed rural America and I was starting to really enjoy the motif. The wrap-around porch was made of a smooth, grayish wood and featured a porch swing; something I had never heard of. It was nice, but after the first summer I knew I was going to need to screen in the porch or be eaten alive by the bugs.

Jack wasn't kidding about the barn, although there was absolutely no way to land or park a helicopter in it. The house and the barn were about the same size, one painted brown and the other beige with a black roof. There were four bedrooms, two levels, and a garage out back for my second-hand blue sedan. There were hard floors almost everywhere and I rapidly discovered the joy of sock-skating around the house.

If I'm cold, he's probably cold. Why is it so cold?
You haven't turned the heat on, genius.

I reluctantly sat up, accidently catching myself in the mirror that sat atop my dresser. My bedhead was truly epic since we chopped off my locks to a smart pixie cut. I could never have worn the look in the field; my hair was constantly in my face or flying off my head. My new nose was at best neutral compared to the old one: it seemed a little too thin and just a teensy bit mousy. It was different though, and that was the important part.

Why did I sleep in here? I hurried to my slippers and robe and slunk out of the master bedroom to tiptoe down the creaky hall. If you remember just the right sequence of steps, you can get down the hall without making a sound. If you're not awake enough to do that, you curse the floorboards. I peeked in on my little prince in his nursery. It's a whopping seven feet down the hall and I couldn't manage to leave him for most of the first months. *Oh right,* I remembered as I saw the twin bed that was half-covered in spit-up and half-covered in new clothes from online retailers. *Laundry day.*

I gathered up the laundry and headed for the washing machine closet. Pax could sleep through a war, so I never bothered to be extra-quiet. I checked my phones on the kitchen counter; I had two cell phones to keep track of on top of a baby. The red one was the emergency hotline number that could get me talking to someone within two rings; the gray one was my personal civilian line.

Both spent most of the time gathering dust. Most of my human contact was through a DOD contact, running errands in town, or Colonel Sanders.

After I stopped giggling over the fact that his name was Colonel Sanders and he lived in Kentucky, I quickly grew to appreciate the retired army colonel. He was introduced to me as an old friend of Deuce's and seemed to make it his mission in life to keep an eye on me. He and his family lived just across the border; probably a twenty minute drive on the state roads, and Pax and I sometimes went for Sunday dinner. He recently learned how to text, and my phone reflected the skill.

Ding dee-dee-dee! My phone pinged at me. Sammy Sanders woke up early and he probably thought it was past time for me to be up. I don't use an alarm clock: Pax is the only thing I get up for.

"Need 2B N ur town this am," the text read. "Can I bring u coffee?"

My plans of the day included a trip to the library to switch out books. Time to sit and read was new to me and I was slowly devouring every book in the Mystery section of the local public library.

"Sure. When?" I texted back and started making oatmeal. Pax always starts crying when I'm cooking and this morning was no exception.

Ding, dee-dee-dee! Ding, dee-dee-dee! My phone dinged about an hour later and I reassured him that the security system was disarmed. The cameras were eternal but the laser-radar-whatever the system was could be armed or disarmed. There were unique and unexpected modifications all over the house. I pity any run-of-the-mill burglar trying to break in.

Knock! (pause) knock-knock! Sammy Sanders was at my front door and I put Pax in his playpen in the living room. A few minutes later, Sammy and I were watching Pax roll himself over while sipping coffee on the couch.

A thought had been pecking at me and I decided to charge forward with it. "Sammy,"

"Yes, Penny?"

"I don't mean to be rude, but why are you so generous to me? You opened your family, your home, your time," I swallowed the lump in my throat.

"Ah," Sammy set his coffee down and braced his elbows on his knees. "I know what you did."

My heart sank like a stone. *Crap on a cracker. Shit. Wait, what? Which, "what I did?" All of it? 24*

bodies? The death, the wars, the hacking, everything?
"Um."

"Al-Qaida. You gave me, my country, the world a gift we can't repay. I fought them for years with everything I had and finally burned out and retired. But you did it. You got the man who attacked Americans on American soil and the world noticed. Terror cells are going to think twice because they're going to know, now, that we'll get them."

He's talking about Bin Laden! Whew! "Bin Laden and his men stole my only family. It's just me and Pax now," I sighed and returned to the coffee.

"Not if I have anything to say about it. You're a hero, and heroes don't get left behind." There was an awkward pause until he cleared his throat. "Besides, what else is a rusty old vet like me going to do?"

"You have a son whose college homecoming is soon and isn't your daughter about to get her learner's permit?"

"She got it," he admitted gruffly and started a monologue about the wonders of having a teenage daughter in the south. I restrained myself into only smiling with my face hidden.

Marion Sanders looked every bit the sixteen-year-old girl she should, especially gawking around in my doorway. She and Sammy came by on the last Saturday of October so I could have some me-time. Marion is beautiful, dark-skinned like her mother with short natural hair permanently pushed back by a hair band. I knew she had baby-sat for neighbors and friends for years, but I felt better with Sammy present.

I had honestly considered just going to one of the upstairs bedrooms and taking a nap, but I steeled my resolve and went for a cross-country run and explored my surroundings beyond the porch lights. Every time the leaves crunched under my shoes I felt brief guilt at making such noise. The world was quiet, cool, and calm and I decided to run the boundary. I paused a few times to gasp for breath and hate my out-of-shape body, but I made it to the top of the hill. There, I leaned against one of the hickory trees. In the silence I waited and heard the quiet sounds of mechanics in my immediate area.

"Hello?" I called, only half expecting an answer. I knew I was fairly close to the perimeter of the safe zone and suspected that there were cameras, microphones, and other detection devices nearby.

I circled the objects in the area, studying the trees, rocks, and bushes for anomalies. It took a few minutes and I had just decided to climb a tree when something dinged.

"Ding?" I wondered quietly and a voice came from behind me. I spun ready to engage but no one was around.

"I wondered how long it would take," a young man's voice spoke quietly.

I know that voice. Where...who?

"Are you okay?" he continued.

"I'm fine. Out for a run," I said quietly, casually leaning against the trunk speaking.

"It's me, Kmetz," Jimmy Kmetz, wonder nerd, identified himself. "You tripped my sensor."

"What can you see?"

"Anything I need to. I watched the man and the girl come earlier, Samuel Sanders and his daughter, Marion Sanders. You know she got her learner's permit recently? She seems like a sweet kid, spotless academic records and she does community service through the family's church."

"How are you doing?" I asked.

"Good! I finally got to move back home. The commute's rougher but at least I'm back in civilization. You're sure you're okay?"

"Me? Sure. I'm just talking to a tree. I should get back," I excused and left the area after a furtive scan to ensure I hadn't been seen. I walked the rest of the way, studying my surroundings with a suspicious eye. I think on some level I expected R2D2 to jump out of a ditch.

I dialed the code for entry and the noises of children's interactive toys greeted me as I walked in the front door. Pax was shrieking in delight and hitting as many buttons as possible. Marion had him supported in her straddle and he was smacking three different toys at once. It was calamitous and joyous and she encouraged him enthusiastically.

"Who's that? Who's that? Is that Mommy? Is that your mommy?" Marion asked Pax until he looked up for me.

Holy crap, he's so cute! Pax responded by shoving his foot in his mouth and toppling over on Marion's leg.

"We can stay a little longer if you'd like to take a shower. Yolanda always said that she'd take a nap and a shower if she had any time when the kids were young," Sammy offered.

"Sweet! You don't mind?" I checked.

"Of course not!" Marion replied honestly. "Besides, I need some time to change his diaper."

I seized the opportunity while thanking the stars that Marion existed in my life.

My life fell into a pattern; a luxury I hadn't been afforded since my teenage years. I went to town a few days a week for groceries, mail, and book/movie exchanges with the library. I saw Sammy and/or his family at least once a week. I started trading time with Marion; her babysitting skills for my teaching her to drive.

The Sanders family took me in for Thanksgiving but when Marion started begging me to go to Nashville with her for Christmas shopping I had to lay low for a while. Making excuses was better than trying to explain to a sixteen-year-old that I can't make unexpected trips or leave the direct area without a military escort.

I did go on the occasional adventure, but everything was planned ahead of time so an escort could be arranged. I was quite disappointed to find no familiar faces in the first escort group as we went for Pax's check-up plus Christmas shopping.

Christmas is very disappointing when there's no one to celebrate you. Pax couldn't understand any of it but he greatly enjoyed trying to put the few ornaments our miniature tree held into his mouth. He also found great joy in shoving the tree over, insisting that I pick it up again, and repeating.

The night after Christmas the red phone rang. Pax was asleep in his room so I jumped over the counter, grabbed the phone, and flipped it open while jerking my silverware drawer open to retrieve the hidden Glock.

"What's the situation?" I asked while rushing to clear the house on my way to Pax.

"Your phone is dead," a man informed me, "I won't ask where you got that gun."

Probably not an emergency. Hallway clear, ohthankgod he's fine. Wait, what? "What?"

"Your cell phone is dead; we couldn't contact you so we peeked. Stand down, Penny," the man directed.

"The house is secure?"

"Yes, now will you please charge your phone? And watch the safety on that thing."

"Turn off the camera, I'm in my sweats!" I hissed at the phone and headed back to the kitchen to find and plug in the cell phone. "Happy?"

"Ecstatic," the man on the other end replied dryly. "Thank you and, you know, Merry Christmas." He hung up before I could verbally assault him.

"Day late and seriously lacking in sincerity," I muttered and started putting things back to rights in the house.

"Happy New Year!" Marion greeted me through the front door before I had even opened it. "Thanks for letting me stay the night."

"Thanks for coming, Sammy, are you coming in?" I called to the car.

"Just for a minute, Yolanda and I are heading down to Nashville for the night," he replied and carried a duffle bag in. "Are you having someone do work on the grounds?"

"Why?" My adrenalin fired.

"We saw a truck on the side of the road, it looked kinda beat-up. It was next to your mailbox, no one in sight."

"I'm sure it's nothing. Don't you want a cup of coffee?" I asked him aggressively and got them both in the house. "Stay for a minute, please," I picked up the red phone and made a call. Sammy talked to them for a moment and then handed the phone back to me. "Yeah, we'll let you know." I hung up the phone in frustration. "Twenty to forty minutes. Nice bodyguard team!" I jerked the silverware drawer open and pulled out the gun. "The house is hard to penetrate, but the windows are not bulletproof."

"Your con; what do I do?" Sammy asked while silently herding our children into the kitchen to play on the floor.

"Let me pull up surveillance; count the bogeys, get locations," I recommended and the black phone rang. "Hello?"

"It's Jimmy Kmetz," he announced, "I've got a man on your property line; he's not tripping the system yet but one of my cameras picked him up."

"Where and what is he doing?" I demanded.

"Two o'clock, top of the hill, about a hundred and five yards from the barn door. Do you want me to call it in?"

"I already did, they said they'd be here in 30 minutes. Can you stay on the line?" I asked and put my earpiece in. "Is the area otherwise clear?"

"Yes."

"Alright, can you watch both him and my house?"

"Yup, are you going after him?"

I shrugged on my camouflage jacket and told Sammy to lock the door behind me.

"Are we still clear?" I asked Kmetz very quietly as I skirted the barn.

"Yes, and I can see you too. Belle, the man is just sitting on a log. The family is fine, run about twenty yards due east."

I followed his guidance and quickly realized that I was still wearing my fluffy pink house slippers. *Well it's not exactly ideal; bunny slippers, nothing but a BB gun and security that apparently has better things to do.* I climbed the hill from the far right, nearly falling on the leaves from the lack of a real shoe. *There he is. Can a BB gun make a shot from here? I have no idea how far these stupid things shoot! Probably around a .22. Here we go! Of course he's wearing a hoodie.*

"Stay where you are!" I demanded, approaching from his right and aiming my weapon at his head. The man raised his hands slowly and flipped his head back to knock the hood off.

"Don't shoot him, I think its Jackson O'Neill," Kmetz informed me helpfully as though I needed help recognizing Jack.

"Son of a --," I exclaimed and my mommy auto-correct stopped me.

Jack looked me over while maintaining a totally neutral expression. "You wore your slippers?"

I lowered my weapon and tucked it into my pants. "What...?" I couldn't form the words.

"I haven't tripped your perimeter alarms; what gave me up? The people in the car?"

"He's retired military and she's adorable. Why are you here?" I blurted.

"Are the boys in black coming?" Jack asked.

"Talk to the tree," I told him and circled around him as he stood and waved to the nearest camera. "Cancel the backup, please. If I need to I'll just shoot him myself. Thanks Jimmy."

"Do you want me to go? I wasn't sure if you wanted to see me or if you hated my guts or didn't want to deal with the memories," Jack rambled a bit. "I was going to wait by the mailbox; I still remember most of the borders and the set-up here. I didn't have a phone number for you. I was actually just sitting here thinking if," Jack stopped.

"Are you armed?"

"No. I'm basically a civilian right now. Do you want me to go?"

"Jimmy, is there anything I should know?" I asked Kmetz.

"No, he's still him. He's been traveling as far as I can tell; if you give me a few minutes I can send you a file on it." Kmetz replied.

"Thanks Jimmy. I'm going to call Sanders and let him know we're coming." I hung up on him and dialed Sammy to tell him to stand down. Jack and I started down the hill, treading carefully in my torn-up slippers.

"Those ridiculous things are in no condition for this terrain. Can I give you a lift?" Jack asked and I was happy to oblige. We tore down the hill like a couple of teenagers.

"All clear, Sammy, we're okay. An old colleague of mine dropped by and got cold feet," I explained as we entered. "Jack, meet Samuel Sanders and his daughter Marion."

"Sir," Jack shook Sammy's hand.

"Penny, let me call Yolanda, we may need to change our plans," Sammy stated.

"Jack, why don't you explore the house? Give us a moment," I requested and Jack disappeared.

"Sammy, Colonel, I completely understand if you don't want Marion to stay the night. This was frightening, but it's over now. Jack was with me when I was working; he was my bodyguard and caretaker and there is no person on earth I feel safer with. He was hand-picked by your friend. I checked with my people; he hasn't gone rogue or anything. He's been traveling, taking some time off since we disbanded. I don't know exactly what he wants or needs; if he's just here to say hi, or if he'll stay to dinner, or if he needs a couch."

Sammy sighed heavily and frowned. "Let me make a call." He headed outside and Marion and I took Pax back to his toy kingdom, commonly known as my living room.

I overheard some phrases through the window and gathered that he was talking to Deuce. Pax started crying and I heard Jack coming down the hall.

"Where's your changing table?" he asked as he joined us.

"In Pax's room and, about half the time, on that side table over there," I replied while picking up my stinky son.

"You can tell his potty cry?" Marion blinked at Jack. "You must know each other really well."

"Jack is a very good friend. He helped take care of us when Pax was born. I think he may have changed more diapers than I did in the first three months," I explained and changed the diaper.

"Penny," Sammy returned, "I'll talk to Yolanda, but I'm okay with it. Are you still willing to host Marion tonight?"

"Of course. We'll be fine; I'll take excellent care of her." *That's right, Jack. I can take care of myself, my son, and my favorite teenager.*

"Marion?" he asked.

"I want to stay, daddy."

"Jack, you come highly recommended. If Clipper says you're alright, you're probably alright. Good night, all."

Sammy left and Marion took over Pax and put the first movie in to kill time toward midnight.

"I'm going to start the sausage balls and mini pizzas," I excused and Jack followed me into the kitchen. "So," I left it open for him.

"Yeah, I've been traveling, you know, the little RV thing. It was too much like being in the field, so I quit. I had some former Army buddies in this area, I liked it and there are some great universities so I applied to a few of them. My semester starts in a few weeks. There are no vacancies in any hotels in the area tonight: New Year's Eve is apparently their busiest night. I realized I was just a few miles from you. Could I sleep in the barn tonight? It seemed like a cold night to just sleep in the truck, and,"

I cut him off, "No, you cannot sleep in my barn, Jack."

"Fair enough," he retreated, "It was good to see you're doing so well. Take care of yourself," he turned to the door.

"Jack, stay here. The house has more than enough room. Do your laundry, take a shower, a long shower," I added and he grinned. "I think Marion is going to sleep in my room tonight, I sleep with Pax half the time anyway."

"Really? You're sure?" He acted like he was an imposition.

"Of course. House rules: if I point a gun at someone, they either get shot or they get a hot meal and a warm bed. Go on then, get your stuff," I sent him off and stashed my gun.

"You get satellite here?" Jack asked quietly as we sat in front of the television watching the crowd in NYC. It was about an hour to midnight; Pax was sound asleep, Marion had nodded off in the chair and Jack and I were left on the couch.

"Yes; I thank God for the children's channels. Anyone who says they never leave their kid with a television is lying," I confessed. "Do you want to connect to the Wi-Fi?"

"No, all I have is my cell phone. I probably need to get a laptop for school, but I gotta find an apartment first, and maybe get a proper car."

"The excitement of our lives is just staggering," I joked dryly.

"What's it been like for you?" Jack asked curiously.

"It's quiet, mostly; every time I blink Pax has grown out of his clothes, and I'm shockingly close to quoting some of his favorite shows verbatim."

"Sounds boring."

"I...I think I like it."

"Good."

I got up to stretch my legs and hopscotch my way through the hall to check Pax. I couldn't get the stupid grin off of my face: life was pleasant.

Penny Oswald exists; a woman who is kind and loving and has friends who really care about her. Here, in the backwoods, I'm shielded by trees and guarded by science. The non-stop war is beyond my reach but my personal missions were accomplished.

"Hey," Jack peeked in through the open door to the nursery, "Are you okay?"

"Of course, why?"

"This is all...I can't picture you being happy like this."

"It's just peace, Jack," I admonished lightly, "I'm fine with it. For the first time since my childhood the world and I are at peace."

"And you're okay with that?" He was starting to look dead sexy in the doorway and I brushed past him into the hall. I caught a glimpse of us in a mirror and my eyes glinted back at us.

"Hmm?" I blinked, distracted.

"You're okay?" he repeated.

"Of course," *For now.*

*****

I feel so privileged to entertain you and thank you for reading this story. I write because I believe that life is a series of stories waiting to be written, read, lived, and enjoyed. I absolutely adore my readers and gain more inspiration from you than you know.

If you enjoyed this book please take a moment to review it online and recommend it to your friends and family members. I would love to hear from you on Facebook as Victoria Helen Rose.

Works by Victoria Helen Rose:

Transatlantic (2014)

The Belle's Revenge Series

Beauty, Fury, and Lies (2014)

Killing Waldo (2015)